PRAISE FOR

MICHELE HAUF

About *Flawless:*

"An exciting read from start to finish."
—*Romantic Times BOOKclub*

"This action-packed romantic suspense
(is a) gripping thriller."
—*The Best Reviews*

About *Once a Thief:*

"...unrelenting suspense and action will keep
readers entertained on every page."
—*Cataromance*

"Incredibly gripping, Hauf's lyrically
spare voice is bone-chillingly appropriate
for her edgy, almost noir story."
—Nina Bruhns, award-winning author of
Hard Case Cowboy

"An absorbing and totally mesmerizing
read that I simply could not put down."
—*Romance Designs*

Dear Reader,

Join Jamie MacAlister as she thrills at speeding along the Parisian freeway, wind in her hair, tunes cranked and… gunfire in her wake. Yep, the heroine of this story gets her kicks by driving the getaway car. It's all about constantly being on the edge. And driving away from everything that has ever hurt her. Now Jamie has decided to turn and face those haunting demons and right the wrongs she's been a part of. It's not easy going clean, but she's made of determination and drive, and a lot of girly stubbornness.

As a writer, this story was a challenge. I'm not what you would call a car person. Heck, I still can't find my own car in a parking lot after a mere ten minutes of shopping. But, as when Lance Armstrong said, "It's not about the bike," this story is not about the car. It's about learning to push beyond your limits and to take a chance. I believe we are each, in our own manner, strong, fierce and brilliant. Have you discovered your inner strength?

Michele Hauf

P.S. Watch for characters from my last Bombshell book, *Once a Thief,* to appear. And more about Ava will be revealed in my next Bombshell story!

MICHELE HAUF

GETAWAY GIRL

BOMBSHELL™

Published by Silhouette Books

America's Publisher of Contemporary Romance

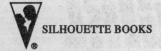

SILHOUETTE BOOKS

ISBN-13: 978-0-373-51421-2
ISBN-10:   0-373-51421-2

GETAWAY GIRL

Copyright © 2006 by Michele Hauf

www.SilhouetteBombshell.com

Printed in U.S.A.

Books by Michele Hauf

Silhouette Bombshell

Once a Thief #49
Flawless #62
Getaway Girl #107

LUNA Books

Seraphim
Gossamyr
Rhiana

MICHELE HAUF

has been writing for more than a decade and has published historical, fantasy and paranormal romance. A good strong heroine, action and adventure, and a touch of romance make for her favorite kind of story. (And if it's set in France, all the better.) She lives with her family in Minnesota, and loves the four seasons, even if one of them lasts six months and can be colder than a deep freeze. You can find out more about her at www.michelehauf.com.

To my husband, Jeff. For a few months I showed
an interest in cars and speed, but, well, it's over now.
Sorry, I'll never really care about which driver is in
the lead, or which NASCAR track is the fastest.
But I'll always care about you.

This story exists because of the great help I got from a
couple of people. Jim Crider, aka AutoJim, tried his best
to educate this non-car person on the basics of speed,
gears and car lingo. I know, it was overkill to do the
donut more than once, but I still think it looks cool.

Thanks to Kurt Hauf, for also attempting to fill
my brain with the logistics of all things car. Of course,
all mistakes or wild inaccuracies are completely my fault.
What do you expect from someone who buys her cars
because they're "curvy and not square"?

Laura Vivanco was my Scottish connection.
Many thanks!

To my son, Jesse, I'm sorry I didn't use NOS in the car.
Yeah, it would have been cool, and so "fast & furious."
Maybe next time.

Chapter 1

I may not always know where I'm going—or even why—but that's fine. It's the journey that rocks my world.

The back door of the car I sat in, a charcoal Audi A8, swung open. Glancing in the rearview mirror, I eyed the masked face that popped inside the backseat. Two dark eyes sought my calm stare.

"Pickup?" the urgent male voice questioned. His French accent made it sound like *peek-up*.

"Three passengers?" I volleyed back.

"*Oui,*" he gasped. "*La lapine?*"

"Yes. Are you being followed?"

The hiss of a gunshot zinged past the passenger side window at the same time that the man snapped, "*Oui!*"

Behind him, still on the sidewalk, a female's nervous squeal prompted his resolve. He slammed an insistent palm against the headrest of the passenger seat.

"Get in!" I urged.

The man slid across the leather backseat. A woman clothed in a pink velour running suit followed. Her face was masked with a black hood, and her hands were bound before her with thick, dirty rope. Shoved into the center of the seat by another masked man, she murmured frantically.

Another bullet pinged the back bumper. So it was going down like this? And here I'd thought today's pickup would be different.

I laid the accelerator pedal to the floor. The last man in closed the back door. The woman cried out a mournful note.

The Audi peeled across the ancient cobbled street that wound through the narrow 2nd *arrondissement* and passed behind the seventeenth-century walls of the Bibliothèque Nationale. The building was no longer used as a library; modernization, you know.

With an eye to the rearview mirror, I surveyed our wake. Two figures dressed in black and wielding guns fired at our retreat. I winced as a bullet nicked the upper glass of the backseat window. A spiderweb cracked across the entire window. Good thing my trusty BMW was in the shop.

Had it not been five in the morning, the gunfire might have attracted the city police. As it was, the street was relatively quiet as the city began to stir and sniff the aroma of coffee, *baguettes* and street sweepers' soap. Excellent driving conditions. The sweeping vehicles that sprayed down the walks were about the only hazard to watch for.

"Location?" I called to the backseat.

I knew the drop-off location—had already entered it in the GPS—but I needed to verify it to ensure I'd nabbed the right pickup. An added precaution. Likely the threesome were *not* innocent bystanders. How many hooded passengers fleeing gun-toting thugs were there to be found on a Paris street corner?

"Gare du Nord!" one of the masked men offered in clipped French. *"En avant!"*

Right answer. Wrong attitude. I'd *en avant* them as quickly or as slowly as I desired.

The address would take us to the train station in the 10th *arrondissement*. Not far from here, but a twisted route of turns and narrow streets. The traffic would be moderate because the real work rush didn't kick in until after 6 a.m. An added bonus was that I could exceed the usual slow pace of about nineteen kilometers an hour.

Adjusting the driver's side window down a few inches drew in the greasy-sweet fumes wafting from the *pâtisserie* across the street that zoomed by. The bakery served up delectables in waxed pink boxes tied with white string. Should I mention my fetish for *pain au chocolat*? It's all about the ritual. Test with a few nibbles, then tongue out the middle, then devour—quite opposite my philosophy, which was devour first, then test.

I'm a reactor, you see. Diving in—and asking questions later—is my forte.

Petrol runs through my veins. Speed is my fix. The road speaks to me. I love this city and its every twisting, cobbled road. A lifeline, these streets. And like a network of life-giving blood veins, I know every street like I know the entrails of my BMW 5 series. The Audi is merely a fill-in until the Bimmer is finished up in the shop.

I lowered the window halfway, another two inches, to allow me to hear sounds outside the vehicle. While concentration was key, I needed to hear everything, from car horns to pedestrians to—

Another gunshot drilled the air. It didn't hit the Audi. Eyes darting left to right and forward and back, I performed constant periphery surveillance. *Merci,* there were no pedestrians on this narrow road.

Shifting into third, I navigated the narrow shop-lined rue Vivienne that would spit us out onto a five-way exchange along the busy rue Montmartre. It was tricky at this speed. But the solemn brown Peugeot that had attached itself to my tail wasn't about to let up.

While keeping one eye to the road, I checked the auxiliary mirror installed above the passenger side at the corner of the ceiling, angled for a view of the backseat and observed the hooded woman. Each man held her by the upper arm. The pink jogging suit appeared girlie soft and prim next to the heavy canvas hood tugged over her head. Nervous moans muffled behind the hood competed with th *schuss* of outside noises. I'd seen this before. Nothing nev They never removed the hood while in transit, but n because revealing the route would compromise their ide tities. It seemed to keep the abductee a bit calmer, like on of those hooded falcons.

Abductee. That's a harsh word for this situation. The me in the backseat? They were the good guys. Soon enough, th frightened woman's adventure would come to an end. And would be responsible for making that happen.

I swerved sharply onto the avenue.

"We've less than ten minutes before the drop-off," one of the masked men insisted in perfect English.

So state the obvious.

I glanced in the mirror at the man.

The dashboard clock flashed 5:13 a.m. The pickup had been delayed five minutes. Not on my part. The passengers had been late. I had been revving the engine, prepared to depart, when the warehouse door had slammed open and out ran my passengers. Numbers Three and Seven, I knew. Today's client always used numbers to identify their agents. I liked the anonymity. That's why I, Jamie MacAlister, was known to my clients only as *la lapine*—the rabbit.

The rue Montmartre was clear, save a few vehicles spaced far enough apart to allow easy passing. Rosy sunlight shimmered on the silent building windows as we sped by. Beyond and straight ahead, the domed ceiling of Sacré Coeur sitting on the hilltop, one of the highest points in Paris, glittered like a bronzed rose.

Stepping on the brake, I downshifted, then angled sharply into a left turn. One of the men in the backseat swore. I love a Frenchman's oath, no matter how nasty. The accent gave it élan. That's French for enthusiastic self-confidence and style. See, this Scottish lass has been studying.

The smell of petrol spurred my adrenaline. It was a sweet perfume, like the expensive kind the Vendôme vixens purchase by the ounce—and for the five euros I laid out per gallon of petrol, it was a comparable comparison.

On the sidewalk, a toddler, clad in striped pajamas and clasping a dog's leash, dropped his mother's hand to make driving circles with his gripped fingers and revving noises with his sputtering lips. The white poodle yipped and began to dance around the mother's feet, effectively wrapping her ankles with the leash.

I had to smile. Gearhead that I am, I completely understand a child's fascination with cars and speed. Pa had taken me to my first street race when I was four and ever since, my veins had been infused with motor oil.

Now to navigate the rue La Fayette at a moderate speed,

yet shake the tail before I got too close to the drop-off. It wouldn't do to send off my passengers and leave them to battle the bad guys. My job required a clean drop, no ragtag bringing up the rear.

Behind, the Peugeot took the corner and, in the process, nicked the front quarter panel of a slow-moving green coupe. They were determined not to lose me. As were all tails. Were they not, my job would become obsolete.

Funny how the journey never changed, even though the destination had. Did I mention I was working for the good guys now?

Ahead, the traffic thickened. The train station was always busy. Clutching the steering wheel with a comfortable, sure grip, I manipulated the faithful Audi into two-lane traffic that would choke us to a snail's pace if I allowed it.

That wasn't about to happen.

The Peugeot kissed my bumper. One of my passengers gripped the headrest. With a frantic look at the cracked rear window, he then swung a masked gaze up to the rearview mirror. Wide, dark eyes met mine.

I never offered the oft-sought reassurance. Who had time to play babysitter?

I held the man's querying eyes briefly, but a flash of sunlight struck the Peugeot's lion rampant hood ornament and redirected my attention. A hand holding a gun jutted out from the passenger window of the tail.

"Down!" I ordered. *"En bas!"*

The passengers dropped their heads. Keen. This crew knew how to take orders.

A jerk of the steering wheel forced a red Vespa scooter onto the sidewalk, clearing a space in the far traffic lane. I fit the Audi into the spot the idiot scooter should not have filled.

Paris and its relentless attempts to insinuate motorized scooters into the traffic!

Another gunshot roused a few screams from pedestrians wandering the sidewalks. No hits to the Audi—at least, none I had heard. But what kind of idiot continued to fire around innocents and witnesses?

Behind me, the female now clutched one of the masked men's hands, her bright pink fingernail polish chipped, or, likely, chewed ragged. She must have been through hell.

I was determined to end it quickly.

This lane moved slower. The boulevard de Denain lay less than a mile up—my target. The Peugeot began to pull parallel to the Audi. You had to love that boat of a Peugeot, though, it was a beast to handle compared to this slick little number.

With one eye on the road and the other on the passenger-side mirror, I spotted the gun. From this distance, I couldn't determine the make of the weapon, only that it looked large enough to do serious damage. The shooter wore a black facemask and jacket.

Why did they always wear black? Villain couture sorely lacked panache. The occasional blue, or even a subtle violet, would really spruce things up nicely.

A survey of the backseat noted the good guys also wore black. I smirked. Two months ago, who ever would have thought *I'd* be working for the good guys? Perhaps I should put in a requisition for a black suit myself.

Nope. I preferred skirts that didn't constrict when sitting behind the wheel and loose blouses.

Giving a piston-charge chew to the peppermint gum lodged in my cheek, I worked my jaw as I revved up courage.

Scratch that. Courage wasn't required to wheel the getaway car—it was one hundred percent raw female balls.

And mine are big, thank you very much. Gears, grease and drive, that's what I'm made of. If I'm not behind the wheel, then somebody had better check me for a pulse.

"Keep your heads down!"

Maneuvering left, I nudged the Peugeot, which made it swerve long enough for me to squeeze in ahead of it. A massive garbage vehicle led the line of growing traffic.

Glancing to the car on my left, I made eye contact with a handsome man on the passenger side, sun-tanned arm dangling as he tapped the car door to tunes I couldn't hear. An Italian? I ran my fingers through my wavy blond hair and blew him a kiss. He returned it and gestured to the driver of his car. A space opened up for me to slip in front of them, leaving the Peugeot veering behind the garbage truck. Love those Italians.

"Seven minutes!"

"Keep your knickers on," I muttered. If there was anything I hated more than an armed tail, it was a backseat driver.

Fitch had updated me on street conditions this morning, not through on-the-road scouting but through her cyberconnections and access to Paris's traffic control. The place de Roubaix was under repairs and traffic cones blocked the dirt road, so the direct approach had been my only option. This route took me straight toward the train station, which offered a bit more traffic but would do.

The windowed facade of the Gare du Nord loomed ahead and flashed like blue water in the sunlight. Nine statues representing important European cities beckoned passengers from high above. Once I'd known the names of each of the cities, but I didn't care anymore. Been there, done that. On to the next adventure. I wasn't one to stick around and get comfy.

Navigating the right lane, I eased the Audi dreadfully close to the chrome bumper of a parked delivery truck whose nose stuck too far into the driving lane. Delivery vehicle drivers drove as if they ruled the road. That attitude—I'm bigger, so get out of my way—never works with me.

Eyes keen to my periphery—there were children walking with their parents—I gunned the Audi to an intersection, then turned off on the rue Perdonnet and hit the gas.

With no sight of the Peugeot in the mirror, I pulled up to the curb before the train station and idled. I couldn't read the clock on the face of the station from this angle, so glanced to the GPS display.

"Five minutes to spare." I pressed the automatic lock button and secured all doors. "Payment?"

The first man who had entered tossed a brown envelope onto the front passenger seat. I pressed three fingers to the rumpled package—just thick enough to be right.

Pressing the tracker pad on the laptop secured below the dash, I keyed a checkmark over the Bibliothèque pickup. Paid. My records were updated, and the fail-safe keyed into the door-lock system was overridden. Should I ever take a bullet to the head before receiving payment, the system was designed to spurt dye onto the passengers and keep them safely ensconced within the vehicle until the police (called by an internal phone system) arrived.

"The Faction is appreciative," the other man began.

I put up a palm to stop him. More details than I needed—or wanted. "I lost the tail, but that doesn't mean they won't get unlost. Run!"

The backseat was cleared in a breath. The first man assisted the woman as they emerged onto the sidewalk. In the process, he slipped off his mask, as well as the hood over the woman's head. Tall and slender, she managed a silent grace even as her handlers rushed her into the train station.

The Faction is appreciative.

Today's passengers were from the underground rescue ops known to me only as the Faction—their identities were but code names—thus, Three and Seven. The Faction rescued kidnapped dignitaries and royals, and intervened in covert criminal affairs that posed greater danger if police were to get involved. They operated outside the law, but their intentions were honorable. And Max Montenelli had approved them as a client.

Good enough for me.

Stuffing the envelope of cash into the glove box, I shifted into gear and drove away from the train station at a leisurely pace. No sign of the Peugeot. It was probably still trapped behind the garbage truck. And should they arrive any time soon? No longer my problem.

Rolling the driver's window down completely, I stretched an arm along the door and managed the steering wheel with two fingers crooked over the right spoke. Swirling the radio dial, I selected an appropriate song on the one station that played American hits—Bowling For Soup's "Greatest Day"—and cranked the tunes.

Good choice. I believed everyone had her own theme song, a song that defined her. It could change with wisdom, experience and life.

Another successful pickup. But different from any pickup I'd ever made in the past. This one had been legit. I had begun anew. The journey had just gotten a lot brighter.

Singing along with the words, I had to agree that this was my greatest day.

Not a bad theme song to have, eh?

Chapter 2

"Taken?"

Sacha Vital did not move. He stood at the center of the small modern office, his hands calmly at his thighs. A silver Dior suit jacket hung impeccably from his shoulders. Black pearl cuff links weighted the sleeves. Asian vanilla scented the mist that fogged from the corner fountain. The floor-to-ceiling windows let in a muted white light, softening the room's steel furnishings, and the hanging mesh baskets of ivy soaked up the sun like beach bums at Cannes.

Taken. The word fell like a bomb. Two weeks of preparation scouting this target—a lazy Spanish villa nestled between treacherous mountains only traversable by foot—and but eight hours the mark had been in hand. The reconnaissance crew had arrived in Paris an hour earlier. The exchange had been planned to the minute—and now?

"Taken."

Sacha skimmed his fingertips along the cool surface of a round granite ball placed precisely in the center on the glass-topped desk. Tap, tap, tap. He spread his entire hand over the stone, seeking his peace, fighting the rise of anger.

More thugs than actual thinking entities, two of Sacha's employees, Jacques and Thom, stood back by the office door. They would not speak until asked a direct question. They knew better. He'd charged them with watching over the princess following the exchange near the Bibliothèque Nationale, keeping her fed and comfortable, and not to touch. He didn't operate that way. Damaged goods never provided as much satisfaction as the return of the complete package did. Besides, he'd witnessed, on more than one occasion, the result of returning a damaged package.

I will never be like my father.

But sometimes a man was pushed over the edge, and he had to take a reluctant step toward dubious rather than fall completely under the surface, never to emerge.

Taken.

And he could guess exactly who was responsible. Wherever he went lately, that damned Faction lurked. He'd smelled them on his trail for the past few months, but until today, they'd clung to the shadows like the rodents they were. Had they been on to his operations? Did he have a snitch in his employ?

Thom, his shaved head bowed but his gray eyes darting up and down, sought Sacha's reaction. He looked like a puppy that had chewed the corner off a couch—and was dog enough to realize it was a bad thing.

Sacha supposed this was what a man deserved for hiring idiots.

Hell, they weren't idiots, they'd just been…outsmarted.

Admittedly, the twosome did not think well on their feet. Instructions had to be fed to them in a constant stream of communication.

Note to self: hire college graduates in the future. *Corruptible* graduates.

Who was he kidding? The future would never be as the present was. It could not be. It would not be.

Fingers growing tense upon the round stone, Sacha lifted them from the cool surface, and immediately, a fist formed.

"The Faction?" Sacha wondered, crossing his arms and pressing his forefinger to his upper lip.

Jacques nodded. "I believe so."

Not his favorite opponent. Yet an opposition he had made plans for. Sacha had placed backups surrounding the pickup in anticipation of just such trouble. And snipers on the roof.

"They strolled into the warehouse and toddled out with the princess in hand?"

"It was an ambush. There were…" Both men looked to one another. Sweat on their foreheads beaded like teenage acne. "Many," Thom finished.

"A dozen," Jacques added, a bit too unconvincingly.

Sacha had arranged for six perimeter guards. With such a valuable package, he should have doubled their numbers! But when had the Faction ever put more than two or three men in the field? The smaller their number, the less obvious.

He eyed both men. Thom shuffled his feet. Jacques studied a non-existent speck on his forearm. Liars?

"A dozen men. Yet, the two of you returned to me remarkably unscathed."

"They hadn't weapons, that we could see."

Sacha lifted a brow. The Faction was not averse to artillery, should it be called for. And if his men had been armed…

He could read a lie like a hawk. Thom and Jacques were lying to cover their own asses.

That damned Faction. They had become his nemesis of late. The Faction operated as a fringe covert rescue ops; their only interest was helping those innocents who daren't consult the authorities for aid. Modern-day Robin Hoods romping about Europe, they were. But they didn't steal from the rich; they stole from the criminals and gave back to the rich. There was something wrong with that scenario. The Faction was a self-serving organization that operated under police radar, just clever enough for their own good.

But had they been clever this time?

Sacha suspected the princess was not safely on her way back to Spain. And if his suspicions were true, that left him little time to reclaim her before it was too late and the Faction ended up with the information he so desperately wanted.

Could they know his reasons for taking the woman from her home? If they did, that would only verify there was a snitch.

"You gave chase?" Sacha wondered.

Thom nodded, head bowed.

"Well?"

"They had a driver waiting outside the warehouse. He—"

"A driver, eh?" Sacha tilted his head, easing out a sudden kink tightening the vein at the back of his jaw. "Arrange a pickup," he instructed. "I've a package that needs…attention."

"10:15 behind Sainte-Marie des Batignolles." I scribbled the time down on the PDA screen set in the console between the driver's seat and the passenger side.

"The cemetery, yes," I confirmed as Fitch gave me directions. "This is a package?"

"You know it, girl."

"Passengers?"

"Two. No names, but the call traced to the île Saint-Louis. I'm sending a tracer through the wires right now to pick up any abnormal activity. But I think they're cool."

She thinks? I tapped the plastic stylus upon the electronic keypad and pumped a few chews of my gum. "You know I don't do same-day pickups, Fitch. Too risky. You'll never have confirmation before then. It's less than an hour from now. What's up?"

"Fifteen thousand big ones, is what's up, sweetie. Euros, that is." Fitch's Tennessee twang echoed out from the radio—the cell phone attached to the dashboard relayed to the radio speakers so I could speak hands-free. "That's a big payoff."

"Who is willing to pay so much for a mere pickup?"

My usual pickups asked a standard five thousand euros. I wasn't greedy, but I wasn't a fool, either. I did this for the money—and the rush. But the fact someone wanted to pay three times my usual price made me suspicious.

"I'm not driving the old game anymore, Fitch."

"I know that. You're straight as a stickpin now. Nothin' wrong with that."

So why did Fitch's tone make me feel guilty?

Plastic drinking straw stuck in the corner of my mouth, I twisted in the driver's seat to swing my feet outside. I stepped onto the pavement with my left foot. The Audi sat in a parking lot outside the Forum des Halles, a mall area that was fronted by lush gardens, that always beckoned me during my down time. I had stopped to buy a plain crêpe with just a touch of cinnamon, and Orangina Fire—with a straw—my favorite snack.

Scrubbing a hand over my hair, I sighed and looked off

toward a flock of gray pigeons attacking a bronze statue's head. "It doesn't feel right, Fitch."

"Trust me."

Fitch hadn't failed me yet. The feisty Goddess of All Things Cyber had served Max and me for years as the go-through for all our pickups. Fitch had so many computers and mainframes and ports and wires on her barge, I always felt lacking while looking over the electronic jungle. I like technology, but if it doesn't involve grease and gears I don't want to take the time to learn about it.

Nearing her fifties, Fitch raised a literal jungle on the deck of the barge tethered to the left bank of the Seine and jogged ten miles daily. She was one hundred percent no-nonsense American smarts—Fitch's description.

Her extensive connections made it easy for Fitch to identify and screen all prospective clients. Also, she had a connection to the computer in my BMW and Max's Audi, and could follow me with GPS or by tracking me on the cell phone. My pride and joy was currently in the shop, getting a few treats, such as a plasma ignition system, dye packs for the security system and bulletproof metal plating beneath the body.

Hey, a girl's gotta watch her back, no matter what the destination. And my new journey was all good. No more questionable criminal activity. This getaway girl was now clean.

With a sigh, I dispelled the unnecessary apprehension. I tugged the partially macerated straw from my mouth. "Fine, Fitch, I trust you." We rarely spoke in person anymore. Safer not to be seen together. Though I feared few repercussions from the bad guys. Fitch did her thing; I did mine. No need to start partying together. "Drop-off?"

"The south reservoir on the Marne."

Beyond *la périph* and out of the immediate city. Of course, the cemetery sat in the shadow of the *périphérique*, which was the freeway that circled Paris—some called it the Ring Road—but the Marne was the opposite direction from the pickup. "That'll be extra for the mileage. You told them that?"

"You want extra beyond the fifteen thou?"

I chuckled and stretched my arms out before me in a pulling yawn. "Guess not. Size of package?"

"Small. Handheld. Sensitive data that will—"

"Enough."

Details…complicated things. Details painted a trail. And a trail to Jamie MacAlister did not exist.

All clients first went through Fitch, and she screened them carefully. Jobs even hinting of the illegal would no longer be accepted. Likely the package the passengers carried contained timely information, which needed to be shuttled quickly and discreetly. I could go there.

"I told them you'd be outside the cemetery at the east gate at 10:14 a.m. They verify the drop-off location, and you're on your way."

"Got it." I clicked off and leaned back to check the dashboard clock. 9:35. I needed but twenty minutes to make the location.

Sipping the last spicy ginger and citrus drops of Orangina, I then crumpled up the crêpe wrapper and tossed that, along with the small teardrop-shaped glass bottle, out the window. A mesh wastebasket chained to a street sign caught the refuse.

Stepping out, I went around to sit on the boot of the car. An initial heel check confirmed my black- and white-checked Vans hadn't picked up any stones that would scratch the chrome bumper. Swiping a few bread crumbs from the knee-length black crinkle skirt I wore, I then lay back, propping an arm behind my neck and my head on the cracked back window. Bulletproofing had prevented the entire window from shattering, but it would need to be replaced, if not for protection, then for the image I wanted to present to my clients.

The sun beamed across my exposed belly. The short button-up white silk blouse rode to just below my breasts. I never buttoned the bottom three buttons. I like freedom of movement, and there's nothing wrong with being sexy—even clocking one hundred and thirty kilometers an hour.

Closing my eyes I took a few moments to breathe and prepare. To shuck off any tendrils of anxiety and lose myself in the moment, and the puffy clouds overhead. Made me feel like a kid again, to stare at the clouds and pick out a fat-bellied bear or a big round daisy. It was important to retain a childlike wonder and to be resilient. Resilience got me through a lot of hard times.

Memories of hot summer afternoons spent running through the sprinkler with the rest of the neighborhood kids were always welcome. I wondered what had become of Stacy MacPherson, the dark-haired rogue of the bunch, who'd always play the pirate or the sneaky one-eyed, one-armed villain. Had he found himself a gorgeous bride or had he become the fat bald man who nursed a pint nightly at the corner pub? Or Robin Fergus, the eternal hostess and mother, who always tended her "children" whenever we had played house in the backyard. She must have a large brood by now. Certainly they were all named after birds, as she had oft liked to name her baby dolls.

Did they ever wonder what had become of Jamesina Mac-Alister? The girl who would fix their dented and flat bike tires and who insisted upon driving the make-believe limousine when the pretend family cruised to the pub? Could they even imagine she had moved from her pa's tiny little house in Crieff, Scotland? That she operated a covert transportation service?

I shouldn't use the word *covert* any longer. I didn't drive criminals now. It was all on the up-and-up.

I am a *professional* driver, thank you very much.

My pa, a mechanic, had fueled my passion for all things greasy, geared and fast. Ewan MacAlister had encouraged me to tear apart my first engine when I was ten. It had literally bottomed out from an old field truck, but the joy of disassembling the network of rusted pipes and gears and desiccated grease had only been surmounted by actually reassembling the thing.

I had driven my first illegal street race at fourteen, and gained reprimands from Pa. "You'll drive your poor pa to an early grave!" he'd often lamented when I'd return home with wind-tousled hair and an exuberant replay about the race spilling from my lips.

That day I'd begun to relentlessly seek anything that put the wind in my hair.

A year following Pa's untimely death—he'd slipped on spilled beer in McNally's Pub, and the fall had taken his life—I had almost driven myself to follow him.

Twenty, alone, and without a single close relative, I had sought a new perspective. Adrenaline had been sucked out of me following Pa's death but like a junkie, I had wanted it back. I had needed it. Was it an attempt to forget my pa, the only family I had ever known? Maybe.

So, I set off for France and had bummed a job in a chop shop. I like to mod engines, but wasn't much for bodywork. And forget those fancy computer chips—I prefer working on good old-fashioned engineering, and leave the complicated stuff to specialists.

Why Paris? No reason, really, beyond the allure of the big city, and the secret racing circuit, I had heard, was huge. The illegal street races were initially difficult to find, but I'd soon scented them out like a bloodhound after a thief.

The feel of raw horsepower under my control is the ultimate. To master a metal beast and make it move as if it were an extension of my own limbs? Nothing like it in the world. But risky. A rollover during a midnight race had resulted in a broken collarbone and the gearshift through my leg. I now sport a keen scar on my left thigh, and had been thinking of tattooing over it with a flaming gearshift. Just thinking. I'm not sure I could handle the pain of the needle.

After a year of fending for myself and surviving on the race money I'd won, I had been turned on to a more controlled driving experience by a charming Italian of African-American descent. Man, but his green eyes could still make me swoon to think of them. Did I mention my love for Italian men?

Maxwell Montenelli had suggested I master my furious desire for speed by introducing me to driving as a profession. Yes, like driving for profit. That meant a bit more money in my pocket, which led to a bit more food, a bit more clothing and a bit more home.

A girl can easily be seduced by a bit more.

Professional driving put a whole new spin on what I had once thought about control. Mastery came only with subtlety, an awareness of my surroundings and a supreme connection with the machine. I had to learn to drive all over again. To dance behind the wheel. The car only did as the driver directed it. Accidents should rarely be blamed on faulty mechanics, only on stupid drivers. Max had once compared mastering a car to a computer. Information in, results out, equals performance. Put in faulty information, you get faulty performance.

I pride myself on superior performance.

I worked for Max four years, taking jobs without regard for the danger or the morality. I'd been young, and had only wanted to please Max. But after countless rounds of cleaning blood and other body parts from the backseat, I'd had enough. I tired of the criminal element Max worked with and six months ago, finally summoned the courage and told him so. Seems he'd known all along the criminal life was not for me. Max suggested I continue to drive, but for the other side. He knew of a covert rescue op that might be the thing—the Faction.

But Max had never gotten an opportunity to introduce me to the hard life. (That's what we of the criminal persuasion call living the straight and narrow—the hard life.) Two months ago—the morning following my twenty-fifth birthday—Max died in a car accident. I still suspect it was a hit by the Network. It had to be. Max was the best driver on the road. And the Network wasn't something you simply left.

If I had insisted Max spend the night celebrating my birthday, instead of allowing him to leave early for "business," might he still be alive?

That was the question I tossed over and over in my brain. He'd been antsy and wired that evening. Had I been paying attention, I might have noticed he hadn't drunk a thing. But I had found my own birthday celebration—sex with a handsome stranger—and hadn't thought about Max until I'd gotten the phone call from Fitch the following morning.

The fact I hadn't been marked as a suspect was a blessing. *La lapine* was a ghost—a quick ghost. Luck had a thing about following me. I didn't mind at all. But I'll never get cocky. My profession requires a hard edge, calm head, and in-the-moment thinking. Business is business.

But the rush had died after seeing Max lying on that cold steel morgue table. I'd felt like a little girl that day, waving goodbye to something that meant more than the world to me.

Two months later, I was now feeling the need for a bit more. Actually, it's my pocketbook that's been yawning widely of late, in need of filling. That's why I'm behind the wheel today. The first job I've taken since Max's death.

Makes me feel good to know I could help people simply by driving them away from the bad guys. It is a small repayment for the four years of illegal activity I'd happily engaged in while learning the ropes from Max.

I ran a palm over the charcoal paint curving toward the taillight. This car had belonged to Max. It's all I have left of him. Save the few photos I had snuck out from his dresser that morning I'd met Fitch to search Max's place for clues.

An airplane cut the sky in the distance. I guessed, from its downward trajectory, it headed into Charles de Gaulle. I followed the flight until it crossed over the steeple of Notre Dame and buzzed the little island of Saint-Louis. The Seine rippled with the wake.

Max had always told me to stop and see the beauty. Like the silver ripples on the Seine or the rosy blush of a sunrise. Max had been good folk. Just because he worked for the bad guys didn't mean evil ran through his veins. Born into a family that ran weapons in dozens of war-ravaged countries, Max had known nothing else and had been looking to leave the criminal element, as well. He'd once said to me, "This is all I know, but you, you can be better."

Max would send out a hooting cheer from his grave to know I had taken a step in the direction that called to me— legitimacy.

And Ewan MacAlister just might smile.

Chapter 3

Friday, 11:14 a.m.

"Location?"

One of two male passengers who had slid into the backseat relayed the correct drop-off location outside the city. The other—shorter, but dressed in the same unimaginative black business suit—remained stoic behind matching black wrap-around sunglasses. The sky was overcast. Sunglasses were *de rigueur* for my clients.

I checked the rearview mirror. The men had exited a plain brick business building nestled between a glass-fronted cheese shop and a pottery store. Understated elegance, this neighborhood, it sat across from a large cemetery shadowed by lush ash trees. The risk of gunfire was just that—a risk. And yet, the hum from the nearby freeway could mask nefarious deeds.

There didn't appear to be anyone sidling covertly down the cobbled sidewalk. No rain of bullets. Could this be an eventless pickup? How delightfully refreshing after a morning dodging bullets.

I gave a cursory glance over the suit coats of each of the men in the backseat, looking for visible weapons. I wasn't about to become complacent in my new role. Even the good guys packed heat, because there was always a bad guy willing to take whatever they had away from them. The small black case held in the hands of the one who hadn't spoken couldn't hold anything larger than a good-sized dictionary.

I smirked at my straying thoughts. I doubted either of these two even cracked open a book, let alone a dictionary.

"Let's go, *conducteur*!"

"Keep your trousers on, *messieurs*," I calmly stated.

A tilt of the rearview mirror did not reveal any detractors. No bush snipers, not even a covert agent walking an inconspicuous dog.

Then, without missing a beat, I asked, "Payment?"

I never asked until arrival. But this time …something made me prompt for it up front. Call it intuition.

A thick white envelope landed the front passenger seat. The paper conformed to a shape that matched the euro banknote. I didn't touch. But I didn't enter the Paid confirmation into the laptop either.

Another glance in the rearview verified the quiet surroundings. What did I expect, sitting outside a graveyard?

Satisfied for the moment, I shifted into gear. "We're good to go. *Messieurs*, buckle up, *s'il vous plaît*."

Even with no noticeable tails, I would not yet count my chickens. The enemy always lurked, either around the corner or as a sniper on a rooftop.

Fitch was jacked in to the Audi—I knew the way—but it didn't hurt to have backup should I gain a tail and my attention be distracted.

The road to the drop-off was a straight shot beyond *la périph* to an abandoned construction site that fed into the Marne River. What the passengers did from there was not my concern. I had merely to drop them off and drive away. Likely, they had another car—or perhaps a boat—waiting.

Twisting the silver dial on the dashboard, I adjusted the air-conditioning. It was too chilly, even with a long-sleeved blouse. Shuffling on my seat, I then stretched my left foot between shifting from third to fourth. Something distracted my focus. I felt…antsy.

I quickly dismissed the notion to turn up the tunes; I never played music with a client in the car. Besides being unprofessional, it kept me from hearing any whispered comments. My clientele was elite, but that didn't mean I let my guard down. After feeling a few surprise gun barrels to the skull, a girl eventually learns.

As I approached the freeway on-ramp, my uneasiness did not subside. The men in black were quiet. Too quiet. They didn't even talk among themselves. I thought to jostle them a little as I sped onto the on-ramp. I overtook the far right lane with a deft twist of the wheel. The passengers' heads swayed to the left.

Not a complaint.

Ah well, they were probably nervous. Though what about, I could not guess. Not a single offensive vehicle had been spotted. We were not being followed.

So, why the need for a driver?

Must be academics. Yeah, I'd driven a few legit rides in the past. Max had all sorts of connections. I have learned that sometimes the show had to go on, so long as the cash sat right beside me. Scientists, especially, loved the drama of the getaway scenario.

The freeway traffic flowed easily and I released a held breath. Why was I so uptight? Sure, I'd been out of the game for a few months, but I wasn't rusty. Just chill, Jamie. It's like riding a bike—at one hundred kilometers an hour.

I smirked at my thoughts. That'd be fun to try, riding a bike at that speed.

Twenty minutes later, I exited and took a two-lane through the suburb of St-Maurice. My passengers remained silent, their focus out the side windows. I hate passing through the suburbs, so many stops and lots of pedestrian hazards.

Soon enough, the countryside appeared. I turned onto a road that paralleled the Marne River and took us away from the clutter of traffic.

"Stop!"

Alerted by that sudden command, I eyed the men in the backseat. One of them clutched his gut and didn't look well at all. Sweat beaded his forehead. Motion sickness? Of all the bloody— Worse things had occurred, but I was so not going to let this one get sick inside. I hated cleaning duty.

I shifted down and pulled over to the side of the loose gravel road.

"Merci," the other man said. "We will take some air."

They exited, the silent one towing the black case out behind him. The tall one leaned over the graveled ditch and began to gag.

"Lovely." I closed my eyes, but shouted out the window, "Stand far away from the car, will you?" Palm caressing the stick, I prepared to shift into gear—when a familiar sound made the hairs all over my body prickle.

Gunfire? Way out here?

I remained in the car. Yes, my passengers were my priority, but so was my arse. The driver never leaves the vehicle; it's a good rule to—

Another shot sounded and I saw a brief spark flash in the rearview mirror. I swung my head outside and looked down the rear of the Audi.

The silent man still held a gun pointed at the shattered left rear taillight.

"That was not necessary! What the—?"

I went quiet as the gun found a new target. Me.

Chapter 4

"Out!" The thug with the gun opened my door and gestured with his weapon. When I balked, he pressed the barrel above my left ear, none too gently, and shoved.

"Fine." I swung out one leg, and then the other, slowly straightening to stand. I hated being forced to go against my instincts. But new instincts were kicking in that screamed, *Be careful, play along,* so I did.

Instinctively splaying my hands near my shoulders, palms facing out, I assessed both men. Both were nondescript, with receding brown hair. Neither was thin; one was a little pudgy in the jaw. Both worked out, to judge from their bulk, but not excessively, for no muscles bulged beneath the black suits. They wore long black leather coats, so *Matrix* five minutes ago. Black pants and shoes. Not polished, the shoes.

Thing Number Two had had a remarkable recovery. He hadn't even been sick. The only idiot here was me.

And I'd had such a good start today.

"Step this way." A wave of the gun prompted me to move to the left toward the back of the car.

I hate having a gun pointed at me. It had happened twice before in my notorious career. A dead stop in the middle of traffic—police or gun-toting tail close behind—usually took care of that problem. This was the first time it hadn't occurred while I was driving.

I am not stupid. I know a gun wins over no weapon at all. But I wasn't close to giving up.

The silent one leaned in to the front seat. Behind me, the boot popped open with a powerful *thunk*. My heart dropped with the same *thunk*.

Now Thing Number One casually walked around and placed the black case upon the open boot.

"Watch the paint," I warned.

He then opened the case and took out a lasso of white rope. Nothing else inside the case. He tilted it to the ground and kicked it across the dirt.

Gaping at the slide of the empty black case across gravel, I took a step back. The Audi's cool steel quarter panel melded to my thigh.

There was no package? This could not be happening.

Less then three steps behind me, the driver's door hung open. The keys were still in the ignition. I could get far with a shot-out taillight. But I wouldn't get nearly as far with a bullet hole in my head.

"What is this?" I asked. The silent one approached me, rope dangling teasingly. "Who are you? Who do you work for?"

The click of the trigger, ready for business, alerted me. The hard round barrel pressing into my skull silenced further protest.

Could I bargain with them? My life for the car? Easy getaway for them. Had they plans to abandon me and take off with the Audi? Go for it! The car was worth fifty thousand euros. Merry Christmas!

"Hands down," the one with the rope said.

"But—"

He gripped my arm and roughly spun me, locking my wrists together behind me back. I barely had a moment to gather my wits. Wits, come together! *Yeah, we're right here, but we don't like this situation any more than you do.*

A mantra Max had taught me zinged through my thoughts. *Always be prepared for the worst.* A driver had a blind spot—his or her back. That's why he should always be armed. And yet, this *greatest day* had seemed so promising that I'd foolishly left my apartment this morning without even considering a weapon.

The worst had not come for years. As a result, I had become complacent. I could throw a great left hook and also kick, scream and defend, thanks to the rough crowd I had hung around with in my teen years.

Right now, I was too surprised to consider defense.

And what would I pay for that lack of surety? Rape? Murder? Both?

"There was no package," I muttered as Number Two shoved me around the back of the car. No, not in the boot. Would they shoot it full of bullets? I dug in my heels. The gravel crunched. "Tell me what is going on!"

Male grunts seemed sufficient exchange as the man with the gun pocketed his weapon and bent to grab my ankles.

"Where are you taking me?"

I managed a kick, but the angle was off and the rubber soles of my Vans did little more than smudge the knee of his pressed pants. I began to squirm, but a thought—conserve your energy—overcame me.

"Tell me!" I protested. My last bit of confidence left with that shout, but I did get an answer.

"Back to the city. Now, shut up, *demoiselle*."

The nerve of him, to address me like a snooty waiter trolling for a tip. Back to the city? Really? Why?

I didn't care. I could work with back to the city. I relaxed my tense posture and sunk into the rough hands of my kidnappers.

Dumped in the boot, I landed on my shoulder and let out a yelp. Instinctively, I stretched out my legs to a semi-bend, but couldn't move them straight. If the backseat were down, I might stretch out completely. Could I get into the backseat from here? What good would that do me? Without a weapon, it was a ridiculous option.

The slam of the boot lid ratcheted my heartbeat to a thunderous pace. I winced and realized I'd bitten my lower lip. Blood tasted bitter on my tongue, but not as bitter as the situation. I thought I'd scream, but kept silent. And listened.

No conversation on the outside. Completely dark inside. Save for the shiny illumination of the release tag dangling above my head.

"What luck."

I rolled my shoulder across the heavy felt floor of the boot and eyed the fluorescent tag. God save the Queen. Unless the Queen's hands were bound behind her back and she couldn't reach the bloody tag. What good was a release tag if one couldn't touch it!

Relax, Jamie, my wits soothed. *They are taking you back to the city. Just wait it out until the time is right.*

The red glow of the brake lights seeped through the felt

lining. If I could kick out a taillight, I might stick out a toe and attract attention as they drove me to some undisclosed location. If they were being honest about returning to Paris, my chances rose measurably.

If they were being honest. When did I start trusting the bad guys?

They hadn't shot the boot full of holes. One thing to be thankful for. Maybe they were drawing straws to see who would do the deed. Had I been singing that this was my greatest day only hours earlier?

Poor choice of theme song.

Now I heard footsteps crunch the gravel outside.

The passenger door opened. I angled my head toward the rear seat. Muffled voices echoed from inside the car. The ignition—I hadn't switched it off—suddenly revved. The shift of gears ground horribly. Bastards. I'd get them for touching my car. Max's car. I'd never gotten a chance to say goodbye to him. This was the only piece of Max Montenelli I still had.

Without this car, I was alone in the world.

A sickening rock of movement notched up my panic mode—but just a tad. Never let them take you to crime scene two. Unless, that place is in a populated city. I closed my eyes, praying my intuition would get me out of this mess alive.

The force of movement rolled my body and my face smashed against the scratchy felt covering the taillight. "Ouch."

Now to wait. Twenty minutes would place us back in the city. Situation? Grim. New theme song? Queen's "I Want To Break Free."

Suddenly the radio began to blare. A few stations crackled as they sorted through various easy listening songs and finally landed on a raucous beat by Ministry. "Jesus Built My Hotrod." Oh, the humiliation.

The sudden notion to slip my bound hands under my feet made me smirk despite the rattle of my teeth as the vehicle peeled across loose gravel. Prepare for opportunity. Right.

With a painful squeeze of my shoulder blades, and by sliding one foot back and over my wrists and then the other, I managed it.

Hands now in front of me, I reached for the tag. Should I pull the release, the boot would fly open. The Audi had picked up speed. We'd returned to *la périph*, if my guess was right, but it was difficult to determine with the frantic music blasting my senses. If we were on the freeway, now was no time to jump out. I'd be crushed like a *pain au chocolat* on the tarmac, or worse, splattered onto the hood of a semitruck.

Was that a worse scenario than being crushed? Why did my mind even want to compare gruesome to grim?

This music was too loud! My fingers shook and I wanted to scream.

Think *pain au chocolat*, Jamie. I would live to devour another.

But before that, I'd make it hell for Things One and Two to chew with missing teeth.

"Wait until they slow down," I murmured, trying to hear my own voice. "Just be calm, Jamie."

Sooner or later, they'd have to stop for a stop-and-go light.

The urge to beat at the boot door led me to take one frantic punch. "Ouch." Pressing bruised knuckles to my mouth, I closed my eyes. Thankfully, the erratic tune came to an end and a slower seventies' anthem began to wail across my frazzled nerves.

What the hell was going on? Who were Things One and Two?

Was this how it would end?

Jamesina MacAlister had become a getaway-car driver. For years, she had driven all sorts, from thieves dashing away from the scene, to thugs transporting weapons and/or money to secret railway docks or helicopter pickups. Only when her mentor was killed did she finally step back and examine her rocket path to Hell.

I thought wistfully of those childhood friends who had likely settled into domestic bliss. Baldness be damned. I'd take domestic right now if it was handed to me in a plain white envelope.

Was this my punishment for wanting a bit more? (I hadn't *wanted* a bit more; I genuinely *needed* it.)

The car began to slow and I listened fiercely. The radio went quiet. Horns honked and the chugging exhaust of a city bus sounded nearby. We were in the city. Where didn't matter. Somewhere on the Left Bank, which could be in the university area.

The Audi slowed to a stop. Time to rock this tiny little boot.

Wasting no time, I grabbed the release tab. As the car stopped, the forward motion plunged my body backward. The boot flew open. Gripping the edge with bound hands, I stretched one leg up and over, and landed the tarmac in a crouch.

A Renault waited in line behind the Audi. The driver rolled down his window and shouted to me, "Mademoiselle, you are kidnapped?"

Close, but not on my watch. I waved at him to reassure, but my bound hands only made the move a desperate plea.

I saw the worried driver frantically punch numbers into his cell phone. The police would soon be on their way. Not my scene, even if I had turned over the leaf just this morning. Obviously I hadn't flipped the bloody thing over far enough.

I dodged around the back of the car and stopped. Thing Two exploded from the passenger's side. His left arm swept out, but there was no gun. He wasn't completely out of the car. I had two seconds…

Spinning on one foot to swing around my leg, I kicked high, connecting the rubber sole of my shoe to the side of the thug's jaw. I landed solidly, assuming a defensive stance with fists before me in a double—yet bound—threat.

Thing Two took the kick with a snap of his head and his arms flailing out. He wasn't down—but I wasn't finished. Hands still bound, I couldn't punch, but I could stomp. I crushed the arch of his left foot. An elbow deflected his left fist, but I felt the pins and needles in an electric burst. Twisting at the waist, I lunged around with another elbow, aiming for his solar plexus.

Taking a hit to the ribs, I chuffed out breath, but used the backward motion to bring up my foot to ratchet between his legs. I delivered a superb groin shot. Yes! The judges award *la lapine* a perfect ten for her performance.

Thing Two went down.

The driver leaned across the passenger seat and introduced a gun to the performance.

"I'm out of here."

I swerved around the open car door and dashed behind a moving van parked at the curb. I managed a glance at the Audi. The driver had begun to turn around in the intersection, door open, causing a literal jam of four vehicles. Thing Two— *Monsieur I'm Not Really Sick*—staggered to his knees, clutching his groin. I should have laid him out, but I had been going for speed and escape.

Kicking a small moving box out of my way, I decided to take a chance, and ran through the yard where the packed boxes were being dispatched. The hornbeam shrubs were high, which disguised my path, but likely not for long.

Avoiding a moving man clad in white jumper and wielding boxes that towered higher than his head, I skipped up the front steps and dashed through the empty house. The smell of disinfectant was overpowering. Someone must have owned pets. Someone protested in what sounded like Arabic—but I don't speak the language, so it's a guess. Sunlight at the far end of an empty kitchen signaled the back door.

Something about this job stank of my past. The criminal element had infested my newly sanitized domain. I knew the feeling, the stench of wrong. I had had an initial moment of unease when picking up the men.

Not legit, kept ringing in my brain.

Why hadn't I trusted my gut?

Slapping the back screen door with both palms, I forced the steel-framed door outside. I flew down the back steps, dodging the cement fountain dried to a green crust around the base of a gaggle of naked cherubs. The backyard was enclosed by more of the high hornbeam shrubbery. Normally, I can appreciate a nicely trimmed shrub, but…

Risking it, I ran straight for the bushes. Bound hands blocking my face and arms, my legs fought against the pull of the resilient and scratchy branches. I dragged my feet through closely spaced trunks. Glossy leaves slapped my face, fruitlessly attempting to hold me back. This was so grim!

Emerging on the other side in a faltering walk-run, I got my balance back. I huffed and paused, glancing to the wall of shrubbery. "*Merci*, there were no thorns."

A quick study determined I'd not have time to wrestle with the rope about my wrists. Grease blackened it in places, making the rope grip tightly.

The back door slapped against the outer wall of the emptied house. Things One and Two were on my scent.

Time to kick it into high gear.

to face losing any of these people. Though I was getting myself deeper into trouble. I decided to hole up until I caught my breath and could think through all of this safely.

Chapter 5

Twenty minutes must have passed before I slowed my full-out-gasping-for-breath pace and reduced my strides to a walk. I was in the 14th *arrondissement*. My home was close by. I lived in the relative quiet shadows of the *cimetière* du Montparnasse.

I know, what's with the cemeteries today? Was it some strange sort of foreshadowing for my life? I didn't believe in woo-woo stuff, so I trudged onward, putting that ridiculous thought out of my head.

No sight or sound of either Things One and Two, or Max's Audi, for ten minutes. I could be in the clear.

Could be.

But I wasn't willing to risk it. So I turned a sharp right, zigzagging as I had been, taking the alley behind a row of small antique shops. No straight lines, and keep away from the main streets. Just like driving.

Huffing from exhaustion—I was not in such good shape

that a three-kilometer dash didn't tax me—I was encouraged only slightly that home was close.

Striding out to the sidewalk before a flower shop (*de rigueur* in this neighborhood. Cemetery. Get it?), I followed my body's need to wilt and bent at the waist, catching my palms on my knees.

Whew! What a workout. The thing about the French was, they didn't do gyms or diets. They didn't need to; they had that whole live-pleasurably-die-right thing down pat. So I had been ignoring my workouts for years. I was trim and ate like a horse, but this body now screamed for a nap.

There are people walking by on the sidewalk, staring at your bound hands.

Right.

Scampering across the cobbled sidewalk, I shuffled down the block toward my building beneath the blessed shade of ancient lime trees. Sunlight speckled the sidewalk here and there. I checked my perimeter. No charcoal Audis. No henchmen on foot.

Dodging to the right, I insinuated myself onto the steps of my building. Emery, the concierge, buzzed me in without comment or even a look—so I saved the smile. He always had his nose buried in the latest Stephen King novel. Oddly, he looked very much like the horror writer with his thick brows and evil yet goofy grin.

Thankful the lobby was empty, I trundled across the marble tiles and into the elevator. Pushing the five button for my floor, I then collapsed into a corner.

Never had the cool slate tiles of my apartment felt so welcoming, so homey and warm. I tread through the living room, toeing aside one of dozens of velvet pillows I kept piled in the middle of the floor and went straight on into the cool violet shadows of my bedroom. The blinds were drawn, the pale lavender curtains pulled, allowing a soft haze of light to touch the bed, and shading everything in tints of purple.

I eyed the high tester bed. Heaped with bead-embroidered blankets and velvet comforters and sequined pillows in green and violet, it offered a nest of softness. Collapse beckoned, but a hot shower nagged.

Using my teeth, I picked at the soft white rope that had loosened only slightly about my wrists. Gnawing at the dirty knot, the taste of grease didn't bother me so much as the situation I'd allowed myself to be put in. It took a few minutes, but after half a dozen swear words, the rope slipped off.

I rubbed at my sore wrists. "Bloody…unfashionable thugs!"

That was about all the protest I could muster. It had been my fault that I'd allowed myself to land in the situation in the first place. But I still felt it had been a wise choice not fighting getting into the boot of the Audi initially. Whoever had wanted me might not have cared if I was kicking and screaming, or quiet and dead.

Odd, though, that they'd gone through the motions of me driving them out of the city. Yes, but it had worked, hadn't it?

I stripped on the way to the shower, leaving a trail of wrinkled clothing. A shiny chrome-plated tire rim from a Hummer 2, standing between the toilet and the tub, served as a makeshift stool and clothes catchall.

Oh, blessed relief. While my body surrendered to the rush of a hot shower stream, my mind would not allow one moment of complacency.

The pickup had been compromised. Before or after the initial setup? Before. Definitely preplanned, with the rope in the case.

Who the hell were Thing One and Thing Two of the un-imaginative black suits?

Fitch would get to the bottom of it. I'd call her soon as I dried off.

Hell, I hadn't even gotten paid. The white envelope was still in the Audi.

Paid for what? My own kidnapping? There likely had been blank strips of paper in the envelope.

And now I was short one car. Max had loved that car. Praise the girl goddess of gears I still had my BMW.

No time to linger in the shower. I had a mystery to solve.

I towel-dried and went naked into the bedroom. Digging my toes into the ultraplush purple carpet bedside, I glanced to the googly-eyed kitty clock on the night table. I had modded the thing by attaching inch-long false eyelashes and a carbon piston ring that served as a crown.

"One o'clock," I murmured. Eight hours had passed since I'd left this morning. And in that time I'd performed my first legit pickup and had gotten kidnapped. And lost fifteen thousand euros.

Wait, make that twenty thousand euros! The money from this morning's pickup was still in the glove box, and that five thousand was likely real. "Buggers."

I cursed because I really did need the cash. Two months of not working had eaten away my finances, save for a small emergency stash. A bit more was required for my survival.

Riding a shiver that raced from my neck to my extremities, I noted it was not a chill, but more of an inner, something-is-not-right shiver. That same feeling had tapped my skull immediately after the cemetery pickup had climbed into my backseat.

"I've got to stop ignoring my intuition." Though I hadn't ignored the need to ask for payment up front. Hmm...

I was off my game. And what did I expect after a dry spell?

Shrugging a hand through my tousle of wet wavy hair, I paced the plush rug. A scan of the bedside table tripped over a dog-eared erotica novel—I like my reads hot—retro black phone, lamp embellished with more dangling beads than a Cher costume—so I had a crafty streak; sue me—and my passport sticking out of the drawer.

This intuition I wasn't about to ignore. "Right. I'll need my passport, and gather some cash."

I had no closet. I'd purchased a designer's wheeled dress rack at an open market and it held everything I owned on cedar hangers. The pink-striped slip dress was too cheerful. Not right for investigation mode. A black linen suit slinked over one of my sore wrists. Not right, either.

A hip-clinging plaid skirt and a simple violet blouse would serve. I slipped them on and buttoned up the blouse, which stopped just above the skirt and displayed a slice of toned belly. Ease of movement, and plucky. I needed plucky right now.

Hell, I needed answers.

Snatching up a kick-ass pair of scuffed Doc Martens, I paced to a narrow red metal tool case that stood five feet high and served as my armoire. Inside one of the drawers, a pink-and-black *Madame's* powder tin is where I kept my stash. The apartment building's safe was not a consideration. Anything I could pick, I certainly didn't trust. I was no expert lock picker; it was a simple skill Max had taught me. Came in handy when I once used to jack cars for getaway. I ran a much classier outfit now. The thought of grand theft auto, well, it couldn't be justified.

Drawing out a stack of banknotes I folded them and slipped the wad in the small front coin pocket of my skirt.

Boots in hand, I strode into the living room and bending

over the leaf-green chaise longue, I collapsed onto my stomach, cheek hitting the velvet like a rock.

"Suck it up," I commanded my aching muscles.

Trolling the floor, my fingers pushed aside scatters of lug nuts and an assortment of bolts, from head bolts, to manifold bolts, to rod bolts. Finally, I latched onto the phone I'd covered with crystals last fall. (Be it a car part, or tiny rhinestones, I rocked when it came to creating beauty out of junk.) I'd lost a cell phone in the Audi. If the thugs were curious, they might give Fitch a call, but that was the only number I kept stored in that phone. Too dangerous to store all my contacts in my public "office."

Speed dialing number one, I listened as the phone rang once, twice—pickup. Fitch was in? Hmm…her afternoons were usually spent out on deck, tending her plants.

"Fitch. Speak—Jamie?"

Fitch had caller ID. But the surprise in her voice didn't immediately register with me.

"Fitch, something is wrong."

"You're alive! I mean…you're alive?"

What?

That rise in her voice—Fitch was *surprised* I was alive. Then she'd quickly covered with the same words, but as a question.

Sunday bloody Sunday.

I clicked off the phone and stomped my boots onto the floor, catching my forehead in my hands. "What the bloody—?"

Had Fitch ratted me to someone? Who? And why? Is that why I'd just run across Paris with bound hands and fleeing bullets?

Springing up from the chaise longue, I paced a portion of

floor not covered by cushy pillows or car parts. The phone rang. I cast the sparkling crystal device an evil glare. No need to check caller ID. It would be Fitch.

We had been straight with each other for years. I knew Kennedy Fitch, and could read her face like a book. Not that I saw her face all too often, but her voice was like a face. She always answered her calls with a silly mother-like opening, "How y'all doing, dearie?"

That is, when she knew I was calling.

You're alive? Fitch had been surprised to hear from me, no doubt about it.

The phone quit ringing. I stared at it, expecting it to start up again. If Fitch had sold me out, I needed to get the hell out of Dodge.

Dashing to the bedroom, I grabbed a small black canvas duffel bag that I used as a purse, stuffed more cash inside—heck, all of it—my passport, an extra T-shirt, blue jeans…hell, I shoved in the entire contents on top of the tool chest, which included gum, lipstick, iPod, some snapshots, and assorted clips and rubber binders. I tossed in my handy multitool that featured a dozen tools, plus a can opener—never leave home without it. And…

I turned and eyed the bed. Plunging my hand under the mattress produced a 10mm Glock automatic. The only gun I owned. I checked the magazine; ten rounds. I emptied it into my palm and tossed the bullets into an inside pocket in the duffel. The gun was huge, and not easy to conceal under clothing. But if faced with the barrel of a gun, I have no problem evening up the playing field. I should have had it earlier, but like I said, I'd begun driving the straight and narrow. I hadn't anticipated problems with clients.

Boy, was I wrong.

Grabbing my sunglasses dangling from the frame of my bed and hooking the canvas duffel over my shoulder, I ran from the apartment.

Chapter 6

An open-air café stood across from my apartment building, right next to yet another flower shop. I nodded to Emery as I exited and slid the sunglasses over my ears. The lenses were tinted violet and made the world a bit easier to handle.

My iPod was hooked at my hip, and the earplugs hung about my neck. I love music, but rarely listened to it when I was not driving. (Which was only about thirty percent of the time.) But I did use the device to store addresses and phone numbers, and as a backup hard drive—I kept important information from my laptop on it. It was very close to being my lifeline, the little white plastic music box, but I would never allow myself to depend on technology to such an extreme, and so had backups should I ever lose the nifty device.

I walked across the street, my strides long, and kept right on walking past the café. I knew that I should stick around and see who might come snooping, but the risks were too great. I hadn't a clue who might be on my tail. Likely, they would know me before I could pick them out. Unless, of course, they subscribed to *Thug Wear Daily*; then it would be easy.

Another option reared up in my thoughts and intrigued me the way a bungee jump from a skyscraper did. I had never bungee jumped, but the idea of free falling thrilled me. So it was an easy option to take.

Club DV8 was a good fifteen minutes from here—by car. I gave myself an hour on foot. Hell, what was I thinking?

Twisting at the waist, I spied a Vespa puttering casually down the street. Commandeered by a distinguished-looking gent in business suit and eye goggles, he couldn't be doing more than nine or ten kilometers an hour.

I stepped onto the street, dead center, and assumed the position, one hand to my hip, the other pressed to my lips to issue a clear and deafening whistle. The fact that the driver pulled to an idling stop next to me, his eyes glued to my long bare legs, made me smile.

"Can you give me a ride to rue du faubourg St. Jacques?"

"*Oui, demoiselle.*" He slid forward. The shiny white Vespa was a two-seater.

I slid a leg across the motorbike, in front of the man, forcing him to shuffle backward. He released the handlebars with a questioning chuff of breath, but that was all the argument he managed before I revved the bike and we took off at mach speed.

All right, so it was a little speedier than a baby's crawl, but it was quicker than walking. Sure, I could jack a car, but I didn't do that kind of stuff anymore—the hazards, like jail time, overruled the thrill.

I let the man encircle my waist, because there wasn't any

other way to secure a hold. And he wasn't being rude, just resting his palms on my hips. He smelled great, like a fresh shower and just a hint of talcum powder.

The city buzzed about me as we chugged along the cobblestoned streets. White-aproned wait staff bustled about the sidewalk cafés, laying out pristine white tablecloths and setting up the *prix fixe* menus for the afternoon.

Even at a distance I could pick out the sounds of river tugboats tooting to warn of their arrival or departure. I liked to watch the coal tugs unload. Surprising that in this age of speed and technology, there were just some things that proved to be a better bet, like tugboats. Let me behind the wheel of one of those slugs and there'd be a river disaster just waiting to happen. There were wake laws on the Seine, but I'm afraid I'd have to break them.

Yes, you can take the girl out from behind the wheel, but you can never kill the need for speed.

Though it was afternoon, I knew Dove would be in. He lived at DV8. He *was* the club. Dove knew everything and anything about whatever it was that went on, up or down in the city of Paris. He was friend to no man, enemy to none. You could buy him with a drink, and he'd sell you for the bottle. But his accuracy was impeccable.

I'd met Dove years ago, introduced by Max during an all-night rave to celebrate Dove's twentieth birthday. Yep, he was a young guy. Dove had flirted and kissed my chin, leaving behind sticky remnants of Cristal, but he'd kept it to that. I liked him as much as I knew he was not to be trusted.

The club was on the backside of a block that housed trendy university bookstores facing the riverside. DV8 could be picked out among the line of brick warehouses only by the back door, painted silver and with the name of the club scratched into the paint to reveal the red base coat.

Arriving at the club, I jumped off the Vespa, and then leaned in to bracket the man's face with my hands. I kissed both his stubble-roughened cheeks, then kissed my fingertips and pressed that coy little morsel to his mouth.

I think he blushed, but he was wearing what looked like World War II goggles that covered most of his face.

"*Au revoir, mon amie!*" he called as the Vespa scooted away.

I got a kick out of older men. No posturing or machismo required. They were what they had become, and more power to them if they had aged with grace, humor and an appreciation for a desperate woman.

I tried the entrance at the back of the club. Open. But not easy. I wasn't two paces inside when the bouncer appeared from a fluorescent-lit room to the left. His entire frame fit into the hall like a missing puzzle piece.

"Hey," I said. Stupid.

I hooked a thumb at my hip, tapped a boot toe to the technobeat, and, despite the funky rhythm of the French remake of "Ballroom Blitz" pleading for me to dance, tried to breathe normally. I managed a calm, yet stylishly aloof, demeanor. "Here to see Dove."

"Name?"

"*La lapine.*"

Dove would know the name.

The beat attached to my veins and I couldn't resist; I started dancing. Just a little rhythmic shrug of my right shoulder. Then a bounce on my heels. My hips swayed without even asking. If I wasn't driving, I was usually dancing.

The bouncer gave me a slow once-over, his dark eyes drifting from my violet blouse that revealed a coy innie belly button, down the short length of my plaid skirt. Yeah, I'd expected as much. He could look all he liked, but touch? Only if he thought finger splints were fashionable.

Finally he nodded. *"Attendez ici."* Which meant, wait here.

I didn't have to wait more than one chorus of the song when *le He-man* returned, and with a gesture of a hammy hand, led me down the dark hallway. Dime-sized plastic glitter disks hooked to the walls fluttered as I walked by and stepped into an even darker room. Only when I crossed over to the window did the neon lights from the bar shine inside the office and illuminate the far side.

A man sat cross-legged upon a round red velvet couch the size of a bed. A red- and silver-striped shirt hugged his thin torso, unbuttoned messily, and likely misbuttoned on purpose. Wide cuffs flopped upon his equally wide hands, but thin, cigarette fingers tapped to the frantic call to blitz in *la salle de bal.*

Dove was neither heterosexual, homosexual, bisexual or even metrosexual. The man, as Max had once proclaimed, was omnisexual. At the time, I hadn't asked for clarification, but my mind took me to different scenarios featuring rooms filled with gasping and moaning naked people of all sexes, ages and sizes. And then, the inevitable farm animal sauntered through the image.

I forced my thoughts back to the man on the couch, sans four-legged sex partners. I wasn't about to go there. I could not conceive going there.

I would *not* go there.

"La lapine, it has been a time," Dove said in a flirty whisper. He always spoke in whispers, a bit of the drag queen enunciating his actions. His movements lithe and fluid, he bounced up to his knees and leveled his gaze with mine. "Two years?"

"About that."

"Pity about Max."

"Yes."

Had he and Max…? Maybe. I'd always assumed Max was hetero, but he had been very chummy with Dove on the few occasions we had visited him together.

"Reports say Max was found crushed between the steering wheel and the seat back. Interesting you disappeared immediately following the hit."

My jaw dropped open. This was the first time I'd ever heard the word *hit* spoken regarding Max's death. I'd suspected as much, but no one had alluded to it, especially not the police. And never before had anyone insinuated *I* might be involved in Max Montenelli's murder.

"Don't look so ghosty, girl. I know you're not the bloodthirsty type." Dove smiled like a sated vampire. "Max was good to you. But a sweet little thing like you can't be a runner forever. So, to what do I owe the pleasure?"

"I need some information."

"Who doesn't?" A flick of his hand and a woman, whom I had not noticed lingering in the shadows near a neon-pink floor lamp, appeared with a bottle of Grey Goose. Dove took a swallow of the vodka and offered it to me. "What are you offering for the desired information?"

"Cash." I knew Dove's currency.

"Cash is always good."

Initially thinking to refuse the alcohol, a sudden urge struck me and I reached for the bottle and swung back a healthy swallow. The chilled liquor burned all the way to my belly, but it felt bloody good after a morning of forced calisthenics.

"Cash," Dove repeated. "But maybe you'll join me and

give us a kiss?" He patted the velvet couch and leaned back, stretching out his long, thin legs wrapped tightly in black leather. He taunted with a sexy pout, like a sweet placed upon a velvet cushion.

The vodka dizzied my brain but calmed my apprehensions. A few more drinks and if I sat down, I'd never get up. And man, but Dove would look keener than a movie idol to this lass who had gone without sex for months.

"Sorry, Dove." I handed him the bottle. "I'm in a bit of a hurry."

He pouted. Had I thrown away my only chance at information?

"I hear you're on your own now. I don't think a pretty little girl like yourself should be telling anyone what to do."

"I'm not telling you anything, Dove." Not until he spilled first. "You know I respect you. I've just…hit a bit of a wall."

"Uh-huh. Walls hurt." He patted the couch again, a subtle plead. "I hear you've gone legit."

All right, so I'd play up to him. I slid onto the couch, propping on one elbow and leaned into his vodka- and bergamot-scented air. "Anything wrong with running with the good guys?"

"It is if your path scampers across the wrong good guy."

Wrong good guy? "What do you mean by that?"

"It's just something to slosh around in your mind, pretty." He blew at a bit of my hair, sending it in a wispy flag across my cheek. The contact startled me. Sent a wanting flush straight to my groin.

"Listen, Dove, I need to know if you've heard anything about—" I trailed a finger along a red stripe slinking up his silk sleeve "—me."

He quirked an interested brow. His mouth, while thin, moved like a snake into and out of a grin.

I smoothed a hand back through my tangle of hair. Yes, tangled. Which was the very reason I avoided turning and facing the opposite wall, lined with mirrors. Cripes, I must look a mess. I sat up, quickly losing the urge to seduce.

Standing, I gripped the air in frustration. "I've almost been kidnapped."

"Almost?" Dove let out a shriek of laughter. "That is too splendid, bunny darling. Almost kidnapped! Now that you mention it, you are looking a bit…tousled."

Tousled. If only. More like a harried rabbit. *La lapine dépravée.*

"You really should see about a proper haircut, and a bit of blush would do a world of good."

Makeup and couture was so not my thing. Even the tube of lipstick I'd shoved into my bag was fake. Didn't the chunky boots give away my tomboy charm?

"The clothing is fine," he continued his review of my pitiful state, "but ditch those hideous army boots. You've such a marvelous body, woman. So flirty and tight—"

"Dove." Said tight body twisted toward him, inexplicably seeking the erotic mojo the compliments gave me, while I battled to keep to the plan. "Tell me what you can. You know everything."

"Well, yes, that is true." He tapped his pouty lips with a manicured fingernail and smoldering brown eyes tried to read my gaze. "But I haven't heard anything about you, my precious little bunny rabbit."

I hoped he could read my displeasure in the dim light.

"Seriously," he offered. Standing, he strode past me, brushing my shoulder with the lightest of touches. Like a cat, slinking along, he moved stealthily. Stopping suddenly, he leaned over my shoulder and murmured, "Although, a few phone calls might change that."

Good boy, Dove.

I dug into my skirt pocket and handed the folded cash over my shoulder. Not my entire emergency savings, but close. Dove leaned forward, not touching the money. His wince notched down my hopes.

"I've more," I offered, but hadn't wanted to make such a bold move. Or spend quite so much.

"You'll have to find more, darling, because those few bills won't even line my pussy's litter box." He glanced to the woman who'd resumed her post in the corner. "Meow, precious."

"Will you make some calls right now?"

"As you dig for gold, darling. Go on, dig, dig."

Stretching in a slow-motion glide, he again landed the couch with such élan I almost wanted to hold up a card with *10* written on it. Dove picked up the white phone at his side and, arranging his long-thin-duke body across the velvet, began to make calls.

Dove's theme song? The Killers' "Somebody Told Me".

I wandered to the window and used the flashing strobe light from the bar to sort out the bills as Cheap Trick began to want me to want them. A couple hundred-euro banknotes should keep him happy and leave me enough for food and petrol—life's only two necessities.

Oh, to be liquid again. Max had taken care of a good chunk of my money, and, following his death, it remained a mystery where he'd stashed it all. It was that *bit more* I needed merely to survive.

Survive.

This was on-the-run thinking. The realization hit me so hard that I winced.

I was on the run.

The notion was so new to me. Sure, my very job was running away from the bad guys. But it wasn't as if the bad guys had wanted me, only my passengers.

I didn't like feeling out of control. This scrambling for a single breath. I needed to get back behind the wheel, to breathe and relax. Behind the wheel, confidence reigned; I ruled the world. Outside of a vehicle? I was a bipedal mess.

Dove called two people, making vague leads, and didn't use my real name. *La lapine* was the only name any would know me by. I was the only freelance driver in the city, that I knew of. All other drivers were attached to underground connections and big-name Mafia.

Max had felt it important I remained free, and yet I knew I was attached to a larger organization that I'd never met or learned too much about—the Network. They were the top name on my list of suspects in Max's murder. They hadn't contacted me following Max's death, so I assumed I was out of their fold. Yet I believed the only real way out was the way Max had gone. So I'd keep an eye out over my shoulder.

After the third call, Dove hung up. Stretching his leather-clad legs across the red velvet and spreading his arms the diameter, he eyed me with a predatory smile.

"So?"

"Cash?"

I handed the stack over to him. He didn't count it, merely flopped it near his ear. "Sounds like desperation to me, honey sweet."

"It is," I wasn't afraid to admit. Truth tended to attract more bees than sticky lies.

He nodded and leaned forward, elbows to his knees. "There is a mark on you, but nothing lethal."

"What?" I choked. Okay, so it wasn't as if that announcement should have been a surprise after a ride in the boot of my car—but it was. Could it be what I've feared? The Network had finally decided to take out Max's girl?

"You...have a name?"

"You ever hear of Princess el Sangreito?"

Sounded like a brand of Spanish tequila. "What about her?"

"Hmmph." Dove flicked away a nuisance hair from his cheek. "Seems you fucked someone with your most recent pickup."

"But that was just—"

"This morning. Word travels fast, sweetie."

So it wasn't about Max. "Not lethal?"

"Right. Cross out *dead* on the Wanted Dead or Alive poster."

A sickening chill tightened my muscles. I swallowed back a shout, then calmly asked, "Who ordered it?"

"Can't say."

I leaned over Dove's prone figure. "Can't say or won't say?"

"Probably could...but won't. You know my position, bunny darling."

"I know." Friend to none. Unless the cash flowed much more freely than I was willing to allow it.

I sighed and stood.

Shrugging both palms over my scalp, I allowed the information to sink in. Someone wanted me not dead, but in hand? Because of the pickup this morning. I'd fucked someone? Not intentionally. Who? A princess? I suspected Dove knew that someone's name.

When the Faction called, they never gave details, nor did

I press for them. That was Fitch's job. The less information I had, the better. I was just the driver.

Who had the woman in pink been? And—this might be the important part—who had the Faction taken her from? That had to be it. Was it the woman's family? Was she connected to dirty dealings? Underground figureheads? Mafia?

Things were getting grimmer by the moment. But a silver lining did exist. At least I wasn't wanted dead.

"Okay." I stepped backward toward the door. Flashes of stark disco light danced across Dove's cigarette body. "I've got the answer I wanted. Thank you, Dove. Always a pleasure."

"You know it was all *my* pleasure, darling. Do take care!"

I exited the office, closing the door behind me. Take care?

I stood, breathing deeply, trying to get my bearings. The bouncer loomed across the hall from me, arms crossed over his chest. How could he do that, cross those short muscle-bound arms over such an expansive bit of pecs?

Fingering the doorknob behind my back, I offered *le He-man* a sheepish grin.

Dove knew. *Friend to all, enemy to none.* Which meant—

I opened the door and stuck my head inside the office. Light from the dance floored jittered in yellow flashes across the red couch. As I suspected, Dove held the phone to his ear, his finger poised mid-dial.

"Give me five minutes, please, Dove. Just a head start, okay?"

He set the receiver back in the cradle and raised his arms over and behind his head. "Sure, darling. You deserve it. Run your tail off, bunny rabbit."

And so I did.

I hit the street running. My destination? The underground garage in the 13th *arrondisement*, just down the street from the parc de Choisy. I needed wheels, fast ones, and a connection to Fitch.

The streets were packed with tourist traffic as I rounded the corner and passed a bookstore that had set out what seemed like half its inventory on sidewalk shelves. I hated August—the worst month for driving, all the natives fled for the south of France, while tourists set upon the city like a plague of locusts.

Shoving between a pair of chatty women discussing Proust, I walked swiftly down the sidewalk, taking in the peripherals as I did.

Probing the duffel slung over my shoulder, I extracted my violet sunglasses to shield me from the brilliant sun.

It didn't take a rocket scientist to pick out the red Mégane that clipped my path at a sure pace, one of those nice new jobbies with the glass moon roof that folded down back into the boot. Sweet car.

Grim situation.

Two dark suits sat in the front of the car. Standard thug couture.

I had to hand it to the bad guys—it did make my life a bit easier being able to pick out the danger so easily.

But could I outrun them?

Chapter 7

I used to lay awake at night, staring up at the beamed ceiling, wondering what Pa had meant when he'd called the mother I'd never really known a wanderlust. Always running away, he'd comment in a quiet voice not necessarily meant for me to hear, sort of dreamy or maybe even lost.

I did retain one distinct vision of her. A tall, slender woman standing outside in the yard, hand skimming the tail fin of a fifties' model Nash Metropolitan. With a scarf tied around her head to tame her curly black hair and long fingers tracing the chrome, she looked like a model who advertised washing machines on the television. She waved to me. Diamonds about her wrist glinted in the sunlight. I marveled. And then she slid behind the wheel and drove out of my life. Never again to be seen, save in memory and nightmares.

I'd never seen my glamorous mother physically run, but now, as I pumped my arms and tried to give the tail the slip,

I thought of that nameless woman who I never had opportunity to know. I must have been four or five that day the Nash rolled out of the yard. She'd driven away from me—run from my wanting heart.

Jayne, that had been her name, with the extra *y*. Like Jayne Mansfield, Pa had once said. I hadn't known Jayne Mansfield at the time, but now, yes, I think like Jayne Mansfield, for her memory was darkly glamorous.

Unfortunately, my thoughts didn't lend to me paying attention, and by the time I realized I was running west, away from the garage where I could snatch my BMW, it was too late to turn back.

The Mégane squealed around a corner. Then—luck, I love you—it oversteered and missed the intersection, instead sliding noisily into the wicker tables and chairs of a café. Petrol scented the air and screams punctuated the chaos.

I dashed down the street and didn't stop until I'd reached the tree-lined walk that fronted the Seine. I decided to forgo the garage and my car for the moment. It wasn't due to be picked up for days and I was troubled about the phone call with Fitch. It was time to look into the matter. And where would answers most likely be found? Fitch's place.

The cyber goddess's place was but a few blocks off. Wherever a person could see the river, they would eventually find Fitch. Usually she moored the barge in the shadow of the Eiffel Tower, but on occasion she'd move north a mile or so.

The bells in Notre Dame struck four o'clock. Tourist traffic and the booming megaphones from the *bateaux mouche* bussing along on the Seine busied the late afternoon with a sensory overload. In the summer months, the river was colored green from algae. Not conducive to a refreshing swim. I'd keep these land legs behind the wheel where they belonged.

I found Fitch's barge moored near the pont de la Concorde. Half the deck was walled with an iron frame and thin glass to create a Victorian terrarium. Fitch liked plants, and plants liked her. If I so much as glanced at a living green object, it wilted. Which probably goes a long way in explaining why I'd been banned from the greenhouse. I didn't even touch! The flower just…broke, somehow. At least, that's the way I recall it.

Crossing the river, I found a bench along the quai des Tulieries and waited. Behind me, the fabulous royal gardens buzzed with tourist overflow. I had no plan to chat with Fitch right now. My intentions were more devious.

There were lights visible in the main living quarter on her barge, so I dug out a stick of peppermint gum from my duffel, popped it into my mouth and began the wait.

A cavalcade of Segways motored past me, a small tour group of six. The futuristic two-wheeled human transporters always gave me a giggle. Just walk, will you?

About forty-five minutes later, the lights in Fitch's barge blinked out. I squished down on the bench until my eyes were level with the top of the iron railing that bordered the river.

Skipping across the dock connected to shore, Fitch's spiky red hair beat at the air with as much attitude as was packed into the petite senior. The plant-loving hacker took the sidewalk paralleling the river in a full-speed power walk. She kept in shape, and I'd once noted her body looked ten years younger than it should.

Allowing a full five minutes to elapse, I then, assuming a natural air, strode across the street and took the steps down to the riverfront as if I lived there and had every intention of simply walking onto the barge. The city was alive, the bridge peopled with tourists and residents blended in so seamlessly that no one even noticed me.

All business, I palmed the foreign shape in the outer pocket of my duffel bag. The Glock. Just in case. I'd done enough running for a good while. From here on out, I was in defense mode.

Stepping onto the barge deck, I was always startled not to feel it rock like a moored boat. Silly me. I liked to drive, but on solid ground, thank you very much. I'd never developed sea legs, which is why I planned to stay on the continent a while longer. I'd taken the Chunnel from England to France, but to even think back about riding *beneath* all that water…?

I surveyed the glass walls of the terrarium. Spotless. Fitch must spend hours washing the ten-foot-high paned windows. Inside, green shadows stalked along the glass and reached for the ceiling. Succulents were Fitch's passion. Not cactuses, as she'd once corrected me, succulents; big difference. Sure, if she said so. They were all squat, green and looking like something you could only find in a desert.

Drawing out a small leather case from my canvas bag, I selected two lock-picking tools. I rarely used them—and they weren't strong enough to work an automobile door lock—but one never knew when they might come in handy.

Bending before the door to the main living quarters, I again scanned the area. A speedboat zoomed past, loud music blaring and scantily clad women shimmying their hips for the rich young Frenchmen who ogled them. Waiting until the racket sailed by, I then listened for a moment. No movement or sounds behind the door, so I slipped in the pick tools and began to work my magic.

Maybe not so much magic. A bit of luck was always welcome. Twisting the torque bar, I mined for the inner pins of the lock. Two pins gave easily, slipping up to sheer level, but the third proved more elusive. An overhead security light blinked, drawing unease to the surface. It was broad daylight. No need to worry. I piston-chewed my gum, which always ratcheted up my confidence.

I shouldn't risk so much time at a pick. "Yes," I whispered, as the final pin slipped up into place.

Still kneeling, I twisted the knob and pushed the door inside. Peering into the cool shadows, I first surveyed the doorframe, looking for laser sensors, anything out of the ordinary. Fitch, of all people, would secure her place like the Louvre. Not because she needed to, but simply because she could.

The door swung for a while before hitting a table. The impact loosened some DVDs and sent them falling. I lunged inside and caught a handful of black plastic cases before they hit the floor—thus proving the lack of a set security system. Laying on my back, and using the ambient green light from all the computer hardware, I squinted at the titles—Martha Stewart reruns, all of them.

"Oh, Fitch, you need a place in the country where you can grow fields of flowers." I smiled as Adam Ant's tune "A Place In The Country" fixed itself in my brain as Fitch's theme song.

I reached and closed the door, then, remaining in place, scanned the rest of the small room for alarm devices. Thing is, the room was so heaped with junk that an alarm, if set to scan or trip, would hardly serve its purpose because it was most likely blocked. Confident the room wasn't hot, I drew a small flashlight from my duffel and began to search.

"And what do I need to find?" I murmured as I navigated a pile of tangled electrical cords.

I tried to stand, but my boot toe hooked under a white cord.

I toppled, yet caught myself from splaying out like a fool by slapping a palm to the edge of a desk.

How did the woman get around? Who would have thought such a snappy, organically creative mind could be such a slob. This place hadn't been a disaster when last I'd visited, which had been a few years. Unless, she'd had unwelcome visitors who had trashed the place?

Didn't figure. Fitch would never have left it like this.

Maybe.

Hell, I didn't know the woman as well as I should. Everyone changed. (Or at least, tried to.) This may just be normal to Fitch.

I glanced over a literal Star Central Command of computer equipment. Fitch kept everything on her computer. When she traced a call, it was all done through the computer.

"She must keep records of all calls."

Dancing my fingers over the bamboo spikes of an aromatic oil air freshener released a pungent wave of lemon and mint. I drew in a breath and nodded. I was doing this—breaking into and entering the house of a woman I had, until now, trusted. I was stingy when it came to trusting women, not sure why— oh hell, you know why. The only woman I'd ever trusted had driven away from me.

Wanderlust. What a foul word.

I made my way over to the desk of tiny blinking red and green lights. The entire desk was set up with monitors and hard drives and scanners and plastic boxes that hummed with fans and motors and drives. I couldn't begin to guess at what each did. Aside from an engine, the iPod was as technical as I could manage.

Bending before the keyboard that looked to be the main

one, I tapped the space bar. A widescreen LCD monitor brightened to display a background of two naked men going at it.

"Oh, Fitch." I tilted my head, perusing the men's position. "Is that even possible?" Of course it was. And it was happening right before my eyes. "Plants, Martha Stewart and gay porn. Hmm… Change that theme song to 'Whip In My Valise.'"

There were some things a person should not learn, even about their closest friends.

And that was the pity. I didn't even know my closest friend, *and* she may have turned on me.

Avoiding looking at the naked men, I sat before the monitor and perused the keyboard and various accoutrements attached by twisted cords. A camera, I think, perched atop the monitor like a one-eyed owl. I didn't know if it was on; it probably was. If I was being recorded I'd better make this snappy. I'd worry about an excuse to offer Fitch later, if she ever questioned me. Hell, I now had blackmail material.

Possessing but rudimentary computer skills, I was glad Fitch owned a Mac, the kind I had learned on. I doubleclicked the icon of a rose in the upper right corner—just above a naked man's foot—and up popped a window of documents and programs. I scanned through them, feeling more and more that this was a mistake.

What *was* I looking for? And why did I think I could extract any information from Fitch's files? She was the expert. Fitch—

Behind me, the door clicked and creaked open.

Instinctively, I sank to the floor, tucking the canvas duffel to my gut and sliding my hand inside it.

In strode Fitch. The room wasn't dark by any means, but I hoped to blend in with the mess. Had she forgotten something?

"I know someone's in here," she announced. "I got me a thirty aught six."

Slipping the Glock into my palm, I stood, twisting at the waist, and aimed. "It's me, Fitch."

She startled, catching a palm to her breast at the sight of my gun. "Fuck me."

"I think it may be the other way around. You fucking me, Fitch?" The aforementioned thirty aught six was brazenly missing. Scare tactic. "How did you know I was in here?"

"You tripped an alarm." She pointed to the messy table and shoved aside some clothes to reveal a phone. It had fallen off the cradle, a green light blinked on the panel.

"Don't—" I crossed the room, gun held purposefully "—move a muscle."

Fitch placed her palms outward and high above her head. Too high, but I wasn't about to get picky.

"Oh sure, holding a gun on the defenseless old granny? That's not very PC of you."

"You're not defenseless, you're a black belt karate master. And as for being a granny…?"

Fitch made a bold move, lunging a foot to reach for the phone buttons with her big toe, revealed by walking sandals.

I squeezed the trigger. The blast startled us both. The monitor over Fitch's shoulder sparked and blinked out.

"Damn it all!" Replacing her hands in the air, Fitch then whistled. "Someone has been practicing since I last saw her."

"If you're implying I'm a lousy shot, I don't know who you've been watching target practice."

"You just missed me by a mile, sweetie."

"In—" I was about to say *intentional*, but why let on I'd never think to cause her harm, even if she had screwed me up the river.

"You know why I'm here, Fitch. Who is it?"

"Who is who?" She dropped her hands to her sides. Drawing a gaze over the smoking monitor with the bullet hole through the screen, she again whistled. "You know how much it'll cost to replace that thing?"

I maintained aim. I'd like to rip her head off for turning on me. Still, I hadn't confirmed that, so I was holding out hope.

"I bet it'll cost a lot less than it took to buy you away from me. What's screwing your friends run nowadays? A hundred euros?"

"Come now, Jamie, don't be catty. A hundred euros would barely get me a dinner and a bottle of wine. Unless I go for the cheap stuff—"

"Someone tried to kidnap me this morning, Fitch. The last-minute pickup wanted me, not a ride. And I know you were surprised to hear my voice when I called. Now, I need a name or—" I switched aim to the large computer on the floor under the desk, guessing it was the mainframe, "—the computer gets it."

"No," she hissed softly.

Oh yeah, I'd guessed correctly.

"I don't understand," I said. "I thought I paid you well."

"Jamie, love," Fitch said patiently. She made to step forward, but the spilled DVDs kept her in place. "I'm not proud of ratting you, but sometimes a woman's hands are more valuable than another paycheck, if you know what I mean."

"You actually believe whoever is threatening you will let you live after I'm dead?"

"Now, I don't think they want you dead." I could only gape at that gentle admonishment. "I would have never agreed to the pickup if I'd suspected something like that. Not my choice. You've gotta believe me, darling."

No, Fitch was an independent operator. She chose her jobs, she kept her nose clean. If someone was making her do this, they had to have really put the screws to her.

"I need a name," I insisted.

* * *

"It's a wrong—" Sacha Vital made to flip the cover of his cell phone shut. Someone must have dialed a wrong number. He heard a female voice speaking in the distance. And another voice, but he couldn't determine the identity for the muffled static. Neither was talking to him.

He pressed the phone to his ear, straining to hear bits of the conversation. He recognized the southern accent. Kennedy Fitch. And—sweet score! The other voice must belong to *le lapin*.

"Turn down the radio!" he commanded his driver.

The car went silent. Sacha could hear bits and pieces, but not enough to figure the content of their argument. Didn't matter. The call could only be coming from one place. He knew she operated out of a barge. Speed dialing, he formed a plan.

The phone clicked on. "Thom?"

I watched Fitch worry her lower lip. She had sold me out. But only because she'd been threatened. Sunday bloody Sunday. What to think?

"You know I've always been truthful with you, Fitch."

"I know, damn it! Don't be pulling the big sad eyes trick on me. I am impervious."

"Cold-blooded, more like. Max would have sooner died than endanger a friend."

"Oh!" Throwing up her arms, Fitch surrendered dramatically. "It's someone you'll recognize as soon as you lay eyes on him," she finally offered. "But you won't *know* him. Damn it, I don't know what is going on; I had thought I'd curtailed him for the other—"

"You're going to have to give me more than that."

"Cain't," she twanged. "You know how it is."

"I thought you were on my side?"

Fitch shrugged. "I am. I just… I value my fingers. They serve me well."

"Someone threatened to…?"

"Chop them off. Bit by bit. See the slice right here on my index finger?"

I did. And the cut had to have been deep, for it clearly showed a thick red line of dried blood. I couldn't ask her to risk so much.

"So you see?"

"I do. Hell, what am I going to do? Something is up, Fitch. I'm not safe." I pressed a hand over my heart, but maintained aim with the Glock.

"Oh, damn it all to Kentucky! I'm not about to sacrifice you, sweetie. You've heard the name Sacha Vital?"

I wasn't sure. Sounded familiar. Max had bandied about a lot of names in my presence, knowing I never wanted to pay attention. All I've ever wanted to do is drive. "Elaborate."

"Vital's father is a notorious kidnapper. He's taken royals and politicians in his illustrious history. He's also big into white slavery. Left his mark all the way from Mexico to Brazil to Tokyo. Right now, he's sitting in a high-security lockup in New York City. But rumor has it the son, Sacha, has continued the family's criminal legacy. I just got a name; I didn't meet him in person. You know how I work."

All digital. Conversations were usually voice-altered. Which didn't explain the cut on her finger.

"Why would a kidnapper want me?" I dropped my aim and stuffed the gun in my bag. Fitch wasn't a danger to me. But I wouldn't let down my guard.

"Best thing for you would be to hop a plane to the States and never look back," Fitch said. She shrugged and slapped her palms to the backs of her hips. "Vital's hot for you after you spoiled the biggest take he could have brought in."

As Dove had alluded, yet he hadn't given me a name.

"So it was Sacha Vital's take I screwed up this morning? So sorry," I said. "I saved one more woman from white slavery."

"Vital had every intention of returning her to her family, or so he says."

"You believe what some criminal tells you? He's a professional kidnapper, Fitch. Max told me never to trust—"

"Yes, yes, Max told you everything. He's dead, Jamie. And Max's enemies have now become yours. As well as mine." Fitch sighed and shrugged a hand across the back of her head, redirecting the red spikes heavenward. "I'm trying to keep my head above water, myself, dear. I like this whole—" she did air quotes "—*doing good* kick you're on. Makes me want to do good myself. But I was persuaded most effectively. I didn't suspect foul play, but I also didn't arrange—"

"What made you think it was going to be legit if Vital arranged it? What, did you think it was all going to be roses?"

"Jamesina MacAlister!"

She never used my full name unless I touched that one nerve I knew she possessed.

"Well, if this guy is the father's son, how do you know Vital is an enemy of Max's?"

"Just a guess. But will you listen to me? I didn't arrange a pickup with Vital, even though he requested it."

"Well, he found me. And stuffed me in the boot of my car. Nice talking with you, Fitch. Thanks for nothing."

Time to leave. I got what I had come for. The name of the person behind my kidnapping. Not that it was any help. I wouldn't know what to do with this information until I dug deeper. And did I want to dig and risk tunneling right to my new enemy's door?

"*Arrivederci* and *shalom*!" Yeah, I deserved the snotty send-off. But Fitch's tone softened and as I stepped out onto the deck I heard her say, "Keep your head down, kiddo."

Anger carried me across the barge deck. Jumping to shore, I twisted to slip by the two men who strolled the quai, but one of them caught me by the arm. Hard.

Oh, Sunday bloody Sunday. Why had I not immediately been alerted by the standard thug couture?

Before I could utter a protest, the sweet stink of chloroform filled my senses and blackness took over.

Chapter 8

"That is *le lapin*?"

Thom nodded. "But he's a *she*, boss. *La lapine*."

"I see that." Sacha hated the French masculine/feminine idiosyncrasy and never did get it right. It was enough to make anyone feel, and sound, like an idiot. And, obviously, place the wrong sex to a person.

He stalked about the body of the woman tied loosely about the shoulders to the back of a steel chair. He just couldn't believe...

Once again, his hired idiots had proved themselves incapable. "You nabbed the wrong woman."

"Oh, no," Thom protested, rather boldly. "We followed her, boss, right after you called. Picked her up as she was leaving the hacker's barge. She's the one. The rabbit. Wasn't so fast when we got our hands on her, though."

Sacha stabbed Thom with a piercing glare. The lackey took a step back and suddenly found interest in his shoes.

"Leave," Sacha directed, and Thom backed quietly from the room.

Only when the door closed, and it was he and the unconscious woman, did Sacha let out a breath. Slowly he counted to three. He tapped his thigh, three times, and smoothed a palm over the lapel of his suit coat, taking in the silken detail of the craftsmanship, the fine threading. He eyed the stone on his desk.

No, don't need it. I can do this without a focus object.

Exhaling again, he relaxed his shoulders. *Just release it.*

"You?" he muttered as he bent and squatted before the woman.

Blond hair twisted and wavered from crown to shoulders in a nonexistent style. Long legs sprawled before her, knees bent and ankles crossed over one another. She liked her skirts short, and her body worked the tight top for every inch. The outline of a fine lace bra peeked through the small gap where the button clasped onto the opposite buttonhole. 34B, if he was correct, and he most always was. A nice handful.

But this particular woman, sitting here in his office, disturbed him in so many ways.

"I remember you. I hadn't even thought… You're *la lapine?* But—" A shake of his head only further muddled his thoughts.

How had something like this happened? That their paths had crossed so remarkably?

"If I had known, then…" he said to the pretty blonde whose parted mouth looked like two soft pink petals.

Hell, he wouldn't have changed a thing.

* * *

My noggin had been plundered with a spike-headed mace and then stuffed inside a narrow laboratory glass filled with viscous yellow fluid.

Or that was how it felt as I fought my way up from the haze thickening my neck and shoulders and pounding inside my skull. My body swayed, but a hand to the side landed on something hard. Hmm…I was sitting in a chair. Stiffening, I pushed upright, pressing my back to the hard slats of a metal chair. It was very uncomfortable.

I opened my eyes to unbearable brightness. Blinking, I tried to focus.

"Yes, it is morning," a male voice announced.

I winced as each spoken word struck my skull with the dull end of the aforementioned mace. A *familiar* male voice. American? Where had I heard that voice before? And not too long ago…

My eyes were closing; they were too heavy to hold open. My mouth felt dry and tasted…what was that taste?

Situation: grim.

"I've never seen chloroform work so effectively. Knocked you out overnight. But you looked like such an angel while you slept, I couldn't bring myself to wake you. Now you should be refreshed and ready for the day."

Refreshed? The day? Over…overnight?

The accent was American, most definitely. I scanned my memory for any Americans I might have pissed off over the years. Where to start on a list that stretched for leagues? But a list that bore no names, only memories of pickups, for Max and Fitch had kept the details confidential.

I'd always thought not knowing the details a good thing.

But now that I'd been kidnapped—twice—I was beginning to think the more info I could obtain, the more power I held.

Hmph. Isn't that how things go? You never see the light until it's beaming through your eyelids like an enemy laser. But I did know exactly what I wanted—safety. And safe was the last thing I felt.

I opened my mouth, thinking to speak, but my tongue was heavy and felt as if I'd licked a cashmere sweater. And not an expensive one, but one of those cheap knockoffs with the pills and…

Lifting a hand, I realized I was not bound. A lift of my foot slung it upward too quickly and my chunky boot landed the floor with a slap.

"Nope, not tied up," the curious male voice verified. Nice, deep and confident. His tenor worked a strange warmth to the surface of my neck—a *familiar* warmth. Yet I wasn't ready to open my eyes to the enemy's laser.

"You could make a dash for it," the man offered gaily, "if you dare."

Far too much enthusiasm in that remark. He was playing a game? And without telling me the rules?

"You're…you're—" I swished my fat tongue across my palette and drew up a pitiful hint of saliva "—going…to…let me leave?"

"Of course. Dash now, or sit a spell and we'll chat."

Dash. Right. I couldn't even lift my eyelids, let alone make my legs move in a dashing manner. What a sick joker, this bloke. Of course, I expected little else from one who hailed from overseas.

"You're…an American?"

"Brooklyn accent that obvious?"

I think I shrugged, but my muscles were loose and a little

twitchy. I didn't have complete control of my limbs, which frightened me.

His shoes tapped across the floor—*click, click*. Must be marble tiles. The soft brush of fabric over my bare knee indicated he stood close, though I couldn't scent cologne.

"Wha-what do you want from me?" I managed.

"Ah, my precious little rabbit. You have been running about the city rescuing kidnapped princesses."

"A princess? No I…" Dove *had* mentioned a princess. This plot was growing thicker than my tongue.

Was the woman from the pickup this morning—was it still the same day, that horribly *great* day that had seen me dumped in the boot?—had she been a princess? I'd helped the Faction take a *princess* from this man? Well, there was nothing wrong with that. Especially if he was into white slavery, as Fitch had mentioned.

Fitch had also said something else…what had it been?

It all rushed back now. My brain squeezed out from the laboratory glass and plumped as it took in oxygen. I lifted my heavy eyelids. A few blinks restored my vision. I saw the figure standing before me, hands clasped loosely before him.

I think my heart stopped. For certain, my jaw dropped.

You'll recognize him, but you won't know him.

"No. Bloody. Way."

A handsome lift of dark brow affirmed my bleary, sorry head shake.

I did recognize this man. And as for knowing him…

I'd met him on the eve of my twenty-fifth birthday while celebrating at DV8. I recalled being riveted by his greenish blue eyes, charming sweep of dark hair and retro sideburns. And a grin that suggested he knew more about someone than that person could ever imagine. Man, had that been some incredible sex.

But I had never gotten my mystery lover's name…

"Oh, my God!" the words spewed out like vomit. I instinctively knew the answer, but I stupidly had to ask, "Who the hell are you?"

He made a quaint little bow and said, "Sacha Vital."

My world crashed, one hundred and thirty kilometers an hour, into a brick wall. Don't bother to sort through the wreckage; it's a fatal hit.

"*You're* Sacha Vital?" That was the least American name I had ever heard. And why did a stupid name bother me?

"You don't sound pleased. You sounded immensely pleased months ago. As I recall, your exact words were: 'Let's do it again. Quicker.'"

I gaped, unable and unwilling to put to voice my sudden shock and disgust. Quicker. My modus operandi. My need for speed. And if it's pleasure, then give it to me quick and long. And who wouldn't be pleased when a man was touching every body part just so?

Everything Fitch had said about Vital came rushing back to me. I had made it with a kidnapper? "I think I'm going to be sick."

"Really?"

"Maybe. What do you care? Ohhh." I swallowed back my bile. "The floor is just so…spotless."

Vital paced the immaculate white marble floor before me, Dior-clad and styled to the nines. To my left, a silvery suit jacket had been tossed over a white chaise. No, not exactly tossed; it looked as if it had been precisely laid there, wrinkles smoothed and sleeves aligned neatly. Everything was clean and white and minimal.

If I did get sick, I guessed it would have been more devastating to the man—messy floor, you know—than a threat from a gun.

The entire room, perhaps a small office, was white. White windows and walls and desktop and furniture. Even the plants were silver. Pale granite balls—yep, they were rocks—sat upon the desk, each spaced precisely. Anal decor for the modern-day kidnapper.

I felt instantly inappropriate in my purple blouse and chunky Doc Martens. And the fact I was worried about my couture made me even woozier.

Following the wave that sloshed about inside my brain, I tilted my head to the left.

"Tell me," Vital said, as he tapped one of the round stones with a forefinger, "what is it about me you think you know? That would make you feel so ill?"

"You're a kidnapper."

"Propaganda."

"Propa—" I managed to right my dizzy head. "You're a known criminal who kidnaps and sells helpless women into white slavery."

"My father. Not me." The denial was so quick and adamant I blinked. This man wasn't about to charm me a second time.

"Criminals, by nature, are liars."

"Oh?" He turned and leaned against the glass-topped desk, palming the dustless glass to each side of his thighs. "And this coming from the ever-so-saintly *la lapine*?"

He had me there. My past record wasn't spotless, nor would I be in line for sainthood any time soon. But I'd never sold women into slavery.

Is that pitiful excuse supposed to clear away all your other sins?

No. But, oh hell, this turning over a new leaf was so complicated!

"You are a renegade vigilante," he offered in that sly Brooklyn accent that was beginning to offend my European ears. "Playing Robin Hood to the bad guys, eh?"

Comparing me to a folk hero? Sounded good to me. I shrugged.

"You, *Mademoiselle La Lapine*, rescued a princess from the rail station and then turned her over to the bad guys."

"I'm just the driver. And I didn't turn her over to the bad guys. The good guys got her." Though, I wouldn't speak the Faction's name; they were keen with me. "Princess or not, she's safe now. Though, I expect the thugs firing at us were your men? In which case, glad to meet you, Sheriff. Just call me Robin Hood."

I did a double take on his glittering green-blue eyes. Yes, damn it, they actually glittered, like those of a gleeful child who holds a secret and won't tell unless you give him a cookie.

"Interesting, very interesting." He tapped a finger against his lower lip. "You think you're playing with the good guys?"

"What do you want, Vital?" I was fresh out of cookies, and even if I'd had some, I wouldn't have shared them with this guy.

"You took something that was mine."

"I am just—" I spoke succinctly "—the driver."

I spread my legs so the hard rubber soles of my boots were to the outside of each of the chair legs. An easy dash to the door. Three running strides. But the shadows of large man-shaped objects outside the whitened windows told me to play it cool. And I couldn't spot my black duffel bag with the gun in it—which should have been easy to see in this white-on-white room—so I sat tight.

"No one takes my princess from me and gets away with it!"

I cringed at the volume of his shout. So the man had a temper.

He leaned over me. His top two shirt buttons undone, and the view offered a peek at what I knew were firm muscles. I tilted my head down and to the side. Not by choice; I was still so groggy. What the hell had been in that chloroform? I'd slept the entire night?

"Why did you take the princess away from me?"

Breathing through the obnoxiously delicious scent of his cologne, I managed to sound halfway forceful. "She wasn't yours to take. No one told me she was a princess. Not that her title should matter…"

I'd definitely been overlooking the value of details. I wanted to survive on my own? Pay attention, Jamie. The players are serious, so I'd better start taking names, position and death threats just as seriously.

"She is Alleria el Sangreito," Vital explained, "princess of an obscure Spanish land."

"If it's so obscure, then why kidnap her?"

"Even the most insignificant souls have been loved at some time or another. Her father is willing to pay millions to get her back."

I felt, more than saw, the fist wringing below my jaw. I wouldn't argue with the man until I knew his capacity to violence. I already knew his capacity to sexual hijinks, and that was—

"That princess was going to net me three million euros. Until you stuck your sassy little chassis into the mix."

"It is rather sassy, isn't it?"

The sting of an open palm to my cheek didn't hurt so much but sounded awful. Bones crunched and spit splattered. I spat—onto the immaculate floor, very near onto an immaculately shined black shoe. "I don't recall you liking it rough."

"I don't recall you saying you were involved with criminal liaisons. I thought you were just another—"

"Easy lay?"

"Exactly." Sacha ground the word out in a curdling rumble.

He twisted and paced back to the desk where he again tapped the middle rock. Thinking? Or just trying to hold back his anger? Oh, wait. He'd already failed on that one.

"I didn't know the princess was—" I sucked in spit, but then realized it was blood "—yours." Bastard.

"I want her back."

I laughed. Couldn't help it.

True, I wasn't bound, but I guessed a dash for the door would earn me lead in the spine. Though I'd yet to see a gun, including mine. Where was that bag?

Sucking back a swallow of blood, I attempted the blasé act. "Just kill me and get it over with."

"Fine." Sacha stopped before me. I coached myself not to look up into his devastatingly gorgeous eyes. "Bullet or blade?"

Sunday bloody Sunday. The man was serious.

"Bullet. Less messy. I'd hate to ruin the decor. It's just so…pristine."

"Thoughtful of you. But the bullet would be a lot messier than a carefully placed blade. Flying debris, you know. But you're in luck, first I've got a few questions."

"Naturally." I focused on his shiny black leather loafers so I wouldn't have to drown in his eyes. Been there, done that, on to the next adventure, please. And if it involved escape, I was on it. "No," I said on a sigh. "You were not the biggest or the longest or even the hardest—"

The second slap served to stir me up from the depths of grogginess and put a sharp focus on the face above me.

Sacha smoothed a finger along his palm. Easing away the ache from the assault?

"You were the best fuck I've ever had," he said and turned to stroll, hands behind his back, a few paces away.

The rocks on the desk remained untouched, but I sensed he stared at them with a Captain Kirk-like intensity. Must resist touching!

"The best, eh?" I said. "You don't get around much? Sorry for you."

"Had I known you were *la lapine*… Hell, had I known *le lapin* was really a woman…"

"French sucks, don't it? I know. Had you known, things would be different. Bummer for me. But I don't deal with your ilk any longer."

"My ilk? Sounds like I run with a pack in the wild."

"That remains to be seen. But I wouldn't be surprised."

"Regardless, I would have never guessed *la lapine* would be living the hard way. Or so you believe. Why the change of habit?"

"I like to be good," I said, forcing a cheery tone. "Also, avoiding jail is keen. Something I guess you're not overly concerned about."

"Have you seen me commit a crime?"

"You've kidnapped and roughed me up."

He didn't answer.

"I need names," Sacha said, approaching me. He eased a

thumb in the palm of his hand. Big, strong hands. I guessed he wasn't done slapping me around.

Bring it on.

Yes, I was feeling loosey-goosey from the drugs or whatever they'd used on me. I'd regret this bravado when the bruises started to swell.

I straightened and focused. This driver hadn't yet given up the checkered flag. And Vital hadn't begun to torture or rape. Didn't seem like his style. Of course, serial killers were charming as hell until you pissed them off.

"Names?" I said. "Of who?"

"Of the Faction."

I snorted a half laugh and lifted a foot to bounce nervously on the floor. There was a bruise on my inner thigh just above the knee. I didn't even want to guess what had gone on while I had been out. Two thugs transporting me from Fitch's barge to—where the hell was I?

"What makes you think I'm working with the Faction?"

"I know that you are. They're the only ones who have been on my ass lately. Names?"

"You know I don't have names. The Faction doesn't operate that way. If identities are given, it's always a number. I can give you a Three or a Seven, if that'll make you happy."

Green eyes leveled with mine. Did they change from green to blue with his moods?

"Do not play with me, Jamie."

He knew my real name? How? Who was this guy?

"You're not behind the wheel now. The bad guys have you. And we're not going to let you get away without raking you over the coals."

"You can slap me around all you like, but I can't give you what I don't have. Come on, Sacha." Well, since we were on a first name basis… "You're a smart man. You know the Faction better than I do."

"Indeed. Numbers for names. Clever, but not foolproof."

He turned and strolled to the far wall where I had noticed the door. Sacha opened the white glass door. Outside, a line of windows revealed the bright blue Paris sky. So it was—my gosh! It was morning? I'd really slept all night? How much chloroform did they give me? Can anyone say overdose?

"She's out there somewhere—" he paced back to stand before me, tall, sleek and deadly "—the princess. Which puts me in the market for a driver."

I didn't move a muscle. A twitch in my left leg, needles and pins, defied my need to remain stoic. This was not sounding like a picnic in the park, or even a rumble in the boot of my car.

"You do owe me," he announced, his eyes twinkling evilly.

"What the hell are you asking, Vital?"

"Exactly as I've stated. I'm in need of a driver."

I scoffed. "I think I'll take door number three."

"Which is?"

"Time to leave." I stood. The door was open. I could taste the blue sky of freedom.

"Whatever you're planning…"

"I don't make plans," I stated, feeling the adrenaline fire in my veins like petrol burning through a fuel line. "I just react."

A fist to the man's jaw took him by surprise. But his body didn't even sway from the impact. I delivered a left to his gut, and he bent with a grunt.

I expected a return punch and crouched, showing him my fists, but he merely straightened and beamed those killer eyes at me.

Not gonna work on this lass. I was so over this man of the amazing sexual prowess. And to prove it, I slashed a boot around and clocked the side of his leg just at his knee. He stumbled. Another punch to his jaw sprayed my face with his saliva.

Sacha Vital went down, and out.

I rubbed my aching fist and studied my wrath. "Cool."

My duffel was now visible behind the desk. I grabbed it and ran. There were two thugs outside the door, one on either side. Neither moved when I passed into the hallway—which should have made me wonder.

"Jamie!" Sacha called.

Okay, so not out cold.

Maybe this was my break. So far, no one had tried to physically stop me, which was freaking me out. And Vital hadn't even offered a fight.

Did I dare run?

My feet had already decided a swift pace was best.

"I'm not going to force you to do anything," Vital called to my retreating back. "I need your help to locate the princess. The Faction has her. They'll kill her when they're finished with her."

Liar. Don't listen, Jamie. He's trying to win you over by making the allies look like the bad guys. Classic villain fare.

I sped up and eyed an elevator. Too slow. To the right was a doorway. I stopped and turned. Sacha stood thirty paces away. A thin red line of blood dribbled down the front of his immaculate suit. If I didn't know better, I'd mark him as a fashion model for Dior, all fancied up and looking like a million euros, minus a couple coins for the blood.

But I did know better.

For a moment, the two of us stared each other down. Then when I felt I might melt and slither to the floor, my better senses activated the flee instinct.

Chapter 9

I hit the street running. Destination? *Home*, is all I could think. Home to Scotland because France wasn't so friendly anymore. Who would have thought going into business on your own would be such a challenge? I didn't need this detour from the destination.

I sensed the thugs were on my tail, though I hadn't seen them yet, nor had they been moving when I'd last looked at Sacha. They were not the same two who had tossed me in the boot. Perhaps these two matched Sacha's outfit better. I could hear the morning wakeup call. "I'm donning silver Dior today. Do wear something in nondescript black, so as not to detract from my gorgeous green-blue eyes."

I had slept with my new enemy. Damn, damn, double damn and all those bloody Sundays. Why did it have to be *him*?

I hadn't gotten his name the night of my birthday. The wine

had flowed; I'd been in my happy place. Sex with a handsome stranger had followed. I'd woken in the morning all by myself, in his big, lush bed layered with crisp white sheets. Everything had smelled like fresh-squeezed orange sprinkled with cinnamon. I hadn't regretted a moment of the all-night tumble.

Until now.

I had had sex with a man who might very well sell women into white slavery.

"This is too grim," I murmured as I landed the sidewalk out front of the nondescript business building where Sacha had held me. I didn't survey my wake or check for street signs. I just wanted to get the hell away from, well...hell.

I walked fast, slinging my duffel bag over a shoulder. I hadn't checked the contents; for sure it had been searched. I prayed the Glock was still inside.

The river was close. I heard a tugboat toot and seagulls flew overhead. About half a block behind me, the creak of a door alerted me to more danger. I spun and spied both of Sacha's thugs but they weren't running.

Weaving through two lanes of traffic, I stepped onto the sidewalk opposite the building from which I'd exited. The street stretched toward the river. The shops were not separated by alleys, and I guessed that there were no back doors.

The thugs had moved to the parked cars and were getting into a black Bimmer.

A car honked and someone yelled, "Hey!"

No time for nasty comments from lusty young Frenchmen. I thought to dash across the intersection in front of a red four-door when the voice called again and hit a pause note in my brain.

"Hey, gorgeous!"

I bent, still tracking a jogging pace, and eyed the driver who had called to me. Hmm, handsome. Young. Male. And waving at me like he knew I needed a ride. He drove a maroon Renault hatchback—big suburban yawn; no speed, no glory—but his dimples screamed for attention.

The thugs pulled the Bimmer into bumper-to-bumper traffic, so it must have been morning rush hour. Not knowing the time or my actual location disoriented me. I had to do something.

And so I did.

Rushing to the hatchback, I slid in the passenger side. "I don't know who the hell you are—and I can't believe I'm saying this—but drive!"

Dimples didn't react, so I tried it again. *"Un conduire?"* I made steering motions with my gripped fingers. *"Tout droit!"*

"Drive?" The man frowned. The confused expression stole his gorgeous dimples. "I was going to pull over there to pick up a mocha."

Another American, yet, with a less abrasive accent. I had only lived in France four years, but could pick Americans out in a Parisian crowd just by their awed stare, tourist jeans and fluorescent T-shirts. This guy was far from fluorescent, wearing blue jeans and a soft gray sweater, but most certainly American. Two in one day? I didn't know whether to dance or start a drive-through embassy.

"Why'd you wave at me like you wanted to give me a lift?"

The dimples returned. "I see a pretty girl, I ask her to have a coffee."

"Bother." I stretched a leg across the drive console and

stepped on his right foot. The car revved, and he groped to handle the wheel.

"What the heck are you doing, lady?"

"Where are we?"

"On the Left Bank, not far from—"

"We'll get mochas on the Right Bank, dimples. I know a great place."

"Really?" He slowed, approaching a stop-and-go light. The black Bimmer was one car behind us. Maybe I should have stuck to walking, but I was still fighting the effects of an all-nighter on chloroform.

But if the man intended to just sit there and argue with me, evasive action was needed.

"Put the hammer down!" I dug in my pack and produced the Glock. I didn't point it at the man, and instead held it down near my gut, finger on the trigger. "You wanted me in your car? Well, now you've got me. Fun first date, huh? Now I've got two words for you." Hating myself for having to do it, I pointed the gun at the man's chest. I had to keep it low, out of sight. "Drive. Quick."

"I'm driving," he said, not yet noticing the gun, but carefully making his way through the intersection. When he turned to look at me, he let out a yelp. "What the? That's a—! Who are you, lady?"

"Just drive. Don't worry about the gun. If you slow down, then you can start worrying."

"This is my car. And that's a-a gun!"

"You're very perceptive. Left!"

He turned just in time. The hatchback squealed, but handled the corner with little oversteer. Our tail remained pinned to us. I doubted we'd shake them unless a real driver took the wheel.

"Keep your eyes on the road, dimples."

"My name's Kevin, if you don't mind."

"Nice to meet you, Kevin."

The side view of his smirk crunched into a gum-baring grimace. "I'd like to say same to you, but I think I'll reserve judgment on that for a while."

"Your prerogative."

"Yeah, well, your gun."

I liked a man who learned quickly.

Kevin navigated another stop-and-go and signaled to switch lanes. "Who are we running from?"

"None of your concern—watch the bus!"

The hatchback swerved, but the rear left fender swapped paint with the corner of the bus.

"Damn it!" Kevin pounded the steering wheel. "Put that gun down or I stop the car."

"Stop the car, and I pull the trigger."

"You'll what?"

"Watch out for the bike!"

He swerved to avoid a bike messenger, who wobbled and crashed into an ad post. The cyclist delivered a furious finger in our wake.

"I can't do this!" he shouted.

"Come on, Kevin, relax."

"Relax? I've never had a gun held on me. I'm a little nervous."

"They're still on our tail."

"They? There's more than one? Anyone ever tell you you're a lousy first date, lady?"

He couldn't be traumatized if he was making jokes. "Slide over, Kevin, or we'll both be chewing bullets."

"What?" He gripped the wheel so hard I thought it would break in half with just a tilt.

"I'm going to switch places with you."

Gun hand gripping the headrest behind Kevin's head, I shifted my body onto the black plastic console between the seats. No stick shift, but my boot heel lodged in a cup holder that rattled with loose change.

"I don't do the passenger side, lady. This is my car."

"Yep, and it's such a precious little number. Gun, remember?" I tapped the back of his skull with the barrel of the Glock. It was a dirty play, I admit it. "I'm calling the shots."

Without waiting for further argument, I slid on top of Kevin's right leg and pressed my left foot onto the gas. Hands firmly on the wheel, the gun crushed against the curve, I sat halfway on his lap.

"Damn it, woman, you're going to get us killed." Kevin slipped out from under me. I lifted up to allow him to get his feet out, and he dragged himself to the passenger seat.

"Repeat after me," I said. "*Vous êtes un as du volant.*"

"*Vous êtes*—a superb driver?"

"You got it." I pressed the automatic door locks. "And don't even think of jumping out."

"Why would I do that? I'm not the one with a death wish."

I did have an unhealthy love for danger. It was all about constantly toeing the edge and pushing myself further. Driving away was what I did best. *Just like she had done... driven away.*

"I have a feeling you won't slow down."

"You got that right."

The seat belt clicked, locking him in place. I did the same. "Here, hold this." I tossed him the Glock.

The tail swung immediately behind us, fishtailing a bit before evening out. A rearview check did not reveal any weapons. Sacha's thugs were determined, I had to admit.

But so was I. Now I was in my element. With a couple hundred horsepower at my command and the whole world as my racetrack, I shifted up gears and concentrated on losing the tail.

"This isn't even loaded!" Kevin popped out the gun magazine—rather expertly, I noted from the corner of my eye. "Who are you?"

"Not your business."

"I have a right to ask questions," he said, irate as hell, and obviously completely over his initial freakishness. "Kidnap victims do have rights."

"You're not a victim. You were the one to invite me, remember?"

He hissed something under his breath.

"Yes, that's what happens, kiddies, when you talk to strangers. Just chill, Kevin. There's a tail following me. Two thugs in pristine black business suits."

"Why? What did you do? Will you at least tell me your name?"

I bit my lip. *La lapine* bounced onto my tongue. Max had given me the moniker because I bounded through the city like a rabbit with a fox on its tail.

I tilted a gaze along Kevin's face. Who could he be? An average man on the street I could seduce for an evening of no-strings sex? It had been a few months since my last man— oh hell, I should so not go there anymore. Look who I'd hooked up with last time—a man who now wanted my arse, and not for any particular sexual act.

I sped through a red light, barely avoiding a crossing sports car. The tail was forced to stop at the light or meet a bright yellow DHL truck in the middle of the intersection. Finally, a break.

"Jamie, that's my name."

"A Scot named Jamie, eh? That is your accent? Scottish? Isn't that a guy's name?"

I smiled at him. "It's my name. Deal with it." Then I shifted into fourth and took the passage at top speed. "Hold on!"

As we sped through the next few intersections Kevin remained silent. His fingers dug gouges in the dashboard and his tongue likely lodged at the back of his throat.

I hated that I'd been forced to bring along a passenger. But he'd invited me, so…there really was no force to claim.

I hadn't seen the tail for a quarter of a mile. The river was close, but it promised tourist mania and knots of tie-ups. If I could cross the Pont Neuf and insinuate us into the narrow labyrinth on the north end of the Right Bank all would be well. Tons of tourists, and snakier streets. Easier to get lost. As we soared, literally, across the bridge, swerving and honking to redirect pedestrians, Kevin yelled, "I hope that's one hell of a mocha!"

What a sweet, stupid man, to flag me down, and expecting nothing more than a chat over coffee. Did he always pick up women that way? Seemed not so much risky as adventurous.

Hmm… I liked this man. What wasn't there to like about dimples and a man who let you drive his car?

"Why the gun?" he asked as I slowed and began to creep into a narrow alley. Far as I could determine, the tail had been lost. "I mean, obviously you're a criminal—"

"Am not." I shifted down and stalked the sidewalks for a café. I'd deliver the man to his mocha in exchange for his co-operation. "I just…tend to attract the wrong crowd."

"So why no bullets?"

"They're in my bag. I hadn't expected to need them. I would fire only as a last resort."

"Oh yeah?"

"And then, only to wound." From the corner of my eye, I saw him nod, accepting. What a day he was having, eh? The man's theme song was probably Daniel Powter's "Bad Day."

"I think you've lost them."

"How would you know?"

"It was a black, seven series BMW," Kevin said. "I haven't seen them since we crossed the bridge."

"You're good. But never get too cocky. Check all angles and even in front of you."

Kevin did so, and I had to smile at that. He'd lost all nervousness over being hijacked by a crazy lass with a gun. The man had definitely earned himself a mocha.

"So do I get my car back after we stop?"

"I am not a criminal."

"Then what are you? 'Cause it seems to me like you've just committed a kidnapping, endangered lives, ran half a dozen stoplights—"

"We call them stop-and-goes here in Europe, Kevin."

"Whatever! And you threatened me with a gun."

"There were never any bullets!"

"Doesn't matter. I was feeling threatened."

"You want me to stop at that drugstore for Depends?"

"Funny, but I'm the one holding the gun now."

"No bullets."

"Right."

Scanning the periphery in the rearview mirror—low threat level—I relaxed and automatically reached for the radio dial. I turned the sound on low. "Do you know you've got the sweetest dimples?"

"So I've been told."

"By your girlfriend?"

"Don't even consider it. You are so not my type, lady."

"What is your type?"

"Not—"

"Criminal?"

"—aggressive."

"I see."

I smiled at him in the rearview mirror, and he smiled back. Our eyes danced for a second. Blue like gemstones, I thought of his eyes. A cat burglar's prize. Certainly a prize I would never transport. Not anymore. Very unlike the green-blue eyes I'd looked into earlier. *I know they changed colors, I just...know it.*

Kevin released my gaze with a sexy smirk and a shake of his head. Oh, those dimples.

The coffee shop I'd been thinking of was still there on the rue Villiot, and it was open. And, wonder upon wonder, there was even a parking slot. I pulled up to park and shut off the ignition, handing Kevin the keys.

"Thanks for the ride, Kevin. You...live in Paris?"

Hell, what was the trouble? He was just a guy. A very nice guy, who had let me drive his car. Brownie points for that, for men were so stingy with their vehicles.

"For the season."

I didn't know what that meant, but I wasn't listening anyway. Feeling my body move to the right—away from the door—I stopped myself.

Had I been close to leaning in to kiss the man? He was certainly kissable. *But you've just survived kidnapping—twice.* Not safe to lose focus.

"Er, right. Thank you, Kevin. I'll be fine."

Forcing myself to leave the car, I tucked the Glock into the back of my skirt and stood by the curb as Kevin slid over into the driver's seat.

For one moment, I allowed my body to sink, to drown in the pleasure of the ordinary. The simple kindness of a stranger. With dimples I wanted to fit myself into.

"Look," he said as the driver's window rolled down. "I can obviously guess you're in some kind of trouble. You don't want to tell a stranger, that's cool with me. But you seem nice enough. If a little stressed." His dimples deepened. "How about that mocha?"

Well, I did owe him one.

Chapter 10

When Kevin slid onto the chair opposite my table, I didn't react. In fact, I slouched comfortably into the velvet wingback chair. Wearing soft blue jeans and a gray sweater, he fit right in with the esthetic of Parisian élan. He felt...safe.

And my guard took a break along with me.

He ordered a mocha and I nodded for the same. I didn't do caffeine, but the occasional coffee wouldn't push me over the edge. Yes, I needed the energy right now.

Ninety percent of me had expected Kevin to call the cops and arrest my arse. The other ten percent was shaking its head miserably. *What are you getting yourself into, lass? Shouldn't you be on the run?*

And why did I have to be on the run?

Seemed to me I could create my own destination, and running didn't figure in that plan. The big bad blokes wanted to mess around with me? Bring it.

Maybe.

"Does someone want to kill you?" Kevin started in as he tapped his spoon on the rim of a large porcelain cup.

I smirked and swallowed a sip of froth. "Nope. Just…talk to me."

"What's wrong with talking?"

"Nothing. We're talking right now. How you doing, Kevin?"

"Not sure." He shrugged his fingers through his short crop of blond hair. Beach-bum hair—no, make that fashion-model coif, but without the posturing. Kevin seemed as comfortable in his skin as I did behind the wheel. "I've just been taken on a joyride by a crazed female toting a gun," he said. "How should I be doing?"

I shrugged and pushed my half-full cup to the center of the table. Play it cool. No need to get an innocent involved. But he already knew far too much.

"So you're going to take on the bad guys, kill 'em all, and win?" he prompted.

"Kevin, my dear, you watch far too many movies."

"I don't think you watch enough. You're a woman!"

A frown melted my teasing smile. "And what has that got to do with anything?"

"Nothing, I just— Who's after you?"

"I don't know. And even if I did, I wouldn't tell you. I don't want you involved."

"Now *you've* been watching too many movies."

Yes, but he was just a tiny bit of a chauvinist. I couldn't overlook the *you're a woman* comment. One mark against the man for that. But his dimples countered strongly. "You're an innocent, Kevin."

"My car isn't. It's been driving getaway of late."

The man could not begin to grasp the enormity of that

simple statement. I wasn't going to explain it to him. Innocent, and keep it that way.

Suddenly he touched the side of my face where I guessed I had a bruise, because the contact made me flinch. Sacha's mark?

"Any parts broken?" he asked, concerned as his gaze darted across my face and down my arms.

I stared at him, unbelieving, but strangely relieved to look upon a friendly face after all I had been through. Fresh, fun-loving and…not eager to kill me.

Smirking, I stroked my thumb along my cheek. "Is there a bruise?"

"Not dark, but there's some discoloration under your eye. Looks like you've had a rough day," he said. "And it's only ten in the morning."

"Only ten? I can't believe I slept all night."

"So what's up?"

I sighed. "It's one of those if-I-told-you-I'd-have-to-kill-you situations."

"I see. Well then, maybe I can tell you some things."

"Like what?"

"Come on." He stood and offered his hand. When I only stared at it, he flicked his fingers impatiently. "You can stay at my place," he offered, dimples deepening, "so long as you guarantee there are no guns—fake or otherwise. And…you walk around nude."

I choked on a swallow of froth. "What?"

He ignited those incredible dimples. "Had to try. Want another mocha for the road?"

"No, now I need food to counteract the caffeine buzz. I need to—why do you think I need a place to stay? And what do you think you can tell me?"

A cell phone rang. I knew it couldn't be mine.

"Wait here." Kevin said, as he mined his back jean pocket for the ringing phone. He walked down the row of tables to stand by the entrance door beneath a constellation of colorful paper lanterns. But I could still hear him. And boy, did I hear him over the quiet murmur of nearby conversations. "Eight."

"Eight?" I mouthed, and turned my surprised gasp away from the man's view. The sudden shock of hearing him use a simple number, but as if identifying himself— "No way. It can't be."

Grabbing my duffel and shuffling about for a few euros, I scattered the change on the table, then rushed over to the door. Just as Kevin was closing his phone, I gripped him by the front of his sweater. "Who the hell are you?"

"I…"

"Did I hear you right? Are you… Eight? I'm not going anywhere with you—" I crossed my arms "—until you tell me who you are."

"All right." He linked arms with me and stepped outside, walking toward his parked car. I followed only because to punch him would never get me the answers I required. We stopped at the hatchback and he joggled his keys before turning to me and saying, "I'm Kevin Grant—also known as Eight—and I'm with the Faction."

Blinking and gaping at the same time, I felt my brain fry a circuit. Really. Just zap! A twinge in my brain made me flinch. I wobbled, but Kevin steadied me by the upper arm.

"Eight. You're…with the Faction?"

He nodded. "And that's all you'll get until we're back at my place. It's a safe zone, I promise. Trust me?"

"I…sure." Truthfully, I was unsure of everything, but I knew the Faction meant trust. It had to. They were the good guys.

* * *

Little caution was taken in returning to Kevin's apartment, I noticed. He wasn't constantly eyeing the streets or the rearview mirror, nor did he check for followers as we made our way to his apartment from a street parking space. Yes, I let him drive. Though you must realize it absolutely kills me to ride shotgun. Unless of course, I'm the one with the gun.

He lived in an old seventeenth-century jobbie; the house was narrow but four stories tall. The fourth floor was his apartment, he explained, as we walked through a courtyard no wider than my arms' span and around back to climb a wobbly iron staircase hugging the brick wall. A hedge of eucalyptus dizzied my brain, and reminded me that I still wasn't one hundred percent after my adventures with Monsieur Kidnaps-A-Lot.

I wondered if that overdose of chloroform was what was making me so drowsy. The dose could have done some serious damage. I wondered if Sacha cared. And then I stopped myself with a pinch to my wrist. Why did I care if he cared?

Oh, I needed to clear my head.

Upon entering Kevin's apartment and padding across the creaky hardwood floor, an incredible sense of arrival fell upon me. *Safety here.* All would be right.

This was the second time I'd felt that way around the man.

"Kick off your shoes and relax on the couch," Kevin called as he disappeared into the kitchen. "You like hot chocolate?"

Hot chocolate? Oh indeed, I had arrived. Even though it seemed my diet was to be liquid for the interim, I nodded. "Thanks."

The place was cozy and…yellow. So yellow, in fact, that I froze, arms stiff and mouth in a hideous frown, as I took in my surroundings. Everything, from walls to appliances, to the curtains and radiators.

"Interesting color."

"It's the previous owner's choice. I'm not much for decorating. So long as there's a bed and shower, I'm happy. I think I'm a little color-blind, as well."

"Good for you." I tossed my duffel to the end of the sofa. "Bad for visitors."

Slipping off my boots, I collapsed onto the thick brown leather sofa without a thought. Closing my eyes, I pressed a forearm over them. Just for the moment, I felt the welling of tears as they soaked into the sleeve of my shirt. I didn't sniffle or slobber. But the tension of the day was pushed out with a good cry. Pa had always told me girls were supposed to cry; it renewed their strength.

Good ole Pa. I twisted the heavy hex nut I wore on my index finger—a gift from Pa. If he'd known how many tears I'd cried over my wanderlust mother, well, he'd have to swim to reach me.

Dismissing the morbid thought of my father seeking me out through a flood of tears, I sat forward and caught my head in my hands.

There really wasn't time to sit. I'd lost an entire bloody night.

What had Vital done with me? My mind briefly went to scenarios of date rape, women waking up the next morning to discover they'd been violated. I didn't want to consider, but—I had to go there—I felt…untouched.

All clothing still in place, blouse unbuttoned appropriately. I had to believe Sacha hadn't gone quite that far. I wasn't feeling any pain, beyond my sore cheek.

Certainly I had enemies. From this day forward, every kidnapping or theft I participated in stopping gained me another enemy. None would learn the identity of the unknown driver. And certainly I never learned whom it was I was stealing a ransom away from. That was a practice that had to stop.

There were only two people in this world who really knew me—Fitch and Max.

Fitch had ratted me to Sacha? Had she alerted him that I was at the barge? Hmm, she had managed to press a button on the phone with her toe. Did the woman have a speed dial to Sacha Vital? To go to her now proved risky. I might call her from a phone booth, far from Kevin's home, for Fitch could track a call like a bloodhound.

My only other option was contacting the Faction. No details; no blame. I had never spoken directly to anyone in the Faction, save for the occasional shout for directions from those who had sat in the backseat. Fitch arranged everything right up until that final call. No names were exchanged. *La lapine* arrived to drive.

Now here I sat in Eight's home. I *had* made contact with the Faction. Rather, they had reached out to me. I think.

"Did you know it was me when you flagged me down?"

"Yes." Kevin strode into the room.

The scent of chocolate drew me upright on the sofa. He pressed a warm cup into my palm and sat next to me. Close. He brushed my hair back from my face and, remarkably, I let him do it.

Sipping the warm brew, I kept my head down for a moment, sliding the hex nut up and down the cup, and trying to figure what it was he'd put in the drink that made it taste so good. Something sweet, but different.

"Mexican hot chocolate," he said as he sat back and crossed one ankle over his other knee.

"It's very good. What is that taste?"

"Cinnamon. You…okay?"

"Keen." I managed a smile—and who wouldn't smile at the sight of the man's dimples? "So—when you flagged me into your car…? You know I am—"

"*La lapine*. I've been keeping an eye on you."

"Why? How? I mean, I don't understand."

"The Faction heard Sacha Vital was upset over the foiled kidnapping. We look after our own."

"But I'm not your own. I'm an independent. And the kidnapping, it just happened this—er, yesterday morning."

"I received a report immediately after the drop-off. Everyone who comes in contact with the Faction is watched until we're confident they're out from suspicion."

"Really." I tucked my feet under my legs and settled into the deep leather cushions. "Sounds like you go above and beyond. I don't know if I like that, being followed."

"We're on your side, Jamie."

"Yeah? So why not rescue me *before* two thugs shoved me into the boot? And where were you when someone knocked me out and took me to Vital's hideout?"

"You spoke to Vital?"

I quirked a brow. Didn't he know that? If he had been watching me… "What did you think I was doing when you picked me up? Going for a morning jog?"

"We saw the thugs take you last night, and my men followed, but—"

"But." Obviously someone wasn't paying close enough attention. "Where is the princess?"

"Not so fast, Jamie."

"Yes, fast. Quick, that's the way I like things. I need details. I need to know you're the good guys. Why didn't you reveal your alliance right away when I jumped into your car?"

"I wanted to ensure you were safe. We don't reveal ourselves unless it's necessary. We're like those Watchers on *Highlander*."

"Ah. There can be only one."

"Right."

I shrugged. "I prefer *Bewitched* and *I Dream of Jeannie* reruns. I grew up on those." Heck, I'd spent a summer pretending I was a genie, blinking my pa insane every time he asked me something. "But how do I know you're an ally?"

He shrugged and stretched an arm across the back of the sofa. "I could ask the same of you."

"What? But you've just—"

"Are you working for Vital?"

I choked on hot chocolate. "You saw the thugs after me. Why didn't you ask them? Sacha actually had the nerve to ask me to drive for him!"

"A job offer?"

I made a dismissive sound.

"What did he ask, exactly, Jamie? I need to know."

"He needs a driver. I don't know what for, I don't care what for. I don't work for the bad guys anymore."

I felt an arm slip around my shoulders as I leaned forward to set the mug on the glass coffee table. "I need to know this is all over. Is the princess safe?"

"How'd you know she's a princess?"

"Sacha told me. Was he lying?"

Kevin shrugged. "No. Of course, she's safe."

"Did the Faction take her from Sacha's thugs?"

"We did during yesterday's snatch and pickup. Aren't you glad we rescued her from the hands of that bastard?"

I don't do white slavery.

I nodded. I was in no condition to think too hard. But if

Sacha claimed not to practice slavery, then who—ah, his father. But Fitch had told me he was in jail. Had the son taken up his father's profession? Stupid question. Of course he had. Why else kidnap a woman? And I had been in his custody, unconscious, for so long.

Why hadn't he sold me to whomever it was he sold his women to? I was no princess, but I wasn't chopped liver, either.

Now I felt the warmth of Kevin's body against my face. He'd pulled me back to sit close to him, without my even realizing it. I should have pulled away, stood up and stormed out of the room. But it felt too right to sit here, wrapped in comfort. So rarely did I feel safe.

"So the princess is safe."

"Of course," he answered.

"With…her family?"

"Let me do a check. Will that reassure you?"

"Yes, thank you."

Kevin stood and crossed the room to the phone on the yellow wall. Having abandoned his shoes, his jeans slouched over his toes giving him a casual aura. I love a man's bare feet, especially just peeking out from under soft jeans. If it's the only bared bit of flesh, I'll take the feet as opposed to a bared chest. Seriously.

He tapped out a number. "Don't blame yourself, Jamie. You were doing your job. And you did it well. My men made it to the Gare du Nord with minutes to spare. The Faction hadn't planned for your further involvement."

"If you mean being kidnapped, I guess I'm fine. A little light-headed still, but…" I sighed.

"Yes?" He spoke to someone on the other end of the phone. "Verify classified mission 3-7P."

My mind worked the code with ease. Three and Seven, along with P—must mean the princess.

"Excellent. Thanks." He hung up. "Miss Sangreito is on a flight to Spain as we speak. Two members of the Faction will accompany her until she's been safely returned to her family."

"Really?" I perked. One good thing to be happy for. Something I had helped make happen. This step in the right direction wasn't all cockeyed.

"It's over." He hooked his thumbs in the back pockets of his jeans and wiggled a few bare toes. "You can sleep here for a while. You look tired. I'm not letting you out of the house until you've rested."

"I can't, I—I just woke up a few hours ago, Kevin. And I really have to be getting back home."

"You don't have much choice. Jamie, you're safe here."

The word *safe* echoed inside my mind, softening and fluttering and loosening my tensions. So tempting. But...

"No choice?" My muscles tensed. "What do you mean by that?"

"That's right, you couldn't possibly know. There was a fire in your building last night. Likely set by Vital."

I was stunned; I didn't care if my mouth hung open. How had that bastard known where I lived? Even Fitch hadn't known! For that matter... "How do you know where I live?"

"Following you, remember?"

I jumped to my feet and skirted around the beechwood coffee table. "I've got to go there."

"It's marked off with police tape. Jamie, the entire building is a smoke pot. I drove by it this morning before I located you. You couldn't gain entry if you wanted."

All attempts to wrap my brain around everything I'd learned about Kevin and Sacha and my home failed. Numbness embraced my body and my fingers jittered. It wasn't even noon, and he was suggesting I stick around and take a nap?

"Does chloroform affect your brain?" I wondered, dizzily reaching for my head.

It was the kiss to the corner of my eye that made me smile my first genuine smile in days. I reached out and felt Kevin's fingers slip through mine. He squeezed. *Safe.*

"Sit back down, Jamie."

And I think I did, but I'm not sure if I sat or if Kevin lowered me to the sofa. A flutter of my lashes dusted the moist kiss still perched at the corner of my eye.

Nice guy.

I think I can trust…

Chapter 11

The scent of cinnamon-spiked hot chocolate greeted my sleepy-eyed wakening. Pale afternoon sunlight streamed across the toes of my boots, toppled on the floor near the sofa, and danced on the yellow wall across the room.

This wasn't my living room. The color was enough to give one a migraine. And I hadn't suffered those since childhood. Where was I?

A clang from the kitchen alerted me.

Right. *You're napping in a strange man's home.*

Said man having admitted to following me—but not close enough to rescue me, twice over. Which should cause some concern, but now that I recalled my adventures, I figured the drugs were what had really worked a number on me.

What sounded like a frying pan clanged on a gas burner. He must be making something to eat.

Sitting up and swinging my feet from the arm of the sofa

to the floor, I shrugged a hand through my tangle of hair. Nature called. I decided to discover the bathroom on my own and so got up and tiptoed past the kitchen. It was down the hall to the right.

The bathroom was a surprise, like a rich Turkish fantasy—in yellow—but gorgeous all the same. A tile-maker's dream. I touched the gilded tiles surrounding the medicine chest and the door swung freely open. Not much inside. Shaving cream and razor. No noticeable fungus creams—a good thing. An open box of condoms-*ribbed for her pleasure.* So the man was thoughtful between the sheets? My neglected libido revved its engine.

Stifling a shiver at sight of my uncombed hair in the vanity mirror, I then tried a finger-scrub with a jot of toothpaste to clean my teeth. I'd left my bag in the living room, but I didn't recall nabbing a comb. Satisfied with my breath, I then peed and, with a toss of my non-existent hairstyle, wandered out into the—wait for this—yellow—kitchen.

"You've got some serious issues," I muttered as I ran a hand down the back of a wooden chair painted, well, you guessed it. "Who lived here before you? Little Mary Sunshine?"

"It grows on you."

"Really? Like what? A fungus?"

Kevin gestured with a spatula toward the stack of pancakes waiting on the center of the table. Drawn more by the steam curling up from the hot chocolate, I slid onto a chair and sipped, but closed my eyes to the bright walls that whispered to me *Kill! Kill!*

"You like raspberry syrup?" he asked, with a slam of another pancake onto the wobbly stack.

"Never tried it."

He sat down across the table from me and shoved the plate of pancakes toward me. "Freshly made. I drive out to Saint-Cloud once a week to buy all my fruits and veggies from a farm. They make a mean salsa, too."

"French salsa?" I forked two pancakes and poured the ruby-dark syrup over them. "You got a thing for hot chocolate?"

"Kinda." He sipped, and to either side of the cup his dimples punctuated a little-boy grin. "Sleep well?"

"Heavenly. How long was I out?"

"About an hour."

"Must be remnants of that horrible chloroform. I was out all night."

"They must have redosed you after initially taking you in hand. That stuff shouldn't work like that, not for so long. Unless you had some sort of allergic reaction."

Redosed? I stretched out my left arm and stroked it with a fingertip. No needle marks. An inspection of my other arm found only a new mole on my wrist. Of course, I'd initially inhaled it. Had they made me inhale more?

Now I was a little freaked. And feeling kind of crawly. Why would they redose me? Why not just question me last night?

"What's going on, Kevin?"

"Not sure. I suspect Vital thinks you're working for the Faction. Maybe he wanted to pump you for information. Is that what he did?"

Not exactly. I was slapped, not pumped. It had been the strangest kidnapping ever. It wasn't as if I knew what the typical kidnapping should be like…though it had happened twice. It was almost as if Vital had given me a head start when I'd made a break for it. Why?

Sunday bloody Sunday. I'd slept with the man. He'd remembered me. Fondly or not so fondly?

Again, why did I care?

Could it have been the reason he'd let me go so easily?

Smirking around a bite of delicious pancake and syrup, I nodded instead of answering the question. I wasn't sure of the answers, and well, Kevin was easy to be around. Too easy, almost. His cashmere charm made me not want to think about the serious things, such as a probable death warrant on my head. If Sacha believed the Faction had snatched the princess from him, he might not sit back and take that one too lightly. He'd already proven to me he wasn't about to let this go.

And yet, he had let me go. Something didn't add up. For the life of me, I couldn't figure what.

Choking on a bite, I reached for the pitcher of ice water, but Kevin beat me and poured a glass.

"So Kevin, are you, like, some higher-up in the Faction?"

"Can't talk about Faction business."

He had gobbled up three pancakes to my one, and forked another two onto his plate.

"Right." Yet, the fact he'd revealed himself to me had broken that rule, yes? I appreciated he'd at least given me that information.

"So how did you get into the business of pickups, if I may ask?"

I shrugged, toying with the final pancake. "I was taught to drive by my first boyfriend. An Italian. Charming and handsome, and always flashing the bling."

He smiled. "So this boyfriend, I take it he was not legit?"

"Nope. And that's all I'm willing to give you. Unless you want to exchange information about the Faction?"

Dimples denting his smile, Kevin shrugged. "Max Montenelli, yes?"

My fork clattered onto the plate, shooting a drizzle of raspberry syrup across the yellow tabletop. Well. This guy was just full of surprises. "I suppose you should know if you've been keeping an eye on me."

"Sorry."

"I'm sure it's all part of the job. I shouldn't be upset. I think."

Why did I feel he knew more about me than Fitch? Uneasiness made me shift on the chair. I sipped the icy water.

"So what made you start working with the Faction? The good guys."

He wanted to chat, but he wasn't giving me a single crumb. Maybe if I just softened him up a bit… "Suffice it to say, after four years driving getaway for all sorts of nefarious characters, I just couldn't stomach it anymore. I've decided to go legit, and have been since yesterday morning."

"Playing the rescuing knight to damsels in distress."

"What else could I do? I love to drive. Petrol runs through my veins. And the runs I used to do, well, they served no good. If I can help someone now, instead of harming, I feel that knocks one of the crimes I've committed from my chart. You know?"

"Atoning for past sins, eh?"

I nodded. It sounded stupid, but it was where I was at right now. Just wanting to do good.

"I can understand."

Could he? I narrowed my gaze on Monsieur Mysterious. So far, all I knew about him was that he'd lied to me and wasn't keen on rescuing the damsel in distress, even though, had he tried, she would have kicked him in the gonads and told him to take a hike. But he could make some wicked hot chocolate and pancakes.

I leaned forward, mug held below my chin to blow at the steam. "Will you tell me how you got involved with the Faction?"

"Nope."

"Had to try."

"The details are not important in this situation. What concerns me now is that we get you on the first plane out of the country. You're not safe in Paris anymore, Jamie. You've got to run."

Nodding, I toggled the fork. He spoke the truth. Sacha Vital may have let me slip through his fingers, but I sensed he'd not lost my scent.

Recalling something he'd said made me wonder: if he needed a driver, why not get Thing One or Two to chauffeur him around?

"Jamie?"

"I'm thinking."

Something inside of me kicked and screamed and protested the idea of stepping back and turning tail to run like a rabbit pursued by a fox. I didn't want to leave. This damsel wasn't a runner. *Nor a wanderlust.* Hell, I was no damsel, either.

"So what do you think?" he asked. "America?"

"Huh?"

"Jamie, you've got to leave town. It's important—"

"I know. I just…" I toyed the fork tip along the edge of half a pancake. "You're very nice, Kevin. And keen."

He turned the most quizzical look on me. Only then did I realize what I had said.

"I mean, well, bloody Sunday—why did you have to come along when this mess fell on my head? You're handsome and charming and, damn, those dimples. Would you not look at me like that? It's as if you're already standing with one foot in the bedroom."

That got a startled lift of his brow.

With that graceless confession, I stood and paced to the window, fists beating my thighs impatiently. The view looked over some cathedral—I didn't know which one; there were tens of dozens in the city. The afternoon sun glinted on a shard of red stained glass.

"I'm not sure—" he started.

"I like you, Kevin."

I hadn't heard him move, but the sudden pressure of his hands moving around my waist from behind stiffened me. I quickly relaxed and settled against his hard muscled chest.

Be wary, Jamie. Now is no time to start cozying up with the first strange man who shows you kindness. He's no Max Montenelli.

"You are an amazing woman, Jamie." He pressed his cheek against mine, smelling like cinnamon and raspberries and subtle cologne. "But right now, it's all I can do to worry about you. I don't want to find out from an official Faction communication that one of our liaisons has died."

I sighed. "I'm such a goof." Then I pulled from his embrace.

Such horrid nonsense comes from lack of sex. Yes, I was blaming my neglected libido on this one.

I was feeling trapped. I didn't want the man to force me away from the city I called home, so I had switched gears quicker than a Grand Prix racer. But what an idiotic shift!

"I shouldn't have said anything. I'm just another client to you."

He grabbed my wrist as I made for the living room. "I didn't mean to imply—"

"Don't worry about it. I have this frustrating tendency to

react. Sometimes my heart leaps before my brain has a chance to process. I like you, Kevin. It's been said. More importantly, I've got a big problem. And I should face it, not run away from it."

"Don't even think about it being a problem, Jamie. The plane ticket and transfer of your personal property will all be arranged by the Faction."

"Personal property?" I smirked and rubbed my arms. "You said my apartment building went up in flames. All I've got is—where is my duffel bag?"

"On the floor by the sofa. Fine. That takes care of your arrangements. You need only get on the plane and forget there was ever a man named Sacha Vital."

I swung to face him and crimped my expression. So efficient. Everything all arranged. He was doing his job. He'd inserted an *easy* button into my journey. But by pushing that button, my entire destination would be altered. I still wasn't sure about that. And I knew the very fact I was so unsure proved it would be a bad choice.

Forget Sacha? The two of us had unfinished business. Namely, recall of events that may or may not have occurred last night while I was passed out and in his care.

"I'm not leaving," I stated. Nodding, the decision grew fierce and final. The warrior inside me lifted her battle weapon—and it looked very much like a gearshift. "I can't. This is my home. America, that's…so out of my realm. No, I will not. I will not allow Sacha Vital to chase me away."

"You're serious?"

I hit him with my gaze. "Dead."

He sighed.

"Something has to be done," I said. "Do you know Vital kidnapped that princess and was going to sell her into slavery?"

"I…yes. Vital told you that?"

"Not exactly, but I know things. Someone has to take Sacha down."

"I agree."

"You do?"

"Sure, but maybe you should leave this to the Faction."

"The Faction is a non-combative group that never makes the first move. They only rescue and redirect. And, obviously, watch. Do they have any plans to go after Vital now that the princess has been rescued?"

Kevin lifted his shoulders, but I stopped him before the movement turned to a shrug.

"You see. Vital is not your priority. But he is mine. I don't know what I can do. I've no evidence against him, but, damn it, he can't be allowed to go free!"

"So what's your plan?"

I shrugged. Planning was not my forte. Peeling in with tires squealing and chasing down the bastard until he confessed his truths was more my style.

"Want to hear my plan?" Kevin asked.

"You have one? Of course, you do. You're way ahead in this game. But *why* do you have a plan?"

"It's a backup, in case we weren't able to save the princess. But I think it can be modified to lure Vital out so we can nab him. I think you should accept that job offer. The one Sacha offered, about driving him."

"Why? And for what crime can you take the man into custody?"

"You ready for this?"

That question scared me so thoroughly, that I choked back a swallow, then nodded.

"Sacha Vital killed Max Montenelli."

Chapter 12

He'd let her go because he didn't want to involve her in his danger. And if she worked for the Faction it would only hurt him to keep her close.

But he'd had to try, at least make the offer to see how she'd react. For some reason, Jamie believed she stood on the honorable side of the line. Maybe that was how the Faction operated, allowing those in their employ to believe only what they had orchestrated. Made sense.

Members of the Faction billed themselves as the good guys. Sacha felt they were comparable to the much more elusive—and nastier—Network. He wished he didn't have to jump into this roundabout game to get to the prize, but his only hope had been taken out of the equation.

And now the clock was ticking.

He'd told Thom to stay close to Jamie and he'd reported back that the woman had, after running from captivity, just settled in for a casual mocha. A mocha? Must be a contact, though Thom wasn't able to snap a photo of the man.

Sacha had to sit tight. His men were on Jamie; she'd gone home with the man. With an address, he could start to dig deeper. It was all he had; it was a path he had to take.

Despondent was a good definition of my overall feeling. Without a home—I took a cab by my apartment; it was ashes—without a car, without any of my things. I wouldn't miss the clothing, the few personal items or even the place. I could always find a home. And though my finances were bleak, I could scrounge up some clothes and food. The basics.

Thank goodness the BMW had been in the shop and not in the underground garage below my place. I did everything with that car. She was my sweetie. I may be living in her, though, if I couldn't take on another job and raise some rent money for a new place.

I needed a bit more.

All of that meant little to me now as I stalked the sidewalk, determined. I was looking forward to the challenge. This warrior wouldn't rest until the prey had been tracked down, run over and pressed into the tarmac.

What I would never get over is Sacha Vital storming into my life and turning it upside down. He had no right. I hadn't done a thing to him, except save a woman from white slavery. So he'd lost a few million euros. It wasn't as though he wouldn't make it up within the week on another deal.

And the Faction had released the princess to her family, so that was all good.

But what Kevin had told me…

Sacha had killed Max? To even begin to think of all the implications shook me to the core. I knew exactly where Sacha

Vital had been the night before Max's murder—with me. He'd woken, left me alone in his bed and had then gone to kill Max.

My stomach roiled to think of it. Was the man really so cold-blooded that he'd just wake up and kill? Kevin had given me details I could verify. Max had died in a car crash. He'd been run off a road and crushed into a bridge. By Sacha. Or maybe his thugs had done the dirty work. That made more sense. Sacha, away from his home that morning, had called to check with his men and ensure the job had been done. All while he slept with the one person who might have been able to save Max.

Bastard.

So I'd listened to Kevin's plan and accepted his offer without a second thought.

With the help of the Faction, I would make Sacha Vital pay.

My pace increasing, I strode the rue de Seine, en route for Vital's office on the Left Bank. It didn't trouble me that I was on my own. Because I wasn't. Kevin had suggested I could lure the fox from his den, saving the Faction from an all-out shoot-'em-up. Besides, Sacha could smell the Faction a mile away, Kevin had added. If they so much as got within hearing range of the man, he vanished like a ghost. They couldn't risk spooking him.

So I was the secret weapon. Sacha might suspect my alliances, but I believed he'd allow me to walk back into his life.

I carried a cell phone Kevin had given me in my bag. The Faction would be a phone call away. All I had to do was get Vital out of the city, draw him away from his comfort zone and the protection of his hired guns, and the Faction would then move in. A simple Sunday drive.

I was aware of the hazards. The journey wasn't worth it

without the bumps and hairpin turns. This lass was up for the ride.

And Sacha Vital was going to get the ride of his life.

The man's office overlooked the Seine. Though I hadn't remarked the exact address, I had only run from the place earlier this morning and knew it was on the quai Saint Bernard. I recalled there were no remarkable landmarks, beyond the tip of Notre Dame topping the building in the distance. I supposed Notre Dame was remarkable to visitors, but having lived in the city for years, it was just another church to me now.

At the corner of the pont de la Tournelle, I found the building. I tipped down my violet sunglasses and looked over them. Looking as if it were held together by nothing more than thin strips of brick between many massive windows, the building gleamed in the sunlight, blinding me with a laser-like precision as I approached at an angle.

Entering the lobby, sans furniture and receptionist, I tugged at my skirt and smoothed down the floaty blouse. My attire wasn't so much a mess as a distraction. Hastily, I buttoned the bottom two buttons—this was a business call. That didn't help much; the silk was wrinkled beyond hope. What I really needed was a shower and change of clothing. I should have changed at Kevin's; I did have jeans and a T-shirt in my bag. Some job applicant.

But I had already won the job.

Now to make Vital believe I was interested.

"She's waiting outside, sir. I'm telling you, this is going to surprise the hell out of you."

Sacha nodded to Thom to allow her in. He leaned back in his chair. A triumphant grin slipped across his mouth, but he quickly hid it behind his forefinger. When Thom had called to inform him their mark was making her way back here, he'd laughed. It was so obviously a setup. But he'd definitely hear her out, no doubt about that.

Jumping to his feet, he smoothed both palms over his slacks and gave a tug to the tight button at the neck of his shirt. A careful twist to each sleeve pulled the organic silk to mid-hand. He picked off nonexistent lint from the shoulder. Primping?

He smirked. The woman was a looker. And sexy. And…a fascinating lover. As well, she was nothing he expected her to be, and everything he could hope for. Ecstatic over her return was the only way to describe his mood.

Back so soon after her spectacular escape? (Not that he hadn't purposefully given her a head start this morning.) He was ready to step into whatever game she offered. The mere fact she was here proved she was up to something—likely or-chestrated by the Faction. After all, she was their driver. A smart person would have high-tailed it for the airport.

But Sacha knew Jamie MacAlister was no dummy. A driver, by nature, had to develop survival skills since their spe-cialty was conveying all sorts of criminals. A gorgeous woman like that had to have a set of iron balls and matching iron common sense.

From this moment on, life would be intriguing, if not downright challenging.

Thom opened the door and in marched Jamie, chin held up and blue eyes fixing directly on Sacha. She didn't immediately speak, likely summing him up. Hadn't changed since this morning, but that didn't detract from her appeal. She must have to adjust the driver's seat way back for those long legs that looked as delicious wearing Doc Martens as he knew they looked in sexy green stilettos. The short plaid skirt was a bit juvenile, but girlie. Sacha like girlie women. The floaty purple blouse, though a wrinkled mess, made him aware of her curves. The thought to undress her—again—could not be ignored.

But it did put Sacha on the alert.

"Miss MacAlister, I hadn't expected you."

"Really?" She tugged a heavy duffel bag from her shoulder and set it on the floor near her feet with a *clunk*. He'd searched the bag and knew that besides a dizzying plethora of girlie accoutrements and the odd tool or two, there was a gun inside. "I thought you had offered me a job? You going back on your word?"

So, she intended to insinuate herself into his life. For what purpose? He hadn't told her why he'd needed a driver. Was the Faction manipulating her strings? Very likely.

Play this one carefully. But quickly. Time dwindled. Every moment he wasted, the princess could be spilling sensitive— and life-threatening—information to the Faction.

"I never dishonor my word, Jamie." He leaned against the desk and crossed his arms over his chest, then, decided to prop his palms on the desk at his hips. More open that way. Couldn't have her putting up her guard against his suspicions. "I'm just surprised."

Arms akimbo, her guard remained fierce. "That I would choose to work for a bastard like you?"

"Bastard?" He rather liked it when a woman's ire ruffled her so brilliantly. A soft blush rosed her cheeks, and he knew it wasn't makeup. *La lapine* was a natural woman. "And just how will your newly-gained charitable morals allow you to work for a man who would stoop so low as to slavery and kidnapping?"

"Let's cut through the crap and jump right to the chase, shall we?" She strode right up to him. Solid in her expression, those pale blue eyes meant business. But was that a bit of hesitation in the flicker of lash that briefly redirected that steely expression to the side? "You're not getting rid of me so easily. The way I see it, you owe me a car and a home."

"A car?"

"The Audi your thugs drove off into the sunset with yesterday morning."

When had Thom and Jacques—? Hmm... No, he'd play along with this one. "As quickly as possible. I'd hate to see the lady without her wheels." Sacha leaned back and drew up his right leg to cross over his left knee. "As for a home? I must honestly plead ignorance."

"Are you going to tell me you have no clue about the fire at my place last night? A fire that burned while I was under the influence of your nastiness?"

"I wouldn't dream of claiming ignorance, but—"

"You fried the place while I sat doped up in your office. What did you give me?"

"Just the chloroform."

"Liar."

Sacha straightened abruptly. The stones were right behind him on the desk, but no, he didn't feel anger; it was more a sense of hurt that this woman would accuse him. "I would never lie to you, Jamie. I will always tell you exactly as you wish to be told."

"Oh really? What did you do to me?"

"When?"

"Last night while I was unconscious!"

"Nothing. You slept on the floor right over there. I only had Jacques place you on the chair just minutes before you came to."

She narrowed her gaze at him.

"Why the disbelief?"

"Did you touch me?"

"Touch—you think I took advantage of you?"

"It's called rape."

"Hell no!" He reeled back and grabbed a stone. Cold and hard, it was just so…hard. Breathing out, he focused and turned back to Jamie. "You think you were raped?"

"Just…asking."

"Wouldn't you know?"

"I don't know. It's never happened before."

"Thank God!"

"Do not express false concern over me, Vital." Arms crossed tightly over her chest, she paced before him. "Tell me about the fire."

A fire. At her place? What was the Faction up to? It wasn't a lie if you honestly didn't know what the hell was going on. "Sorry. Sometimes things just…have to be done." But by whom? "You understand?"

"What I understand—" she leaned in closer so he could feel her breath on his mouth "—is that we've got a business transaction to take care of. You wanted a driver?"

"I do, very much."

"Fine, you've got *la lapine*, the best in the city. One ride, in a brand-new Audi—no, make that a Bimmer. I call the shots. You sit back and enjoy the pleasure of my service."

"And you get what out of this deal?"

"Besides the new wheels? I get the satisfaction of taking you on the ride of your life."

"Will it be the ride to end my life?"

"That's a chance you'll have to take. You in?"

Oh, he was in. This ploy was too intriguing to resist. And if it got him closer to the goal… "I'm in."

"Fine." She noticeably loosened her stance with a shrug of her sleek shoulders and a twist of her neck.

Round one: *la lapine*. But Sacha was not down for the count. Far from it.

"Before I can take you anywhere, I'll need a car," she said.

"Of course. Here." Sacha slipped a cell phone from an inner pocket. It was a spare he kept in the office; no valuable contact numbers in it. Usually he lent it to Thom for the directions he would inevitably call for while on the road. "Take the phone. I'll be in contact very soon with the dealer that'll have a new Audi—"

"I want a BMW for this ride. Three series. All the options: Bluetooth, sports package, GPS, active steering. And make it…Barrique Red."

Sacha liked a woman who knew what she wanted. This driver had driven him once; he wouldn't mind a repeat performance.

"Done," he said. "I prefer the German-engineered automobiles myself."

She smirked. "What, a VW Beetle?"

"Bugatti Veyron 16.4."

That got a lift of brow from her. "Red?"

"You know it."

A noticeable appreciation softened her features for but a moment, then business mode tightened her jaw. "So what's the job?"

"I'll tell you when I'm sitting in your new Beamer."

"Americans." She scoffed. "It's called a Bimmer. Beamers are BMW motorcycles, of which, I don't drive. Got it?"

"You're the boss, lady."

"Exactly. So, I'll wait for your call. But the ground rules are, I only take one passenger. You. No thugs."

"Agreed."

"And you won't talk to me."

Sacha shrugged.

"I can see you understand the importance of silence." She tucked the phone into her pack and slung it over her shoulder, and then spun on her heel.

It was all Sacha could do not to follow her sexy skirt-swinging exit like a puppy to its master. But he did lean forward to catch a bit of hip-rocking action as she strode down the hallway. Nice.

Her home and a car? A bimmer, not a beamer, which was a motorcycle. Right. He knew that. Maybe. Her house had gone up in flames? Hmm… He'd have to look into that claim.

Jamie MacAlister had walked into a fierce battle. Did she have a clue what the Faction had gotten her into? Neither side would be concerned for her safety. In fact, both sides may prefer her dead. Unless, of course, she was just sexy enough to appeal to one of the side's lust.

Which, damn it, she was.

Scrubbing a palm over his scalp, Sacha smiled to himself and turned to the phone on the desk. He had a BMW dealer to locate, and a lot of cash to lay out to satisfy his curiosity. But more importantly, he would not discount the urgency and necessity of finding that princess.

Chapter 13

It was just plain naff, taking public transportation, but after losing the Audi, I wasn't willing to risk the Bimmer. Sacha's agreement to replace the Audi had surprised the hell out of me. I guess I wielded more command than I thought. Oh yeah, when I speak, people listened.

Right.

I slid onto an empty vinyl bus seat. The air smelled like industrial cleaner. Pressing my head to the cracked headrest and clutching the hard seat with tense fingers, I closed my eyes and blew out a breath.

That had been easy enough, securing a job with Vital.

Too easy. He was up to something.

As was I.

Kevin had warned me I'd be stepping onto dangerous ground when I agreed to work with the Faction to take down

Vital. I was in for the adventure, and Max Montenelli most certainly deserved to be avenged.

I powered on the phone Kevin had given me and speed dialed the only number programmed. The Faction could track me through the connection. I relied on the cellular airwaves as my only backup. The line crackled but was answered after the second ring.

Kevin didn't even say hello—not that I expected the civility. "Location?"

"Just outside Sacha's office on a bus. Left Bank, heading west and toward the Right Bank."

"You speak to Vital?"

"We're on. I'm waiting for his call."

"You going to pick him up with the bus?"

"So there does lie humor behind the dimples. No, I've arranged transportation." Why I didn't volunteer the car situation to Kevin wasn't important. Was it? If it was a new vehicle, I had little to worry for traps set by Vital. "I'll call you once I've got a pickup location."

"Fine. We'll be tracking. Good going, *la lapine*."

"Call me Jamie."

"Er, Jamie." Do you think he blushed just a little on the other end of our connection? I imagine he did. "But you'll have to get used to calling me Eight. Can't have Vital hear my real name. Not that you'll reveal your connections to the Faction anyway. Right?"

All right, so no blush.

"Roger, Eight. Over."

I tossed the cell phone into my duffel, then shuffled around inside. There must be half a dozen empty gum wrappers, but no real gum in sight. Why I'd tossed in makeup brushes and eye shadow was beyond me—it had all been part of the stuff I'd shoved inside during my rush to vacate the apartment.

I drew out the lipstick tube. The shiny gold cover was dented. "Grim." Must have gotten clonked by the torque wrench. A check assured the valuable little tube was still in working order, so I tossed it back into the fray.

The iPod was still alive, though it had taken a beating the past twenty-four hours. Popping in the earbuds, I then spun my thumb around the click wheel until I arrived at Playlist, then chose Fun.

Bowling For Soup's "Girl All The Bad Guys Want" began to jingle inside my head. How appropriate. I impulsively tapped the click wheel to shuffle to another song, and then, with a smile and a shake of my head, gave in to the silliness of the song.

Drawing the cell phone Vital had given me from the bag, I flipped it open and made sure it was on. Curious, I scrolled through Contacts, and was disappointed to find it clean of phone numbers. Of course he wasn't stupid enough to put that sort of information into my hands. But wouldn't it have been interesting to find a girlfriend's name? Then again, I pitied the woman who had the misfortune to date a man who sold women into slavery.

Twice now, the bastard had put me under his thumb. But this time, I was up for thumb wrestling.

I vacillated shutting off the phone.

You are not being manipulated, he is. No victim here. You're trying to exact justice for Max's murder, nothing but. And don't forget it.

A sigh to blow over ships sifted between my lips. With it, my muscles softened and I snugged against the hard bus seat. Centuries-old stone buildings whisked by outside. I tuned down the volume with a flick of my finger.

"Max, I miss you."

I had thought to so effortlessly shut out the pain of loss from my life. Twice over. First, with my father's death and then Max. The two most important men in my life, and now I had neither. I missed the comfortable alliance I'd had with both. It had felt good to have a male companion, whether it was my father or my mentor. Both had been strong men, but never harsh or unkind to me.

Now, I battled another strong male.

I wondered how Sacha had known Max. I couldn't recall Max mentioning him, though his profession demanded that he deal with all sorts.

Maybe they hadn't known each other. Was Sacha a hit man? Hired to take out a nuisance driver? Sacha had been fathered by a man who sold women for money. On the scale of criminal careers fostered by parental influence, it was an easy leap to make.

The last time I had seen my mentor alive was the night of my birthday. It had been '80s night at DV8...

I love American '80s music, so the fact that it was blasting my every pore was fitting. I shimmied on the dance floor, taking joy in the swishy click of the beaded lime-green fringe that edged my thigh-high dress. Layers of the beads fell from breast to thigh like a flapper's dress. I'd worn killer stilettos in matching glitter-green. Tonight was all about me, and I wanted every man in the club to notice.

But the most important man danced opposite me. I'd been with Max Montenelli for more than four years. It had been his idea to go out for drinks. We weren't boy-friend and girlfriend, though occasionally we were lovers.

Mostly, we shared a professional relationship, but cared for one another. Once in a while, sex just happened.

Flashing strobes danced across Max's smooth, bald, black head. Jamaican by birth, he had lived in London most of his life, so had a cockney accent with just the slightest smoothness of the islands. Gorgeous green eyes always won him a second look from the ladies. And he wasn't one to walk by without noticing those looks.

Sliding a palm down my arm, Max drew me close. We ground our hips in a teasing promise and bounced low.

"I see an acquaintance at the back of the room," Max shouted beside my ear. "I'm going to say hello."

I nodded, but didn't lose the beat as he spun away from me. But three vodkas and I was feeling keen. Dancing with a partner or by myself, it didn't matter, so long as the music didn't stop. The Spanish rhythm of Madonna's "La Isla Bonita" coaxed me toward the center of the dance floor. Once there, I did a periphery scan of the bar.

Flashing lights and arms swaying high in the air made it difficult to pick out anything, but I did spot Max's head in the shadows beneath the balcony. There another man stood, who nodded as Max approached. I'd never seen him before and, frankly, didn't care.

At the time, I'd thought nothing of it. Max had bussed my forehead with a birthday kiss and whispered, "Happy birthday" in his sexy Jamaican-Brit accent. I didn't mind him leaving me alone. I'm in my element on the dance floor (correction: second element; you know the car is first). I'd remained on DV8's dance floor and boogied for what seemed like endless hours of ecstatic dancing.

Later, I found myself a partner who had matched my every move. I love a man who's not afraid to let loose dancing, just allow his body to move and enjoy the motion. He was handsome and danced as smoothly as a Porsche 911 corners going ninety. We'd spent a good hour on the dance floor—most of it slow dancing—even as bodies tranced and thumped to a raucous beat all around us. Neither of us had asked if the other would like to go home for the night. It had just happened.

The small apartment my dance partner took me to was in the 11th arrondissement, not far from the place de la Bastille, where the famous prison once held cruel reign. The three-room loft, faced with dozens of floor-to-ceiling windows, had been sparsely furnished, so much so that I commented, "You just move in?"

"Moving out," he'd said with a whiskey smile. (Though his drink of choice had been vodka, neat.)

He tugged off his suit coat and shirt (the well-fitted designer kind that I knew was expensive only because of the little black-and-yellow bee embroidered below his rib cage on the right side). The sight of his pecs lured me across the room to kiss the hard masculine flesh. Beneath my brazen, exploring touch, his muscles tensed and he murmured a soft plea not to stop. The taste of him, like salt and vodka and sex, filled my mouth.

I wanted all he could give me, quick, hard and all night long.

Strong fingers glided over my shoulders and lifted the thin glittery straps. I shimmied like a dancer out from under the dress as he lifted it and tossed it aside. Wearing nothing but my stilettos and panties, I coaxed him with a sly finger to follow me, and we collapsed together on a lush, high bed.

Nameless sex with a stranger is hot, and it wasn't the first time I'd neglected to learn my lover's name. There's something about anonymity that destroys inhibitions and tempts a lass to simply take it all, and beg for more.

The next morning, I woke alone amidst a sea of crisp white sheets. It was difficult to emerge from the 900-thread-count luxury, but I was annoyed at being abandoned. I did the usual apartment search—de rigueur following anonymous sex—more out of curiosity than looking for anything. He brushed his teeth with Elgydium toothpaste, had no evil looking creams in the cabinet. Silk boxers were his choice, and the refrigerator stored only Perrier and fruit. There was nothing personal to clue me in about the man who had rocked my world.

I hadn't even learned his name.

I've always deviated from the path. All right, so I've sped right on through the warning signs and on to dangerous territory. And standing at the end of that path were the bad boys just waiting to give me the comfort—albeit false—I craved from a man. No staunch, upright morals for this chick. Leave those business suits at home and wrap me in your arms of leather and steel.

I sighed following the final notes of Cinder's "Soul Creation" pumping in my ears. The chorus claimed that I would want it, need it, love it, and even hate it.

Yes, I wanted. I needed. I wanted a man in my life, but he had to take care of himself. Just loving me and keeping me happy were all I required from him. And sex whenever I chose. Sex is good. Sex is keen. Sex makes life worth living. Sex is world currency.

I'd been on a dry spell since sleeping with Sacha, but that had nothing to do with lack of interest. Was it because my world moved so much faster than most of the men I cruised by?

I tapped my fingers to the beat on my thigh and refocused on that morning following waking up at Sacha's. I'd left the apartment after snooping, thinking he wouldn't return, and drove the Audi home. I knew that Max would call me when he needed his car back and suspected that if he'd gone home with a woman, he didn't need me barging in to hand him the keys and wait for a ride home.

Around noon, I'd gotten a call from Fitch asking me to meet her at Max's house. When I arrived, she told me about the car accident. We both suspected it was murder.

Had Sacha left me slumbering in his bed and gone to kill Max? Why? And how? Max had been peeled out of a banger—not his own. I'd immediately thought he'd gotten a ride home, but reports said there had been no one else in the car. Had Sacha's sleeping with me been a clever ruse to…to what?

Something didn't add up. Max had to have been pursued by a professional driver. It's the only thing I could guess. (And my initial guess had been the Network.) Sacha Vital was neither a professional driver nor a member of the Network. However, that didn't rule out him hiring someone, which had to be the likely choice.

But that still didn't explain how Max had gotten behind the wheel of a strange car.

Pressing the back of my head against the bus seat, I closed my eyes. I would bring Vital to justice. I owed it to Max.

But first things first. I was starving. And likely I smelled

pretty rank after yesterday's adventures. I needed a change
of clothing and some food. I had a T-shirt and jeans in my bag;
I'd have to change first chance I got.

Your apartment went up in flames.

If Kevin—aka Eight—was such a good watcher, couldn't
he have prevented the fire? Or did he take some strange sort
of pleasure in witnessing my pain while keeping tabs on me?
We watch. We don't interfere. That man had been watching
too much television.

Thinking of what I had lost in the fire didn't upset me
overmuch. I had taken anything of value when I'd vacated
after the cocked-up kidnapping attempt. Cash, passports and
ID, a few family pictures of me and my pa, and the photo I'd
found in Max's bedroom when Fitch and I had searched.

I dug into the duffel bag, drawing out the stack of photos.
The Black Crows claimed they were "Hard To Handle" as I
sorted through the few glossy snapshots. My pa held a thin pike
up near his ear. The silly grin on his face told me he didn't care
about the fishing; it was the time he'd spent with his daughter
that mattered to him. Another showed Pa sitting on the hood
of an old Volkswagen Rabbit he'd completely overhauled. I had
raced that a few times and had returned home with a stack of
bills—much to Pa's annoyance. He had never been keen on me
risking my life, yet he'd never succeeded in taming my furious
heart. I had spied him cheering me on during more than one
street race, yet he'd always slip away and beat me home. I
wondered if it had been difficult for him to hold the stern, dis-
approving parent look after I'd return home.

Secretly, I think he was proud of me, but he'd never put it
into words.

I bowed my head, ignoring the race of buildings and pedestrians outside the bus window. The corner of my left eye

burned. With a tear? I don't cry. That's my story, and I'm sticking to it.

It was not easy to relate to those good times now. It wasn't as though my life had changed so drastically, beyond my father no longer sharing my successes and challenges. I held Pa in my heart and always knew where to find him, should I need him. Yeah, he'd been proud. One doesn't have to say it to show it in their eyes.

As for my mother? She could still be alive, but I've never felt the urge to find her. Wanderlust? Hmm, I suppose that could be partially to blame for my need to drive. Driving away from things most important to me.

Maybe.

Oh, bloody Sunday, I didn't believe that gobbledygook. I am the way I am because I'm…me, and not because of any mother I'd never had in my life, or because my pa was a quiet man who'd let his daughter learn from her own mistakes instead of trying to mold her into something she was not.

I hadn't turned out so awful. All right, so I was trying my best to atone.

The final picture in the stack featured a dark-haired woman, probably in her late twenties, smiling more with her ebony eyes than her straight mouth. It was the photo I had found lying on Max's nightstand near the alarm clock, as Fitch and I had pored over his things hoping to find a piece of evidence before the police arrived on the scene. To keep it so close to his bed, well, I figured the woman must have been someone close to Max.

Except for the two of us, Max had never mixed personal relationships with business and had asked me to do the same. He'd known of my penchant for seeking one-night stands and rarely commented on the reckless nature of my ways. I was looking for a connection, Max had once analyzed, someone to replace the hole my pa's death had left. I'd always shrug. Max was no therapist. I just like sex.

I had never guessed Max knew someone who would hold a prominent place so close to his heart. Now, I flipped over the photo and read the name scrawled in Max's tight black script: Ava. A pretty name, but there was no way to determine nationality for the shadowed light made the color photo virtually black-and-white. And without a last name, she would be impossible to trace.

With a shrug, I held the stack of photos up and silently vowed to the mystery woman that I would find her, return the photo, and tell her all I could of Max's never-ending thrill of a life. If that was what the woman wanted.

I replaced the photos in an inner pocket of the duffel so they wouldn't get too rumpled. My stomach spoke up. Yes, I could hear it growl even over the low tones of music.

I eyed the passing shop fronts for an enticing restaurant for something hot and quick to eat when the phone rang. The one Sacha had given me.

"Time to put on the game face," I muttered as I flipped it open and tugged out one earplug. "Speak."

"I'm ready."

"Yes?"

"I'm in a parking lot for the InterContinental hotel on the rue de Castiglione."

"Across from the Tuileries? That's a popular area. Must be plenty of tourists milling about."

"Exactly. If you're not here in five minutes, I drive away in your new car."

"I'm on a city bus." I scanned the street, locating a sign; I was on the rue St. Honoré, not far from the royal gardens, but a longer trip for the many stops along the way. "I can be there in ten minutes. If you don't wait for me, I'll hunt you down, Vital."

Click.

Chapter 14

There was so much static on the line, I suggested Kevin find a new provider. I gave him the meet location, though I had to repeat it twice for him to understand.

"We're being scrubbed," I thought I heard him say through intermittent bursts of interference.

I guessed that was some tech term for being scrambled or spied on by those hacks who drive around trying to tap into WiFi connections. I wondered if I should contact Fitch for a clearer connection. I still wasn't sure if I could trust her. However, now we were both playing for the enemy.

Correction: I wasn't. I never would.

"I hope you've got my back," I said to Kev—Eight—and then hung up. "But if you don't…" I touched the shape of the Glock in the bag nestled upon my lap. "I can handle Monsieur Vital."

* * *

I was wishing Adam Ant had been top of the charts during my prime—I would have liked to see him perform "Desperate But Not Serious" in concert wearing his pirate/fop gear, prancing across the stage, shifting his hips for all the ladies.

I sang along to the tune as I walked the sidewalk en route to the parking lot connected to the hotel where Sacha was waiting.

Was that what I had become? Was I desperate but not serious? Desperate for…something. But not serious about finding that something?

Connection, Max's deep British accent said in the haze of my thoughts. *You are desperate for connection, girl. Can you take it seriously once you have it?*

Why did a ghost from my past seem to hit it right on the mark?

Fine, I'd take the connection part, but please, I did not *need* a man. All that jazz about a man completing a woman? Not on my watch. But it goes without saying that I do enjoy men.

A billowing white canopy covered half the hotel parking lot. I strode down the first aisle, eyeing a few patrons leaving their cars behind while dragging luggage toward the hotel. Tourists. At the far end, near a grove of lush lime trees, stood a tall figure, the back of his head visible over the roof of a shiny new 3 series sedan BMW. My pace increased. This was going to be bloody spectacular.

Well. When the man promised to deliver, he certainly did deliver.

Ignoring Vital's nod of acknowledgment at my approach, I ran my fingers over the slick, deep red paint on the hood of the car. It was so glossy it slipped beneath my fingers like silk, but it was finer than any silk sheets that had ever slid over my body.

"Barrique Red," I said with satisfaction. A subtle quiver trickled through my system. Miniorgasm over a car? It was definitely possible, but I didn't quite get there. Nothing less than driving a Ferrari or Porsche could do that.

"Red? It's brown."

"Red," I snappily corrected.

"Whatever." Sacha toed the front tire. "I thought they'd delivered the wrong car when I saw the color. But if you say it's red…"

It did look like a deep chocolate brown here in the tree-laced shadows, but I was sticking to my guns. "Red."

Sleek, agile and luxurious. Two hundred and fifty horse-power, 7,000 rpms and maximum torque. This pretty redhead would go zero to sixty in under six seconds. I could so thrash behind the wheel. She was designed for fun, but not necessarily a backseat full of passengers. Three could squeeze tightly in the back—not conducive to pickups—but I'd worry about that later. I couldn't wait to hear the roar of the engine as I pushed her to the limit.

Christmas had come early.

"The key is in it," Sacha offered. "I figured I'd let you re-program the start code yourself. It's yours."

You had better believe it was mine.

Not needing to be forced, I skipped around to the driver's side, slipped inside and touched the key. My fingers danced over the sleek dashboard, up over the crest of the steering wheel and then along my thighs to absorb the buttery leather into my very psyche.

The interior was quiet, like a private spa designed only for me, and with buttons, each within tapping range, to please my every whim. Sitting on the cordovan leather seats was like sleeping between 900-thread count sheets. The latter was soft as a baby's bottom, and you know how sweet it is to touch a baby's bottom. (Don't get any ideas. I am not ready to settle down and become a mother. Would I repeat my mother's transgression of abandoning her only child? It was something I thought about. A lot.)

Wielding an anticipatory finger and dancing it about in a few balletic circles, I then pressed the Start button.

"Purr, baby, purr." And I think I purred in response to the engine's call to adventure.

I pressed voice control on the steering wheel. "Radio on." The tunes softly pulsed, and I left the volume low because the pound of my heartbeat was all the rhythm I needed.

Closing my eyes and inhaling, I lingered in the heady aroma of factory-new leather and a pristine engine. "Oh, but I love new-car smell."

Alone in a new car—a car I didn't have to pay for—was the best feeling in the world. The flood of superpowered endorphins rushed straight to my groin; I was ready to settle back and soar.

I hit the door lock button on the steering wheel, but it was too late. I'd seen the hand move in for the kill out of the corner of my eye. The passenger door opened. My spa was under invasion.

But I had a brilliant idea.

"Hold up!" I swung out and skipped around to the passenger side. I had to protect myself. No new-car orgasm was going to alter my perception and put me off my game.

Sacha held a black leather briefcase and stood before the open door.

"Arms out," I said. "You are not getting in the car with me until I'm assured you're not packing."

He spread out his arms. "Go for it."

I quickly patted him down from armpit to waist and down each leg wrapped in dark brown velvet that *cushed* under my moving palms. I stood, hands spread and sort of clutching at nothing to either side of me, as if I wanted to touch some more but knew I shouldn't. Velvet?

"You should check my crotch. Guys always stick the gun there," he taunted. "I'm serious. I am a dangerous man."

Only dangerous to the fashion police. So I did pat down his front and arse, just to prove no man was going to intimidate me. Nice arse, by the way, but I couldn't do any more than lightly touch the front of his trousers.

"Find anything interesting?"

Our eyes met for a coy yet snarky duel. "Nothing that stands out as particularly dangerous. Your case," I said, forcing my eyes to the side.

He set the briefcase on the car roof and opened it up. A bunch of papers sat inside.

"What is that stuff?"

"Business documents. Assorted ephemera. I never leave the office without it. You cool now?"

"Fine." I returned to the driver's side and slid behind the wheel.

Sacha's hand jutted inside the car and brushed off the seat. The perfectly clean, brand-new seat. It wasn't dirty, but he certainly must have thought it was.

Sweep, sweep sweep.

"Come on, get over it."

Finally, Sacha slid into the car and closed the door.

Instantly, the atmosphere took on a new shape. It felt electric and a little heavier, and it raised the hair on my arms. My spa had been invaded, but the enemy wore sensuous cologne, velvet trousers and a come-hither smirk.

"In the back," I said, eyes focusing straight forward and, assuming business mode, hands curling about the wheel.

"No."

He sat staring straight ahead, as well.

No? I frowned. Now was no time to play with the driver. All kiddies must respect their betters.

"All passengers must be seated in the back. This is a job. And you are a passenger. The car does not move until you do, Vital."

"Then I guess we'll have a pleasant afternoon sitting in the car, listening to…what *is* that horrible noise?"

"Only one of the greats." Forefinger hovering over the volume control, I restrained myself from cranking up Billy Idol's "Rebel Yell." Right now, I wanted to hear the man and to have him hear me. Behind the wheel I am a professional.

"Move, Vital. It's either the backseat or the boot."

"The trunk? You intend to stuff me in that little compartment?"

"Not going to work, unless it's in pieces. Don't worry, the backseat will do."

"I'm not much for the back of any moving vehicle," he stated. "I get queasy."

Eyebrow arched in extreme annoyance, I hid a smirk. This well-built, powerhouse of a man got queasy sitting in the back?

"It's the truth," he said. "As a child, I never could make the trip to Batz—where Grandma Lyon lived—from Paris without my mother having to pull over to the side of the road to let me, well…"

An unpleasant image jumped to mind of Sacha leaning over the ditch. I used to get sick when riding in the backseat, until Pa helped me get over it. It was all about following the moving horizon with your eyes. Not always possible in the backseat.

Glancing surreptitiously to the right, I eyed Sacha's fingers, tapping the dashboard. Tap, tap, tap. "Batz? I thought you were American? How long have you lived in Paris?"

"I go back and forth. I was born in Brooklyn. My father is New York to the bone, my mother is half-French, but I've been crossing the sea for decades."

Hmm, he didn't have a hint of French to his voice. Usually when people live abroad for a while, they take on a tinge of the local dialect. I couldn't be sure if his entire life was a facade, a convenient story, or if I really wanted to believe the little boy toddling off to grandmother's house.

For now, I was all for keeping the interior clean.

"Fine. You can sit in the front. But remember the rules. No touching."

"It'll be difficult."

"And no talking."

"Would you like to handcuff me to the door, as well?"

Ignoring his sarcasm, I shifted into drive and the Bimmer rolled silently out from under the white canopy. "If I had cuffs, trust me, I wouldn't hesitate to use them."

"Kinky," he said. I swung a look his way, just in time to catch his wink. "I like that about you, so sexually adventurous."

"You don't know a thing about me, Vital. Most especially my preferences in bed."

"If that's the story you want to go with..." He brushed his palm along the inside of the door, swiping at specks of nothing. "You know it's been two months since I've had sex?"

Oh hell. We were so not going there—two months? So he hadn't had sex since...me?

I shifted, awkwardly, and grimaced at the grinding gears. "Just don't make me regret this, Vital."

"I can't promise you that."

"Didn't think so."

Rolling onto the rue St. Honoré, I tapped out the beat on the steering wheel as I eyed the surrounding buildings, sighting nothing questionable. I would not rule out snipers, placed by either Vital or the Faction. All windows were closed against the brisk late summer wind. A few pedestrians were either walking dogs or younger kids skipping or chatting.

As we rolled to a stop at a blue-and-white stop sign, I turned up the tunes. No tunes while there was a passenger in the car? It was a rule I insisted on breaking, for I couldn't bear the silence with Sacha's overwhelming presence literally seeping through my pores.

The drummer pounded a steady rhythm that I unconsciously matched. Again, that heaviness of being surrounded wanted to invade me by seeping into my mouth and nose and filling me with... Two months? That was such a long time.

From the corner of my eye I noticed something bizarre. Sacha was playing— "What are you doing?"

He paused, mid-chord, right hand formed in a plucking motion. "Air guitar." Then took up the chorus again with an enthusiastic bang of his head and the classic guitar-god face scrunch. Metallica blasted "Fuel" over the radio, and this man...

"You can't do that!"

Bringing his head bang to an abrupt, twisting halt, he winced at me. "Another rule? I saw you doing the air drums. Thought I'd join in." He riffed into a silent scale that would have put the band's lead guitarist to shame.

For a moment, I just stared. It was like looking at a bad accident. You didn't want to look, but you knew you'd be thinking about it for the rest of the day if you didn't. The man took his air guitar seriously.

I tapped a drumbeat on the wheel, then caught myself. "Stop it!"

"No."

"And—" clenching my fingers so I couldn't air drum, I fisted the air in frustration, "—stop talking to me. I am—this is a job. Professional, up, down, left, right, anyway you look at it. Please review rule number one."

Guitar abandoned, Sacha cocked his head my direction and shot me a wondering gaze.

"I said—"

"Rule one! No talking to the driver. You did demand my silence," he blurted. "And you had it. I was playing unplugged, I'll have you know."

"You—"

"You either wish my silence, and thus we spend the afternoon cruising the city with no destination. Or you toss the silence rule, I put away the guitar and you get your answers."

He was acting like a little kid with a superiority complex. A little kid who smoothed his palm over the leather seat, back and forth, sensually—as if gliding it over a woman's thigh. Sort of like he'd done to the stone in his office. And the lapel of his suit. What was it with his touching things all the time? The man was just plain weird.

Idling at the intersection, I tapped the steering wheel—but *not* to any particular beat. "Very well. You can speak, but only when spoken to."

He made a ridiculous motion of pulling the guitar strap over his head and setting the nonexistent instrument down on the floor.

I so did not need this goof. "Where am I headed?"

"West. Out of the city."

"Toward Batz?" Not to grandmother's house! That was south and a long drive.

He shrugged, not a yes or no in that move.

"Exact location?"

"That'll come later," he said, "after we've crossed the Ring Road and cleared the suburbs."

I was about to snap that that was unacceptable, but I stopped myself by twisting my palms about the wheel until I felt sure the leather would tear.

Review the mission, Jamie. The Faction wanted me to get Vital out of town and away from any possible thugs he may have backing him up for an easy pickup. Everything was set. So why argue?

And yet, there was a reason he had hired me. "Are you looking for this princess who is safe with her family?"

"Later."

So he would dole out information to control me. And I really hadn't any say around it. What did I care for his ultimate goal?

"Take the second left and ease onto the freeway," he directed.

If he thought to order me around the entire time—

I twisted on the seat, pulled back my right fist, and delivered a solid knuckle-crush to Sacha's jaw. Wincing, I retracted my fist to my stomach. Damn, but that had hurt. I might have broken skin, but I wasn't going to check until later.

He didn't speak, merely gaping at me as his tongue teased his lower teeth. Those changing green-blue eyes danced between anger and surprise.

Turning to focus on the road, I shrugged and shifted into second. "Had to be done."

We passed through three lights before Sacha finally spoke. "Why do I feel like the victim here?"

I scoffed. "The only time you've ever been a victim is today, and of the crime of fashion."

"What's wrong with the couture?" He patted his brown velvet pant leg.

"The trousers are...retro. It's those stripes on that shirt." Fine maroon pinstripes on a field of blue silk. "So naff."

And since when did *I* rule the fashion world?

Hell, I was trying to keep it light. To draw out everything that was wrong with the man, to satisfy my need to have it all right. Because if I looked the better, then he would still be the worse of us two.

A left turn drew us closer to the oncoming exit to the *périphérique*.

"So stripes don't attract the females?"

"Probably not."

"Hmm, might explain the lack of sex of late."

"Yeah? Well, if you whip out the air guitar every time you meet a prospective woman, that could have some effect on your appeal."

"Right. On the other hand...this advice coming from a pitiful excuse for a Catholic school girl."

I wound up to punch him again. My fist met Sacha's open palm with a smack.

He shoved the shield weapon away and eased his legs out before him as he settled into the seat. "I'd hate to have you break your shifting hand on my face."

"Right." Skimming my knuckles over my mouth, I jutted out my tongue and tasted blood. Yep, broken skin. But I was not about to show my pain. Resuming control, I looked straight ahead. "These hands *are* valuable instruments. Buckle up, Vital. We're off."

"Yes, but we're headed the wrong direction. I said west, through the city."

"I'm taking the *périphérique*. It's quicker."

"But less scenic, and so much tourist traffic."

At that comment I swung a long stare at him. The man cared about the view? Or was he just as goofy as he appeared?

"Keep your eyes on the road!"

I turned my attention back to the street in time to avoid a turning bus. That lack of perception was so not me.

"The best driver in Paris?" he wondered mockingly.

"The best kidnapper in the city?" I riposted.

"Touché. I guess we make quite the pair."

And without another word, I merged onto the freeway that circled Paris. Turning the tunes up and restraining myself from drumming along with Love and Rockets' "So Alive," I figured the freeway would offer some smooth sailing, and lack of conversation.

Until we came upon the ten-car pileup crossing six lanes, which had slowed the traffic to a literal halt. *Un embouteillage.* I love the French word for traffic jam. Such a delicious mouthful—but not a treat.

"Guess we've got time to chat," Sacha offered. He unbuckled and twisted on the seat to look at me. "So, *are* you Catholic?"

"I'm Scottish," I said as sternly as possible, tapping the steering wheel. He was breaking the no-talking rule. "Why do you ask?"

"Well, you've got the sexy-school-girl look going. What do you call that? A kilt?"

"It's a plaid." I smoothed a hand over the skirt. "And you're an arse."

"Touchy. Definitely going to purgatory for that one."

"Not Catholic. Scottish, remember?"

"That's not a religion."

"It is where I come from."

"So that means there's nothing under the kilt—er, plaid?"

"Just a kick, itching for your face."

"Meow."

He tapped his knee. Three times. And then he placed his other hand on the rim of the door and gave that three consecutive taps. The guy had a thing for threes.

"All right then," he said. "Want to reminisce about your birthday night?"

Chapter 15

"I need some air," I said, avoiding the loaded question. There was no way I would allow the man to steer me to a conversation about sex.

The traffic had opened onto an exit ramp, a road through Clichy that I was familiar with. It took us from metropolis, to suburb, to country in less than ten kilometers. The joys of the French countryside. A froth of pinks flooded a field to my left, and a billboard advertised Orangina Fire, recharging my hunger.

"Drive to the nearest restaurant," Sacha said.

Hmph. I wasn't about to agree with the man, the...compelling, charming—no, just a man. But who's to argue?

"We'll get a bite to eat," he added. "I heard your stomach growl when we took the off-ramp. Deal?"

I had hoped he hadn't heard that miserable growl, but I was defeated by my body's lack of self-control. A restaurant would afford a safe setting and plenty of people, little opportunity for Sacha to try something.

"So, you'd better talk, Vital. What's the job? Where am I headed?"

"I'll give you all the information you need after we've stopped. Right there."

The golden arches screamed out from a frontage road to my left. A bloody McDonald's in the middle of France. Only the Americans. I pulled in and was even thankful for the greasy smell of processed food as I stepped outside, away from the haven that had become a dangerous place to my libido.

Lingering by the Bimmer—I had only just got her, and she was so pretty—I felt, rather than saw, Sacha's catty smirk over the roof of the car.

"She's safe," he offered.

"Yeah? Well, I've had a bit of trouble with keeping cars safe of late." I activated the alarm with a beep, tucked the key fob into my skirt pocket and strode into the restaurant ahead of Sacha.

He ordered me a royal stacked with plastic-like cheese and dripping more oil than an early '60s Triumph. A squeeze of one soggy fry spoiled my appetite. The orange juice appeared to be safe. It was keen, I must admit. But the processed chicken pieces Sacha snarfed down looked even better.

"So." I wiped my mouth and slurped back a slug of over-sweetened but ice-cold, orange juice. "Is this job going to require extensive driving?"

"Not if we find what I need."

I watched as he placed the white plastic knife and fork to each side of the white cardboard box the nuggets sat in. The napkin followed. Along with the plastic wrapper—neatly folded in half—and a wet wipe. Everything so…orderly. Just like his clothes, his personality. I wondered if the guy had a bit of the obsessive compulsive thing going on.

Sacha took a sip of his beer and sat back with a sigh and a pat to his non-existent belly. "Okay, here it is."

All ears, I leaned forward expectantly.

"The job is, you're going to help me find the princess."

Why had I thought it could be anything but?

The plastic creaked as I slammed back my spine into the unmoving molded seat. "Vital, are you that stupid? The princess is gone. Returned to her family."

Calmly, he drank his beer, then set it down. Precisely above the white fork, in fact, he made minute adjustments to the plastic cup to make it so. What was with OCD Boy?

"And what leads you to believe she is safe?" he asked. "Did you witness as she was placed in the loving arms of said family?"

"No, but I dropped them off at the train station. And the—" I couldn't reveal my connections to the Faction. He had to know I was working with them, or at least suspect, because he'd suggested as much when he'd questioned me in his office.

"Certainly that proves she is safe." His tone mocked, as did his eyes; they tinted to a pale, cold blue. "That the Faction took her directly to the train, kissed her on the cheek and waved her off. Think, woman. What proof do you have?"

I started to mouth "Kevin told me," but kept it to myself. I had no reason to distrust Kevin. *Eight*! If he said he'd returned the princess, I believed him. What reason would he have to lie? The Faction was the good guys. Besides, I'd been right there when he'd put in a call to check she was safe.

Really? Are you sure that call was about the princess?

I wasn't about to start doubting now. Should I?

I didn't like the way Sacha was prying beneath my skin with a fine razor; it was making me squirm.

"What reason does the Faction have for keeping her?" I countered. "And for that matter, why do *you* need her so badly? Isn't one woman the same as the next in your line of work? As long as she's gorgeous and young, you can sell her—"

"I've had enough of your insinuations that I am a slave trader."

I gave him a silent *duh* shrug, imploring with an incredulous gaze.

The action set him off. Fist clenched upon his knee, Sacha gritted his jaw. I thought his eyes became a vivid green, but it had to be a trick of the afternoon light beaming through the colored windows that decorated the nearby play area.

"Do you always jump to conclusions, Miss MacAlister?"

I flashed a look of surprise at him. A burn of warning heated the back of my throat. "I never told you my last name."

"I make it a point to know the people I work with. And to never make assumptions."

So he'd had me checked out? Then he should know I couldn't tell him anything about the Faction.

Enough already with this princess who was no longer a part of the picture. I wanted to get out with it and ask him why he killed Max. And had I been part of the setup? But that might scare him off. The fact he knew so much more about me than I did about him—we hadn't exchanged names the night of my birthday—pissed me off.

Fitch had to have filled him in.

"Fine. No assumptions."

But that didn't mean I couldn't jump to conclusions. Big difference between an assumption and a conclusion. An assumption was just a guess; a conclusion took more thought and considered the facts. I had few facts on Vital, beyond those that the double-crossing Fitch had given me.

"Maybe you're not what you so blatantly appear to be," I said. "But give me one good reason why the Faction would keep the princess."

"For the information she can give them."

I folded the crunchy yellow paper that had wrapped my sandwich, avoiding the grease that stained half. "Which is?"

Sacha rubbed a palm over his face and adjusted his position on the hard yellow seat, pressing his spine to the plastic in an attempt to distance us, though the small table would not grant such an escape.

"Time to put everything on the table, Vital. You want this ride, you've gotta help me here."

"All right, but prepare to be open-minded."

"I'm—" Hell. Truth? Not as open-minded as I liked to believe I was.

But I wasn't answering to this man, so it didn't matter, right?

Smoothing a hand over the duffel on my lap, I again felt for the gun and drew a finger along the hard outline of both cell phones. Was the Faction close? Surely, they would not swoop in and take Vital in hand here, with all these witnesses and children.

"The princess was attacked a week ago," Sacha explained. He swept a gaze about the restaurant, ensuring our conversation was as private as one could get with a massive glass-enclosed playground teeming with kiddies but ten strides away. "She was almost assassinated—strangled—but at the last moment the assassin pulled back and ran off. Days later, the princess announced to the press the assassin had been a woman."

"What has that got to do with anything? Why would the Faction want her?"

"Because the princess is the only one who can identity the assassin. If it's true, it's very possible this female assassin was a part of the Network."

Stop the train, and let me get off. The Network? Now there was a name I recognized.

I coached my expression to remain glum. This wasn't information I was willing to give Sacha. "Still means nothing to me. Why the Faction wants this Network, I don't care. And you. I don't get you, Vital. Why do you want this woman?"

"Because if the princess can identify the assassin, I may very well have found my sister."

"Your sister?" First he brings the grandma into the picture, and now we're chatting about a sister? What was the man's game?

"That is the only reason I kidnapped the princess. I read the paper and learned what she knew. I simply want to question her. If I show her a picture of my sister, maybe she can identify her."

"How? For what reason?"

"As the assassin."

That took the breath from me. Sacha's sister was an assassin? With the Network?

I lowered my head but looked up at him through my lashes.

"I've been searching for her for a while now," he said. "She disappeared a year ago, and I'd initially thought she was traveling through Europe. That was, until Ma told me she hadn't heard from my sister for months. I've come close to finding her, but never sighting her. I believe she was recruited by the Network."

So much about the Network I did not know. And yet, wherever I went, it followed. Why hadn't Max introduced me into the fold?

The Network was an elite rogue operation of criminals that, while independent of one another, worked exclusively through leads and intel provided by the members. Not at all like the Faction, because that group worked as a unit. The Network joined independent operators.

I'd once been a part of it, or so Max had told me. I'd never learned anything more than that, except all its members were young women, trained by men. Oh, I had suspected the Network was behind Max's murder, which is why I'd lain low for a few months.

Now I knew otherwise, but that still didn't make me want to sleep with both eyes closed.

Would the Network come after me?

Sacha thought his sister was an assassin for the group?

Interesting. But I wasn't willing to spill any more right now. Did he know I was once part of the Network? The man could be playing me. He'd had me checked out—I wasn't sure how deep my trail led, or to whom, now that I thought about it—but I shouldn't think he could get so far as the Network.

This had something to do with Max's murder; it had to. So much connected. Maybe the Network had hired Sacha to take out Max? But then, surely Sacha would have better connections to the Network, and locating his sister would be a breeze. If there really was a sister.

"She's all I think about," Sacha said. "I would have never kidnapped the princess if I didn't believe she is my only hope of finding my sister."

"Why not just stop by for coffee and a chat? Something a little less…illegal?"

He shrugged. "It's all I know, Jamie. When you've been around it all your life…"

Somehow, him calling me by my name lessened my anger.

However, I know it's a method used by terrorists and the like to get on your good side, so I decided to stick to the facts.

"That explains your motive. Maybe. But the Faction shouldn't care one way or another."

"Oh, yes they do. Who do you think killed Max?"

I gripped the folded sandwich wrapper and squeezed it into a ball, if only to keep myself from delivering another punch to his chiseled jaw. He wanted to play it out in the open like this? I could play. "You arsehole!"

Sacha blinked.

"Kevin told me you—"

"Kevin? Who the hell is Kevin?"

Merde. Well, he wouldn't place him to the Faction; they used numbers. "A cohort."

"Another driver?"

"Not your concern."

Sacha's jaw pulsed, and his eyes really did darken to rich emerald this time. "And this Kevin, he told you *I* killed Max?"

"Who else would have motive?"

"Motive? Try the Faction."

I gaped. "And for what reason?"

"For the information Max had on them. Which is the same information I have, thanks to Max telling it to me the night we met at DV8."

"Was that the first time you met Max? How do you know Max?"

"Do you want to hear this or not?"

"Go on."

"The very reason the Faction wants me dead is the same reason they took out Max. And if they can determine that the princess was indeed approached by a member of the Network, then they've got a connection. I suspect the Faction wants to take out the rest of the Network for fear Max told the members, as well."

"Told them what?"

"That the Faction is dirty," he said, lowering is voice to a harsh whisper.

"Bullshit. They rescued the princess from you."

"Yet, you still haven't given me proof you know she is safe."

"Because I…"

Didn't have actual proof, beyond what Kevin had told me. Had I been blinded by the power of the man's dimples? That was idiotic. Of course I hadn't, nor would I allow the handsome face sitting across from me to alter my thinking.

"The night of your birthday I met Max in the parking lot. Just before I entered DV8 and then met you. I knew Max. He was wired and nervous, but I ignored it because I wanted to call in a favor and hadn't seen him in a while."

"What sort of favor?"

"I wanted to know what he knew about my sister—which was nothing—but he promised to check into it. He owed me one."

I lifted a brow. This man—he couldn't be telling the truth. But the information spilled out from him so easily. He had promised only truth. But had he given me any reason to believe that?

On the other hand, he hadn't given me any reason *not* to believe him.

"I saved Max's life a while back. He was driving me to a pickup and a tail attached itself like a leech. A leech with a machine gun. I took them out before they could take out Max."

"How do you know they weren't after you?"

"Because Max named them all and told me they were after him."

"So you guys are chums?"

"No. I hadn't seen him since that pickup. As a gesture of good faith, that night, Max offered me information that would serve until he could look up my sister. He told me about a job he had done for the Faction. How he witnessed them take a kidnapped teenager and, instead of returning her to her family, packing her off on a ship to the far east. They're dirty, Jamie. And if your Kevin is working for the Faction, he's playing you right now."

The yellow wad of paper was too small and compact for me to do it any more damage. I tossed it onto the scuffed brown tray.

Kevin playing me? That would mean the Faction was controlling—no. Max had trusted the Faction. Hadn't he?

"I wonder why Max never…" I stopped.

Max wouldn't have told me about his conversation with Sacha because that was the night of my birthday. No night to make such a dire announcement; he'd wanted me to have fun. Besides, it sounded as if Max had talked to Sacha *after* he left me in the club.

I shouldn't have let him leave alone.

"So you're saying…"

Sacha took the ball of yellow paper and tossed it toward the nearby garbage can—missing by a leap. "The Faction killed Max for the information he had on them."

"Now you're making assumptions. You can't prove it. Why shouldn't I believe you're just making up an elaborate story to protect your own hide? Maybe Max wouldn't give you the information he had on the Network so you decided to retaliate."

Sacha sighed. "You forget I was a little busy that night after leaving Max."

"Yes, fucking Max's girl!"

We both jerked glances to the side. A woman at the far wall snapped her newspaper and, with an admonishing eye, went back to reading. Half a dozen kiddies partied behind the glass wall, each lobbing colorful plastic balls at each other's heads, well out of hearing range.

"Let's go back to the car," I suggested.

Without waiting for the man, I cleared out of the restaurant and strode across the parking lot. Then I turned around and stomped back toward the restaurant. I wasn't going anywhere without a change of clothes.

"Back for ice cream?" Sacha asked as he held the door for me.

"Costume change. I'll be right out."

Inside the restroom, I changed quickly, tossing my skirt and blouse into the garbage. I was too tired to care about toting them with me. The white T-shirt fit snugly, as did the blue jeans. Slapping some cold water across my face, I took a moment to study my reflection. Had I aged ten years in two days? It wasn't my appearance, but my insides that felt older.

Never in my entire career of getaway driving had I gotten involved beyond driving. I didn't chat with clients. Most especially, I didn't stop and have a bite to eat with them. Uncharted ground put me off my game.

And the man was just so…

"Don't fall for it, Jamie. He's dangerous."

I swiped a few droplets of water from my cheeks, nodded in agreement, and then ventured back outside.

I slid behind the wheel and rolled down both windows to feel a cross-breeze over my face. Vital stood outside the passenger door, waiting for me to unlock it. An unsure heaviness settled upon me. Part of the feeling due to the greasy dinner, no doubt, but I couldn't discount the misgivings Sacha had unearthed. Who was lying to me?

I contemplated locking Sacha out, but I was too eager to hear it all.

He leaned in and began to swipe a hand across the spotless leather seat.

"Oh, just get in, will you?"

He paused, palm lingering over the seat. Was it so difficult for him to just sit down? A few more swipes cleared away any minutia I wasn't capable of seeing but obviously his zoom-vision could. Finally, he got in, but kept the door open and one leg out on the tarmac.

"I had no clue who you were that night at DV8," Sacha said. "I can't believe I didn't pick up on it right away."

"How could you have known?"

"A gorgeous young woman driving the Audi you had tricked out to the nines?"

Max's car.

"I could have been a spoiled heiress."

"Not the way you drove me, baby. A spoiled heiress wouldn't know a thing about real sex."

I smirked, and a flash of our night together made my neck burn. I instantly occupied myself with brushing dust off the steering wheel. My goodness, the nonexistent dust fairy had dusted the whole damned vehicle!

Images of that night were unavoidable…

"That one," my nameless lover said with a nod toward my right breast.

I crawled over his bare legs and delivered the requested morsel to his lips. And within minutes he'd succeeded in giving me another orgasm, merely by

Michele Hauf   171

using his mouth and not moving any lower than my
waist. The man was remarkable. I sat upon him and
curled my fingers firmly.

"What are you doing?"

I realized I had a grip on his cock and was… "Shifting? I…like to drive."

"I guess so. Well, drive on, sweetie. Drive it hard."

And I had. All night long and into the morning. I could
only have slept a couple hours.

"According to the coroner's report, Max was killed in the
morning," I said. "You were nowhere to be found when I
woke up."

"I awoke around 7:15 a.m. I didn't have time to get to his
place before he was killed."

"You don't know what time he was murdered."

"7:45 a.m."

I swung him a gape-mouthed stare. "How could you possibly…"

"I was on the phone with him when it happened. I was
walking back from the grocer. I had thought of a few things
I'd neglected to tell Max the night before. One minute we
were discussing my sister, the next…silence."

He had heard…? Impossible. Because I knew otherwise.
"Liar."

"What will it take to convince you?"

"The truth. Your story is remarkable, but there's one problem."

"And that is?"

"Max was killed in a car accident."

Chapter 16

"And why do you believe that? Turn the music down," Sacha announced. "Let's get to the bottom of this."

I touched the volume control on the steering wheel and turned my body toward Sacha.

I was open to this getting to the bottom of things. Because now that some of the pieces had been presented to me— albeit from the villain's perspective—doubts were forming in my mind. And I didn't like seeing only half the picture. It wasn't fair to me, or to Max's memory.

"I went to the morgue to identify the body later that day after I...left your house," I said. "The coroner made a horrible joke about not having to examine the remains because it was so obviously a crash."

"So they didn't look for the bullet hole?"

I gaped. "I don't know what you think you heard—"

"Sounded like a gunshot when I was talking to him on the phone."

That's right, Sacha had said he'd been on the phone with Max. As he'd been walking back from the grocer. Could be a lie. I had no reason to trust this guy.

Filling the passenger side with more than just his body—his presence gave off an eerie vibe—Sacha leaned forward. "So tell me, what kind of car was it?"

"I don't know," I said. "I didn't see the scene. I spoke briefly to the coroner. I didn't ask. Just wanted to get out of there."

"Fair enough. But answer me this: A professional driver shows little concern for the kind of car that killed her mentor?"

"I was distraught!"

But, man, did he have a point there.

Max had been brought to Casualty hours after his death. Fitch and I had identified him in the morgue two hours later. Now that I think of it, shouldn't his face have been cut up from the windshield? I only remember how peaceful he'd looked in death. Eyes closed, bald head still shiny. Sweet Max.

"It wasn't Max's car?" Sacha asked. "You mentioned the Audi."

"That your thugs stole."

"If you say so. But verify, the Audi was Max's car? The one you were driving the other day when you, er, landed in the trunk?"

"Yes. I'd taken it the night of my birthday."

"Do you always borrow his car? Don't you have your own?"

"I do have my own, yet I do—did—often borrow Max's car. He'd picked me up to take me out for my birthday. Later, he said he had some business and wanted to walk, so he gave me his keys and, even later, I drove it to your place."

"So tell me why, if he wasn't shot, Max would be driving

a car—not his own? And, obviously, the following morning, since I did speak to him the next day on the phone."

When he put it that way, it did make me wonder. Add to that the mysterious phone call between the two men that morning and their brief exchange the night before at DV8. That would mean Max had to have hung up with Sacha, gone outside, gotten in a strange car…

"If Max was shot…" Sacha tossed out another idea.

"Of which there is no proof."

"Save the sound of gunfire I heard over the phone. I know what it sounds like when a body drops, Jamie. And Max didn't answer after that."

"So you then just casually returned home after hearing a man get murdered?"

"I wasn't sure. I…you were there waiting for me. I wanted to get back to you, and—hell, I didn't know what to think. And I didn't know where Max lived, so it wasn't like I could call the police and tell them to check it out."

"So you just forgot about it?"

"What could I do?"

"You could have called the police and had them trace the phone call."

"Yeah, and become an accessory to a crime."

"You are so self-centered!"

"Call me what you want. I know it's just your anger speaking, not any particular frustration toward me."

What sort of psycho-babble…?

"What I want to know is, why would the killer make it look like a car accident?" Sacha asked. "Especially if he knew the guy was a professional driver and that anyone else who knew him might question that death?"

"Don't know. I didn't question." I shoved my fingers back

through my hair and tugged. "Damn it! So your theory is, the Faction shot Max, then transported his body to another vehicle and made it look like a crash?"

"Answer me this. Why did you believe it was murder if you knew it was a car accident?"

Finally an easy question. "Because Max is the best driver there is. He wouldn't be so foolish." And at the time, I'd thought the Network quite clever for trying to make it look as if Max had died doing something he loved.

Sacha nodded. "You can be the world's best driver, but that won't necessarily protect you from the idiot drunk driving in the lane opposite yours who swerves at the last minute."

"Defensive driving."

"A long shot."

"Max was a professional."

"Again. Drunk drivers are loose cannons."

"All right! So you've proven your point. Max couldn't have possibly been in the car…alive."

I scrubbed my palms over my face. A dark chill had begun to ride my spine. It trickled up my neck and tightened my scalp. This was the exact state I'd been in upon seeing Max lying dead upon a gleaming stainless steel table. I didn't like it, and I knew the queasiness was fast on its way.

I turned my head and drew in the cool summer air through my nose.

The Faction had killed Max? Had I trusted the enemy all along? Kevin, the infamous number Eight, *was* he playing me?

One way to find out. I paused as I reached for my duffel bag. I knew the phone Kevin gave me was in there. Did I want to blow my cover by revealing my contact? Hmm…

And yet, Sacha's cold-blooded ignoring that he'd heard a murder struck me even harder.

"How do you know so much?" I speared Sacha with a severe look, but I wasn't in the mood to stand good on any implied threat. Curling up into a ball and weeping sounded much more satisfying. "I have no proof you were on the phone with Max. You left me alone in that empty apartment. Which makes me wonder now why it was so empty. You said you were moving. Was that another lie?"

"I did move."

I still glared. "Where do you live now?"

He shrugged. "There's one place in Paris, but I've got new digs outside the city, just beyond the suburbs."

"You could have went to Max's house in the early morning, shot him, and—"

"Max lived on the Right Bank; I used to be on the Left. A good trick on foot, wouldn't you say? I wasn't gone for more than forty-five minutes."

"What?"

"That morning." Sacha ran a hand through his hair, and then tapped the passenger window with his knuckles. *Tap tap, tap.* "I got dressed and walked four blocks to buy pastries and orange juice for us. When I returned I was surprised you were gone. The bed was still warm."

"You...came back?"

I pressed my forehead to the steering wheel. This was too much to take in. And if I didn't process it correctly, it was going to be muddled beyond recognition.

"I left right after waking." All right, *after* snooping through his things—minimal—so the moving claim I could buy. "I didn't check your side of the bed. It could have still been warm. You brought...breakfast?"

"I tossed the pastries."

"Pastries?"

"There's a *pâtisserie* down the road from me. The creamiest *pains au chocolat* in the world. Like eating heaven."

The man had bought the one food that could make me do anything just for a bite. Oh, baby. How could he have known?

"But I didn't want to eat them after what I thought I'd heard on the phone. And besides, you were gone," Sacha said. "I couldn't believe the best thing that had happened to me in years had disappeared from my life."

"Please, don't even try—"

"But—"

"You didn't even know my name!"

The fist he held before his nose, eyes closed, jaw clenched, didn't do anything to soften his image in my book. No flaky butter pastry with two bars of chocolate wrapped inside—yes, two bars—was going to win my heart over the horror of losing my best friend.

Releasing his fist, Sacha turned those frustrating eyes to me. "I've never told you a lie, Jamie."

I thought about that as I studied Sacha's blue-green eyes. They were half and half right now, so clear and boldly defiant of any one color.

He'd answered all my questions quickly and within reason, whether or not I liked the answers. I didn't know whether to be sick over his listening to a murder and then just letting it go without investigation, or to just chalk it up to being a part of the trade. A man like Sacha would never invite the police over for a chat, most especially about a murder.

Oh yeah, he was master of the verbal spar. Had he really been truthful with me?

Why did I not want to trust this guy? As far as I knew, he hadn't lied. He'd confessed to kidnapping the princess and then losing her, and to wanting to get her back. And he knew things about Max's death that made sense. As twisted as his morals might be, it had all been truth.

Who would lie about kidnapping?

"So when was Max killed? I went home after your place, took a shower, then went right to Max's. It was an hour, hour and a half, tops."

"He rang me about fifteen minutes after I left my house. That was when I heard the gunshot."

"My God, he was… When I got to his house…he may have just been there, alive."

That evidence frightened me. Had I just missed saving my mentor's life? Or having my life extinguished, as well? Had I been watched? Followed? How else would the Faction know I was connected to Max?

I'd never asked myself that question. How had Kevin known I was connected to Max? To be watching me, following me. Fitch had been the one to put out feelers to the Faction a few weeks earlier. It was entirely possible the group knew me only because of her.

Maybe?

I pounded the soft leather steering wheel. "Why have I been so stupid about this?" I clenched my fists tightly in frustration to either side of the wheel. I wanted to plant my foot on the accelerator and not let up. But I was aimed at the McDonald's—not keen.

"You've been emotional," Sacha offered in a voice too tender, too understanding for my aggravated state.

I shook my head fiercely, trying to separate the facts from the false reality I'd wanted to believe. And yet, there was still a chance the Network could have sneaked in, shot Max and tried to make it look like an accident.

"You lost someone who meant a lot to you," Sacha said.

"Of course, you weren't thinking properly. And if the coroner said it was a car accident, what reason would you have to question him?"

"Why are you so—" I didn't know what to think of the man anymore "—*not* the kind of guy you should be?"

"Meaning?"

"Meaning, you're…nice, and kind and you're touching my arm."

"Sorry." He took his hand from my forearm.

When he'd placed it there, I didn't know. But the absence of his touch suddenly felt so…empty. Put it back, I wanted to say, but at the same time, a weird shiver skittered through my system. Wanting a confessed kidnapper to touch me wasn't betraying any morals. I didn't have morals. Yes, I did. I just—cripes, they were so new to me. And I wasn't sure what to believe anymore.

"It's tough losing someone you care about. Or not knowing where they are and if they are safe."

He was speaking of his sister, the one he suspected had been recruited into the Network.

I'd always put the Network at the top of the suspect list. Though I knew every pickup Max had made could have garnered him another enemy, the Network held that sort of unknown evil influence.

So we had the Network, which I knew was a criminal operation, and then there was the Faction, a covert ops I was beginning to have serious doubts about. Good guys or not-so-good guys?

I turned and sat staring out the windshield, the bright colors of the restaurant playground blurring as I unfocused my eyes.

We've been keeping an eye on you.

If Kevin had been tailing me since Max's death, why wouldn't he take *me* out? He must know I was in the

Network? And if Sacha's suspicions were correct, the Faction wanted to take out the Network. I should be valuable to the Faction; they should suspect I would have information to lead them to the Network.

Or was this all a clever ruse by Sacha to throw me off his bloody trail of deception?

"We should be on the move," Sacha said suddenly. "Can't risk sitting for too long. I'm going to the men's room." He grabbed the brief case sitting on the floor near his feet. "Can I trust—"

"Pee fast," I said. "I'll be revving the engine."

The moment the passenger door closed, I clicked on my phone and speed dialed Fitch.

"Jamie! I've been worried and wondering if you'd ever speak to me again. Where on God's green earth are you?"

"McDonald's."

"A relation?"

"No." I smirked. I hadn't realized just how tense my muscles had become, and the sudden mirth relaxed me a bit. "The restaurant. Somewhere in the suburbs. Fitch, I need a favor."

"You asking someone who sold your hide to the enemy?"

"I know you weren't given a choice. It would be a difficult decision for anyone facing the threat of losing his or her fingers. And the enemy, well, I'm not sure about him anymore."

A dozen children about waist height were lined up at the entrance to the restaurant. Sacha waited patiently at the rear end for admittance. He even smiled and smacked a high-five to the little boy in front of him.

"I need everything you can find on Sacha Vital. And...the Faction."

"You okay, Jamie?"

"I'm not sure. I'm with Vital right now."

"Hell, you want I should track you? I'm dialing into your GPS right now and if I can get a good satellite shot—"

"That's keen, Fitch, but don't freak about it. I'm here because I want to be. I thought I was helping the Faction. But, well…I need that info from you. Stat."

"Will do."

"Oh, and Fitch? See what you can dig up on the Network, as well."

I hung up, and after a moment of hesitation, dialed another number. It rang twice. "Dove?"

"Bunny rabbit!"

"Just one question, Dove, and I promise you whatever you wish."

"Ooh, tempt me, darling."

"This is for Max."

"All right." His voice changed, all serious. The man had been much closer to Max than I could ever guess. I could sense it in his calm breath.

"Just answer me this: Sacha Vital, the Network or the Faction."

"Darling—"

"Dove."

"Okay. I'll answer."

Chapter 17

The phone rang and I activated the voice control on the steering wheel. This BMW came equipped with Bluetooth, and wirelessly connected to my cell without my even having to work out wires or software or tech stuff.

"Found some interesting morsels for you, sweetie," Fitch said. "You want the Faction, Vital or the princess first?"

"The princess."

"Right. Alleria el Sangreito. The Spanish TV network, Antena 3, reported that an attempt against her life was made a week ago. She was able to fight off the assassin and had planned to give a press conference with details so the assassin could be caught, but never did. She was kidnapped two days ago from her father's villa. She's still missing. Her family is frantic. They hired an underground covert ops to rescue her—"

"The Faction."

"That's my guess—of course there's no mention of any

name—but the unnamed rescue source claims they haven't gotten the princess away from the kidnapper yet."

"Vital?"

"There's no reference to suspects. But it's my guess."

"Christ, OCD Boy has been telling me the truth all along."

"OCD Boy?"

I smoothed a hand over the empty passenger seat, flicking my fingers across the soft leather. "Vital has…a few quirks."

"Ah. Cute, too."

"Fitch."

"I'm just sayin'."

"When did you see him to know that he's cute?"

"So you think he's cute?"

"I didn't say that. I just—I thought you said you didn't talk to him face-to-face?"

"Hold your horses, sweetie—and that desperate libido. I just ran a check on him, remember? I'm staring at his sexy mug right now."

"Fine." How dare she bring up my pitiful, unfulfilled libido? I was not desperate! "What can you tell me about Sacha Vital?"

"Nothing. As in, nothing on him. He's clean, Jamie. Just had the very bad luck of having a professional bad-guy father precede him. He's done small-time stuff. Public records reveal he's been busted for running betting scams and once stole a car, but otherwise…"

Yikes, the man sounded like a saint compared to me. "He stole a car?"

"Sounds like your kind of man."

"Seriously, that's all there is on Vital?"

"That's it. And this picture I'm drooling over? It was taken last year at a charity function in the States to save Alaskan seals.

He's got his arm around a beauty, but he's petting the cute little white seal in the foreground. Ain't that the sweetest thing?"

I wondered who the beauty was, and in the next instant, slammed my fist into the center console. I did not care who Sacha put his arm around. I just…did not care!

"You want me to read through his daddy's list?"

"No. I…no." Some sighs are unpreventable. "Seals?"

"He's listed as a top contributor."

Well, that threw me for a wild and crazy loop. "And the Faction?"

"Ah yes, the illustrious Faction, formed by former Sergeant Cyril Cooper six years ago in an attempt to flush out the criminals who kidnapped and murdered his daughter. All sorts are recruited, including policemen, Special Forces and even a criminal or three. Your Number Eight is one Kevin Grant."

"He did tell me that."

"Right, but they're not all honorable and decorated military men. It's rumored they buy some of their operatives from prison. They officially 'kill' their new member, then they become numbers, and work for the Faction."

"I didn't know that."

"Yep, and scanning Kevin Grant's rap sheet pins a white slavery conviction on him three years ago. Funny, he never made it to the New York State penitentiary where he was supposed to be incarcerated. A freak bus accident took him out. His remains were burned to a char, impossible to identify the body. I wonder what poor soul they got to play the dead guy?"

"Damn!"

"Oh, yeah, and Grant may have worked with Sacha's father a while back. But I can't tell what his connections are to the Network. You know how clean the Network's trail is."

"No, I don't. I don't know anything about the Network. According to Vital, it sounds like the Faction wants to take them out."

"You switchin' sides, Jamie?"

After hearing what Dove had had to say, and now this?

"I don't know. I just...don't know. Just because Kevin Grant has a criminal background doesn't mean he's not on the up-and-up now. The Faction are the good guys, right?"

"Best I can tell. But you keep an eye over your shoulder at all times, you hear me? I'll be watching you."

"Thanks. Here comes Vital. Can you tap into the Faction and locate them? They should be tailing me."

"Will do."

Sacha Vital had a sexy walk. Unassuming, yet with shoulders pulled back straight and confidence lifting his chin. He wore the silly striped shirt with élan and those velvet trousers positively screamed sex. So he was a fashion nightmare, but I wasn't one to throw stones. The dark sunglasses he wore only increased his sensuality. Stubble had begun to darken his square jaw and, along with the sideburns, gave him a rugged, scruffy appearance. Like a bad boy—my favorite kind of male.

As he neared the Bimmer, I tapped the hex nut on my finger against the steering wheel, and vacillated about unlocking the door, but hit the unlock button before he got to the car. He slid in and offered me a bottle of water for the road. I took it and stowed it in the glove box.

Buckling up, he then slicked back a few stray hairs from his brow. "Did you corroborate my story?"

The question didn't surprise me at all. The man was no idiot.

"You know I did. Fitch checked into the Faction and the princess. But there was nothing more on you."

Sacha shrugged. "What more do you need to know?"

Other than that he liked seals and had a stone fetish, along with mild OCD?

He was right. I knew everything pertinent. He had one goal, and that was to obtain the information the princess had on her attacker. It wasn't as if he were a knight in white armor looking to rescue the damsel. No. He wanted her for his own reasons. Valid reasons.

And the few questions that did jump to mind—Why seals? What the hell was in that chloroform? Do you have a girlfriend? You want to do it again? —would never be voiced in this proximity.

"Where do you think she is?" I asked, putting out feelers in this muddle. "Your princess."

"Not sure." Sacha wiped the dashboard of more dangerous microdust. "But you know, I was thinking just now."

I lifted a sly brow, but didn't comment.

"Now, I don't really need her. Drive north."

I shifted into Drive and pulled out of the parking lot. "Why don't you need her?"

"The princess has become superfluous," he explained. "I've just learned some interesting information about my hired driver. If you know a single thing about the Network you probably know tons more than she does."

"I know nothing, only that—" Did I want to give the man the information? Well, it wasn't exactly pertinent. "I only know that I was part of a bigger network of organized criminals. *Was* being the key word. Max is dead, and now I'm living the hard way."

"That your story?"

"And I'm sticking to it." Traffic was light, so I rolled through the Stop sign and headed north. "You wouldn' actually abandon the princess if I did have information that could help you?"

He shrugged. The action stabbed at me. Maybe he wasn't as nice a guy as I had begun to think.

"You still need her to identify your sister. You're hoping the assassin will not be her."

"Right."

"But if we don't find her, no skin off your back, eh?"

Another shrug. Well, it wasn't a quick agreement. Maybe he did have a conscience.

My conscience was doing mad gyrations. *If she's out there, you have to get the princess*, it yelled. And I had to agree. My initial destination must be altered. I wanted to find Max's murderer—and I was so close—but right now, there was an innocent woman in far greater need of my interference.

Could I sacrifice my own needs for that of another? Had I ever done it before?

You're looking to avenge Max; that's a sacrifice. Of a sort.

"Take the next road," he said as I neared an intersection. "It'll place us on a country road."

"Where are we headed?"

"Can your Fitch locate the Faction with her fancy gadgets?"

"Maybe. You think she can pinpoint where they're hiding the princess? Damn! Why am I buying into this story?"

"Because you trust me."

"Did you threaten Fitch?"

"I did. I sent Thom and Jacques in to play thug. But I would have never allowed them to cut her. Promise."

"That your story?" I wondered.

"And I'm sticking to it. How much do you know about Light? Did he cozy up to you? Did he…?"

"He did not." Though I had considered it. Oh! That I had even been falling for the man's dimples and charm. Is a little hot chocolate all it took to seduce me and bring me over to the dark side? "And it's none of your business if he and I had." Besides, I was already on the dark side. Couldn't get much darker unless there was an eclipse.

"I'd be jealous."

I fisted the steering wheel. "You can't be jealous of someone who despises you!"

"Still? Haven't you at least forgiven me for abandoning you, now that you know I came right back that morning? I had chocolate pastries."

So he would play the pastry card, eh?

And if I'd known he was running an errand, I would have remained between the crisp sex-scented sheets a while longer. I admit it! I'd fallen that night. Not in love, but maybe in like. But now that I knew better, this girl was not going to succumb.

Not even to big-eyed seals.

"I'm undecided," I finally said.

"I'll take that over not forgiving. I can't pin the Faction's location," Sacha said. "If I could, I'd go in there and take them out myself. Unfortunately, both the Faction and I need you. And if they need you, then sooner or later, they'll get to you, and then I'll have my chance."

"So I'm bait?"

I eyed the black Mercedes in the rearview mirror. It tailed me. Where had that come from? Certainly not McDonald's. And driving on a gravel road headed out of the city? Wasn't the sort of car one took for a Sunday drive in the country. They weren't close enough to allow me to see the faces. The Faction? Had Kevin gotten a fix on my location? I hadn't called him back since we'd left Paris. I'd intended to, until the details started piecing themselves together.

"If I say you're bait, then I've notched another mark against me."

So he wasn't denying it. And had I really expected anything more?

"Listen, buddy, you've got a long climb out of the negative column before you start scoring points. Why even bother?"

I sensed Sacha leaned across the center console, but my sight remained divided between the road before me and the Mercedes behind me. The silk fabric of his sleeve brushed my hip.

His words were clear and deep, and they hit me like a bell. "Because for one night you gave me freedom from the darkness of the world I've become."

I swallowed and concentrated on the tail in the rearview mirror. Because to even think on that last statement might soften my resolve. He wasn't playing fairly. The darkness of his world? Where did he get that crap?

And yet, my mind flashed back to that blissfully breathless moment after we'd made love for hours. Both of us exhausted, he nestled close to me, his forehead to my breast and his lips teasing my nipple. He'd said something like, "I'd like to lie by you forever. You make me happy. Haven't been happy for a long time."

And I'd thought it was the first time in a while that I'd truly felt happiness, as well.

It had to be the Faction behind us. It was possible to track me using GPS and the cell phone. Fitch did it all the time.

"What are you going to do about them?"

I flashed a look to Sacha, seeing that exhausted lover who'd fallen asleep with my nipple in his mouth. He had sighted the tail.

"Turn me over? Was that the plan?" he wondered. "You draw me out of the city, away from my safety net, and then the Faction pounces?"

I sucked in my lower lip and bit softly. "You expected a Sunday drive in the park?"

He nodded and stared down at his hands, clasped loosely in his lap. "I guess we're both bait, eh?"

Yeah, but could I make the leap and trust him?

I wasn't really sure anymore who had done what, where and why. Trust had been taken out of the equation. Instincts were all that mattered. And instincts made me pull over to the side of the road where an old rest stop had grown over with weeds.

The Mercedes rolled to a gentle stop about six car lengths behind us.

"Sorry," I murmured, surprising myself I'd even said it. But I had, and I meant it.

Stick to the plan. If the Faction was dirty, I'd deal with that when it came. I didn't need Sacha to find the princess.

"They'll take you into custody and turn you over to the authorities. If you're innocent, you've nothing to worry about. I don't want any trouble, Vital."

"You're going to kiss me off so easily?" He tapped the steel briefcase handle between his legs. "And here I thought we had a thing."

"A thing?" Yeah, like sex-exhausted mornings in a big comfy bed. "The only thing we have between us is that…gun! Where'd you get that?"

He wielded a .38 mm. "Had it in my case. Put it in my pocket in the restroom. You should have frisked me again. Didn't Max teach you that? Shouldn't that be getaway-car-driver Rule Number One?"

"Rule Number One is don't talk to the driver."

"Oops." He made a zipping motion across his mouth with two pressed fingers.

Arsehole.

Over a megaphone, a voice crossed the short distance. I pressed the window button to lower it three inches.

"Send Vital out with his hands up."

I looked to the man in the passenger seat. He scored points for being handsome, charming, and a damn good lover. The gun wasn't aimed at me; he had laid it casually across his lap. And he wasn't talking.

I wasn't so sure anymore if he really did kill Max. He had no alibi beyond shopping for orange juice and pastries. But he'd intended to kidnap the princess and had almost taken her in hand before the Faction busted that plot. It had been Sacha's men who brought the princess to Paris from Spain.

And yet, everything he'd given me thus far had been the truth.

Okay, so I had a quibble about handing him over to the Faction. But just a little one. I was in this for Max. And don't forget it.

Time to get this monkey off my back.

"Ready?" I asked.

Sacha turned the gun handle toward me, an effortless surrender. The quibble grew a little larger. I took it, but didn't hold it on him; instead, I laid it on the center console, barrel facing his leg. He leaned forward and slid the briefcase onto his lap.

"What now?"

"There's something I have inside here I think you'll want to see."

"What, you carry your last will and testament around with you? I'm not responsible—"

"How quickly you teeter from one side to the next, Jamie. Maybe I was wrong about you." His jaw pulsed as he punched in the digital combination. "I thought we'd connected that night, but I was a fool. It was just sex. Just…whatever. Time to prove to you, once and for all, how bloodless the Faction is."

"What are you doing?"

In the backseat, a cell phone let out a jingle. I twisted and retrieved it, and clicked on. "This is Five," the voice said.

"Tell them to keep their panties on," Sacha hissed.

"Give us a moment," I said to Five.

Sacha opened the briefcase and drew out a few papers, then deposited them on the floor by his feet. Just scattered them. Quite out of character for OCD Boy.

"You've got thirty seconds," the unfamiliar voice said. It wasn't Kevin, which bothered me for reasons I couldn't touch. He was probably heading the operation from a remote location—but still.

The cavalry was already here. Of course, depending on which side you stood, the cavalry could be either a relief or a very bad thing.

Unsure what Sacha was up to, I snapped, "If you're waiting for a goodbye kiss—"

I choked at sight of what was revealed beneath the felt board in the briefcase.

Sacha lifted the board and set it on the floor. Below, a series of what looked like explosive devices—wired together and measuring about one foot by two feet—were lifted with care. I'd never seen explosives before, but trust me, the first time you lay eyes on them, you'll know down to your quivering toes exactly what it is.

Sacha looked to me and winked.

"You insane bastard."

"It's insurance," he said. "But you watch. I don't think this party is going to end the way you think it should."

Chapter 18

"Hold off," I said as calmly as possible, speaking to Five.

Would a loud noise set the explosives off? Doubtful. But it was a visceral reaction to still myself and speak softly.

"Do not fire. We have a complication."

Sounded as if I were talking to Houston. *We have a problem...*

"No complications," Five returned. Shouldn't Houston be a little more amiable? "Vital walks in ten seconds, or we open fire."

"No!" I jerked open the door and jumped out. I'm a reactor, remember? It may not have been the wisest move, but I still held a morsel of faith in Kevin.

Abandoning the phone on the seat, I raised my hands near my shoulders and splaying out my palms, I shouted, "He's wired with explosives! Do not open fire!"

Behind the dark, tinted windows, the big German machine didn't make a sound, a silent predator I knew could match my

BMW kilometer for kilometer. Utter silence filled the seconds. Time that hurt like a mother.

I searched the windows for signs of movement. Sunlight beamed through the moon roof, casting a haze across the driver's side but allowing me to see through the dark tint. The driver remained motionless, one wrist propped on top of the steering wheel, his sunglasses focused on my car.

"Why are you doing this?" I hissed out of the corner of my mouth to Sacha, but kept my hands high and even offered a weak smile in the direction of the Mercedes.

"My sister is in trouble," Sacha stated plainly. The weariness of the world tainted his deep voice. Right now, I knew the feeling. "And I'm not ready to die. At least not until I've found her."

"They aren't going to kill you. The Faction is—" I had no clue anymore whether or not the Faction was bloodless. Who was I but a middleman who never got the details and should have broken that rule years ago.

"We'll see. Get back in the car, Jamie."

"No—" Just because he called me by my first name didn't mean I had to like him anymore.

He held explosives!

It's not Vital. But I can't say whether it's the Faction or the Network; that information just isn't out there.

Dove's answer. And yet, I had needed to test Sacha. And right now, he was receiving a failing mark.

"This scenario is unacceptable," a voice echoed out from the Mercedes. "Ten seconds. Nine…"

My standing here wasn't doing any good. Dropping my hands, I slid into the driver's seat, turning off the phone and tossing it in the back.

This needed to end, right here, right now.

"Get out, Vital." I needed to be a part of the solution, instead of just reacting. "You may not have killed Max, but that doesn't make you any less dangerous. If you give me info on your sister, I'll do what I can."

"No time. Don't you trust your Faction? Do you think they'd be so stupid to open fire with all the explosives I've got in hand? It would rocket the entire car into flames, killing their target—me. As well, such a move would destroy the driver."

"Five…" echoed out behind us.

They would not open fire. *We just watch.* The continuing countdown rattled what little concentration I could find. Would Kevin allow them to take me out, too?

The first ping of a bullet to the Bimmer's hood worked like an electric shock to my system. They were going to take out Vital. And they didn't care about collateral damage. Maybe I was also on that hit list, but I'd just been too stubborn to believe it.

I believed now. Hot chocolate and dimples. I was such a sucker.

Shifting into gear and turning off traction control, I slammed the door shut just as a bullet skimmed the outer left quarter panel.

"Shit!"

I pulled forward and to the right, then cranked the wheel left and put the hammer down. The car spun. Sacha now faced the Mercedes. I revved, voicing my anxiety with the engine. And then I floored it.

The gravel road made traction difficult, but the Bimmer gripped the loose surface as if she had a death wish. She performed a perfect one-eighty, which I then pushed to a three-sixty. Dirt and dust plumed about us in a tornado. I headed into another doughnut.

Another bullet pinged some part of the car, but I couldn't guess which part. Nor would I take the time. My third spin stirred the dust so high I couldn't see the Mercedes or the road.

"What the hell are you doing, Jamie?"

"It's called diversion," I shouted back. "Hang on!"

Instincts told me to spin out now. Hitting the gas, I sped toward the freeway, leaving in my wake, a choking cloud of brown dust. Thrash time. I wouldn't step on the brake now if you held a gun to my head.

The Mercedes did not immediately follow. Dorothy wasn't in Kansas anymore. A big bad ground storm tornadoed all about the gravel road.

"Impressive," Sacha said. He carefully rolled the explosives on his lap into a thick column. "But they're on us now."

"Just keep your mouth shut, Vital. That was one of the rules, remember? I'm the driver. I call the shots."

"And you always know what's right."

I wouldn't dignify that one with a response. Another punch to his jaw is what he deserved. But I'd refrain from the call to aggression until I could get clear of the tail.

"Hang on! I'm gonna put your tonsils up in your mouth!"

Shifting smoothly, the Bimmer climbed beyond one hundred kilometers per hour. I wasn't familiar with this road, and I hadn't seen a single car pass in the time we had parked. We were headed away from the suburbs and into stark countryside.

The car gripped and pulled. Just as reactive as myself, but smooth and without a conscience. And what a joy to be without a conscience. Been there, done that. Time to get a clue.

Okay, so I'd gotten said clue. Now to make it work after all I'd done to mess things up.

The Mercedes gained. I stepped up the speed. These windows were not bulletproof. One hit to the passenger side was all it would take to ignite the getaway car like a Bastille Day sparkler.

Sacha, meanwhile, rolled down his window.

I pressed the window control button, stopping the passenger window halfway. "Idiot! What are you doing? You're worse than a kid! Keep hands and fingers inside the moving vehicle!"

"I'm going to dump this," he said.

"No!"

"Give me some control, will you? Trust me, Jamie."

I didn't take a moment to think, because I did trust him, damn me. I'd held this man in my arms and felt his happiness. And now I knew that his moral core struggled as much as my own.

"Fine. But your aim had better be more accurate than your garbage can toss."

I lowered his window completely and slowed to eighty kilometers. The man had a plan, and it worked for me.

Utilizing my tail draft to coast up close, the Mercedes quickly gained. A bullet pierced the back window. It hit dead center and traveled through the body of the car, landing the computer screen in the dashboard. *Merde*, the GPS was out. But worse, that jerk had just marked up my new car!

"You ready? Hold onto the seat belt," I directed Sacha.

Swerving to the right shoulder, I saw the gunman poke his hand out the left window. Sacha's shoulders and head plunged out the window.

"Sorry!" I offered. Groping for some part of him to hang on to, my fingers slid over his suit coat, missing pockets. "Hurry, if they get any closer—"

Sacha flopped back inside—sans explosives—and shouted, "Go!"

Now that was a command I would listen to. Gunning the ignition to clear the blast radius, I wasn't about to fall back to see what happened. I didn't have to look. The rearview mirror ignited with a brilliant amber flash.

"How did you— That went off merely by hitting the—" There were no answers I wanted to hear, at least not reasonable answers.

Sacha didn't look back. He wiped a hand across his forehead and rebuckled his seat belt. "Do you believe me now?"

"Yeah." I blew out a breath. "You've never lied to me, have you, Vital?"

"How could I lie to a gorgeous lay like you?"

Despite myself, I smirked. The man was a cad. But he was an honest one. Which meant everything he'd ever spoken to me was truth. Really. And that excited me.

I had just switched sides. *Again*. I didn't know what the hell to label the team I was currently driving for, but it felt right, so I'd cruise with it.

"Where to?" I asked.

"I thought you called the shots?"

"I'm fresh out of ammo. We need a place to pull over and make a plan. Maybe Fitch can work some mojo and track the Faction through the—"

"Through whatever it is Eight gave you to keep in contact with them?"

Nope, not a stupid man. "There's a cell phone in my duffel."

"Of course," Sacha said. "Didn't think they'd let you loose without a connection. Take the next right."

And I did, because I'd assumed my role. Driver. I might not always know the why, but if I knew the where and when, I could get you there safe and reasonably sound.

"That no-talking rule?" I said.

"Yes?"

"I've canned it."

"Good. Got any rules about sleeping with the enemy?"

"Not sure. Convince me you're the enemy, and then I'll worry about the hazards later."

Forty-five minutes later, the sun dashed a jagged crimson line on the horizon as it sunk beyond a hilly rise of field in back of the forested area Sacha had directed me to. I wasn't familiar with any roads beyond the suburbs, unless they were main roadways that tracked between major cities.

This was wild country to me. I half expected to see a wolf wander out from the brushy ditches.

It didn't even occur to me to be nervous a bad guy was taking me to his home to do…bad things to me, until I parked the Bimmer in his garage and turned off the headlights. For a moment, everything was dark. The engine sighed out. The new-car smell had been perfumed with human adrenaline and the faintest tang of male cologne.

As if grabbed from behind, I jumped at the click of metal— the dome light blinked on when Sacha opened his door.

"Home sweet home."

Cripes, why was I so jumpy now? Not the bad guy. In fact, dare I admit this, he was kind of sweet, in a goofy, OCD badly-in-need-of-anger-management sort of way.

"How many homes do you have?" I wondered.

I remained glued to the comfy leather seat, not too eager to enter the house where it would be just the two of us. I knew now why my nerves were twitching. The engine was cooling. Miles of roadway were not streaming beneath my body.

I was facing life *outside* the car. And everything was always a little more challenging when outside my haven.

Sacha stood beside the passenger door. "Two or three homes, including an apartment in Brooklyn. Coming inside, or do you love her so much you're prepared to snuggle up right out here?"

"She is gorgeous." I palmed the leather shift. The damaged GPS looked like a scar on a model's face. I was just glad it hadn't penetrated farther into the engine. We could have been goners long ago. "Just one question."

"Shoot." He leaned down and impossibly green eyes waited for my reply with a whimsical glitter that challenged my desperate need to keep it platonic. And *so* not serious.

"This is what you wanted, right," I asked, "to get me for yourself?"

He waggled a lascivious brow. The cad had come out to play.

"For devious means, Sacha, not for sex."

"You'd rather I torture you, *then* make love to you?"

"Is that what you have planned?" My nerves started dancing the idiot disco, a far cry from the ballroom blitz.

"Jamie, if you thought I had intention to harm you, why did you drive me here?"

I sighed. Because I did trust the man, even if it had taken an all clear from Dove, a spectacular explosion and almost dying to learn that.

So I'm stubborn.

And really, had I any choice? I could have shoved Sacha out onto the ground and left him to the Faction, then driven off into the sunset.

Yeah, I'd had a choice. And I'd made it.

Sacha sat on the edge of the passenger seat and leaned an

arm across the headrest. A move that stretched his suit coat over the hard body beneath. Nice. "Here's my question."

"Fire."

"After escaping from me the first time, didn't you want to turn tail and run as far from the evil kidnapper as possible?"

"Hell, yeah."

"Then why didn't you? Who convinced you it would be a smart idea to become my hired driver?"

Kevin. The man was a jerk, eight times over.

"Exactly," he said, and then stood again. "I think the Faction has put us together to kill two birds with one stone. We going to let that happen?"

"Nope." The garage lights blinked on and I got out of the car. "Our two birds are worth a heck of a lot more than their one stone."

The BMW was dusty and battered, having taken a bullet for the cause, but she was mine. I never give back a gift, no matter what the implications. Pressing my fingers to my mouth to kiss them, I then delivered the morsel to her hood.

"What do you know about the Faction?" I asked as I followed Sacha inside the house and into a starkly white-and-chrome kitchen that was lit by a few fluorescent strips concealed beneath the glass-faced steel cupboards. "Good, bad or ugly?"

"All of the above." He opened the fridge and took out two glass bottles of water. Snapping off the caps, he then handed one to me. "There are no good guys, Jamie, just bad guys wearing masks and chasing the other bad guys."

"But the Faction—I had thought Max approved... They...rescue people." Why I was still arguing their case, I didn't know.

"They do. And ninety percent of the time, they turn the person over to the authorities or the family, if they were hired that way. Doesn't mean they don't have their own agenda. The Faction works for whoever has the big bucks. But it's not always the good guy with the big bucks, if you know what I mean. And if someone pisses them off…then they take matters into their own hands. Have a seat."

I settled onto a plush white sofa in the dining cove. Everything was white, but a nice contrast to Kevin's evil yellow abode. No wonder Sacha was a neat freak; look at his environment. The light from the kitchen cast a pale haze over the dining area, but I was glad for the subtleness. I wanted to sleep.

"The Faction is basically good," Sacha conceded. "But there's always a bad apple in every organization. It's a simple fact."

I bent over and unlaced my Doc Martens. "Did Max piss them off?"

Leaning against the kitchen counter, Sacha slugged back his entire bottle of water, wiped a hand across his mouth, and then said, "He had information on the Faction that could destroy their covert operations. Information he had called to hand off to me that morning of his death. He'd been getting nervous. He knew the Faction was tailing him, and had asked for my help."

My boots toppled onto the pale hardwood floor, and I tucked my feet up under my legs and snuggled deep into the lush cushions. No, don't even think that word, *lush*. Might get too comfy, and even…relax.

"Why you?" I snagged the water bottle between my fingers, dangling it over the floor. "I've never heard of you before— well, I have—but not from Max. At least not as a friend."

"I wouldn't go so far as to call us friends. We were business associates. If we had been more than that, perhaps I'd have known you were Max's girl the night we met."

"Would that have stopped you from seducing me?"

"Memory fails you, gorgeous. It was you who did the seducing."

"Fifty-fifty," I offered. Tilting my head back was a mistake, because the cushions received my heavy skull like a blissful dream. Man, I was tired.

"You wore a sexy little short skirt that night. It was all sparkly. Green, I remember. With dangling beady fringe things that stopped high on your thighs. Woman, your legs are killer."

"We're getting off subject here."

"I know. But you gotta admit, you were dressed to seduce that night."

"It was my birthday, I was celebrating and feeling…"

"Like a million euros?"

I could appreciate his appreciation, but back to the subject. "Why did Max call you?"

"Because we had spoken the night before. Made a connection, is my guess. He understood my quest to find my sister. Maybe he thought he could trust me. Or maybe he simply wanted to spread the danger in my direction, put the Faction on my tail. I just don't know."

"Yet you don't know what it was Max knew that would make the Faction want to kill him?"

"Unfortunately not. We only talked about a minute before, well…you know. But obviously the Faction has placed me as a confidant of Max, and now they won't stop until they have me in hand. I suspect they won't even bother to interrogate me. A bullet to the skull should prove sufficient. They've done it once…"

"And you're not afraid?"

"I'm not screaming for my mommy, if that's what you're asking."

"So you never get afraid?"

"What is fear?"

I felt the couch sink and knew he'd sat next to my folded legs, but I'd closed my eyes, and prying them open felt a tremendous task.

"Fear is knowing your life is in danger," I answered, "and reacting."

"By running like a rabbit? Max give you that name?"

I made a confirming noise.

"Tired?"

"A little." Actually, a lot. Why else would I feel so serene just lying here in a strange man's house? "What's the plan? We can't stay here; they will find us. Besides, if they do have the princess…"

"I've got perimeter scanners that'll alert me to approaching vehicles. I don't know how to find the princess, unless you can put in a call to Fitch."

"I will."

"Good. We're safe for the night, Jamie. I've a guest room…"

"Actually, I'd like to snuggle up right here. This couch is…" *yawn* "…comfy."

"Suit yourself. I'll get you a blanket."

As he left the room, I dragged my loose limbs upright and skipped over to my duffel bag and took out the cell. Fitch was already working on the global satellite imaging, but the trail ended with the burning Mercedes. She would work through the night; I was confident of that.

I wasn't aware of Sacha covering me up. Immediately after hanging up with Fitch, I drifted into a dream of the night when I'd made love with a sexy stranger.

After showering and wrapping a towel about his hips, Sacha padded out to the dining area to check on Jamie. Toes tucked under a throw pillow and hands pressed together and tucked under her cheek, she looked like a little girl curled up on his big overstuffed sofa. A little girl who needed someone to take care of her.

Had she been on her own only since Max's death? Likely. From the little he knew of the Network, they liked to claim their female protégés young and naive. And Ava was only twenty-three.

It was odd that, even though Montenelli had died, someone from the Network wasn't working with Jamie. Or had she escaped their grasp with Max's death?

Sacha doubted it.

And look at the trouble she had found in the little time she'd been on her own.

His guess was she'd scoff at the idea of any man taking care of her. And he knew she was far stronger than she appeared. Behind the wheel, she kicked ass. Physically, he wagered she might hold her own in a fistfight, but not against big hulking thugs such as the ones he hired (but they were basically just for looks). Jamie's skills kept her behind the wheel, but she couldn't drive away from the Faction forever.

Nor could he.

The cell phone she must have been holding was precariously close to falling off the sofa. He snatched it and folded it shut. Then unfolded it. Walking into the kitchen, he checked the call log. Fitch. About twenty minutes ago. To be expected. And before that, no calls made for more than a week. So this must be her phone. Which meant…

Sacha noticed the duffel bag abandoned by the door that opened to the garage. He had no compunctions about bending over it and spreading it open. He pushed aside the iPod that lay atop a scatter of makeup accoutrements and empty gum wrappers. Makeup? He held up a lipstick vial. The woman didn't wear makeup; she was a natural beauty.

Curious, he twisted up the lipstick. Sports-car red.

He twisted the tube until it notched—and started to vibrate. "What the hell?"

The device was a…

"Well, I'll be." Smiling widely, he twisted it back down and returned it to the bag. So the woman carried all the necessities. His kind of gal—independent, fiery and sexier than all out.

There were two cell phones—the one he'd given her…and then this one. Had Eight given this to her? As a means to track her once she had him in hand?

He squeezed the back of the phone and the battery panel fell onto his palm. Ripping out the batteries, he then tore the thing apart, looking for a tracer, anything that did not belong. Not that he knew the innards of a cell phone, but…it looked legit. Replacing the parts and batteries, he then quietly set it on the floor by the canvas bag. A peek around the corner verified Jamie hadn't moved.

Ready to leave it, Sacha noticed a few papers wedged between the iPod and an unopened pack of Black Jack gum. A passport, some euro bills and a photo he recognized—the same photo he'd given Max that night at DV8 before his murder.

"Ava," he whispered, stroking a finger along the shape of the woman's dark hair.

He swallowed hard. Why did Jamie have this picture?

"I will find you. But I hope it's not working for the Network."

His sister an assassin? She'd been closer to Father than he had been, yet Sacha had always had hopes she'd go to college and leave behind the family curse. Dancing had been a passion of hers. When they'd been kids in Brooklyn, she'd dreamed of moving to Spain and learning to dance the flamenco. They had never been close, but that didn't mean Sacha wouldn't die for Ava. Or die trying to save her from the twisted sense of reality their dad had instilled in her naive juvenile heart. The two of them had seen so many things, wrong things, criminal things.

He wished Jamie had information about the Network. Maybe she did, and she wasn't telling him everything? Should he rough her up? Force it from her?

Not his style. Besides, to even think of harming a single hair on her gorgeous head...

You slapped her in your office.

Asshole. He'd been angry, and more than a little confused at the time.

Pressing the photo between his palms, Sacha bowed his head and closed his eyes. Breathing out, he vowed he would harm no woman. Especially not one who intrigued him as much as Jamie. And he didn't need a smooth stone to tap three times to refocus any angry compulsions. But he wouldn't stop delving, prodding her until she was completely honest with him. He had given Jamie nothing but truths.

Time to strip the lies from her facade and get to the one truth that could save Ava.

Chapter 19

I awoke, and exploded into a hacking fit of coughs. Remembering the water Sacha had given me earlier, I groped for the plastic bottle, but the haze of night was so thick and...smoky.

And then I smelled the smoke and saw the flame. The entire kitchen was on fire, and that was just the bits I could see. I heard the fire but couldn't see it.

Jumping to my feet, I rushed into the kitchen. Beyond the doorway a wall of flame whipped madly.

"What the hell?" I jumped as a ceiling beam creaked and snapped right before me. Smoke choked me.

Scanning the room, I faltered as I rounded the kitchen counter and went with the motion, landing on my hands and knees. Down in a crawl position, it was less smoky and I could breathe.

The house was on fire. I don't know how, but I wasn't about to start wondering. I had to get out.

Crawling on all fours, I scuffed the heel of my palm on the strap of my duffel bag. Slinging it over my shoulder, I then crouched and jogged through the house and toward the hallway where there was minimal smoke and no flame.

Where was Sacha?

I kicked at the first door and it opened easily. It was a bathroom. Coughing, I bent double and clung to the doorframe.

And then I heard the sound that could only mean an approaching missile. One of those small jobbies that the bad guys fire out of their handheld cannons. I dropped, flattening myself in the hallway.

"The Faction," I said on a choking gasp.

The missile hit overhead. The explosion of flame and timbers and creaking roof joists seemed unreal, something you only see in a movie. I crawled forward and slammed my body against the next door. It was closed, but not locked. I pulled myself up along the doorframe, shoved open the door and ran inside and did a body slam with Sacha.

"What's going on? Did you hear that?" he asked. "It sounded like—"

"Someone wants us dead. Come on." I grabbed his forearm and dashed back out into the hallway.

Sacha trailed, lagging as he retrieved something from his room, but I kept hold of his arm. "Is that a back door?"

"Yes!" He rushed ahead and bent over before the door, obviously putting on some footwear, but it was so smoky I couldn't be sure.

The back door swung freely and I jumped out onto a brick pathway. Moonlight competed with the frill of flame eating up the roof. Amber sparks rained over the overgrown grass yard.

"You think they're coming in?"

"Not about to take that chance," I shouted. "I don't think they'll risk entering a burning building."

"They could be trying to flush us out."

"And doing a remarkable job at it. Come on!"

I tugged Sacha along. The brisk night air worked to startle me completely awake. Even as I trundled along beside Sacha, coughing on the smoke, I took inventory.

"My shoes!" I hadn't time to grab them from in front of the sofa. "And your…underwear?"

Moonlight poured through the thin canopy of tree cover so I could plainly see Sacha. He wore a thick white terry robe open to reveal striped boxer shorts. I glanced down his dark-haired legs to see a pair of rubber galoshes rising to below his knees.

"Didn't have time to make myself pretty for you," he said, then coughed. "You want my boots? The forest is thick. I don't have an extra pair, or I would have offered."

"I'm fine." Stepping from bare foot to bare foot, I questioned that easy reply, but I didn't want to strip the man of anything else. He must have been sleeping in his boxers. "Just…let's get the hell out of here. You have a weapon?"

"Not unless you consider striped boxers deadly."

Well, now that he mentioned it…

"The Glock is still in your bag," Sacha said. "Hold my hand. There's a trail that goes through the forest."

Behind us, an explosion burst into a brilliant amber plume. Debris flew into the trees, and small particles of ash and leaves rained down upon us.

A coughing fit doubled me at the waist. I had inhaled a lot of smoke, and my mouth tasted like an ashtray full of lit cigarettes.

"You okay?"

"Breathing. Are you?" I wondered as I followed him away

from the destruction. We'd passed through a line of tall slender birch. Behind us, the house blazed and choking smoke filled the air. "Your house just went up in flames."

"So long as you're safe, I'm not worried about a bit of wood and stone. Watch out, there's a steep drop ahead. Hold on tight, and—"

"Whoa!"

The steep drop made itself known. I stumbled. Heels sliding on soft dirt and crunchy leaves, I landed in Sacha's arms. He smelled ridiculously erotic, and I felt ridiculously, well, ridiculous, noting his scent in the middle of the night with the bad guys on our tail and ash raining upon our heads.

"Come on, no time for regrets."

I gripped Sacha's forearm as he walked me carefully down the rocky slope.

"The dirt path is just ahead," he said. "I've been on it once before."

"You don't think they'll follow?"

"Do you know what direction the missile came from?"

"That way. North, I think."

"Then I have to guess it was fired from the road. We're tracking the opposite direction."

"I'm not keen on hiking, just to let you know."

"I suppose you prefer four wheels. Wish I had a pair of ATVs, but I don't. I'll take care of you, Jamie. Jump over this big exposed root. That's a girl."

I landed on what felt like firm, flat ground, and once again, managed to end up wrapped in Sacha's arms. He bowed his head and pressed his cheek alongside the crown of my head. Such a comforting, utterly un-villain-like move. I reacted by hugging him. And when I did so, my arms slid inside the open terry robe and clung to hard, male muscle. He felt so good. Warm, and…safe.

Yes, safe. It had been a while since I'd felt this way. And what a strange time for me to feel it, with bad guys in tow and a fire burning up my wake. Maybe it was the adrenaline coursing through me that cried out for a moment's respite. Maybe I'd just realized that sometimes good things come in surprising packages.

"Thank you," I murmured against Sacha's neck. I nuzzled close. Stubble tickled my cheek. "You feel right."

"You feel frightened. You're shivering. Are you sure you're okay, Jamie?"

"Just a little freaked. It's not every day I wake up in the middle of a fire."

"Yeah. But you saved my life."

"You were on your way out."

"You think so? I was disoriented from the smoke. If you hadn't been there to lead me out…"

Twice now, homes had burned because of me. Who really set my apartment building on fire? The Faction? That would prove how Kevin even knew to tell me about the fire in the first place.

"You'll survive," I murmured. "Just, let's get going. I'm not keen on taking one of those missiles in the back."

The forest was thick, as Sacha had warned. The path was littered with jutting rocks and loose pebbles, and was no wider than a man's shoulders. Lining the path, thick brush and the occasional prickle bush popped out from the dense cover of trees.

I thought I'd like to have some shoes—even a pair of oversize men's galoshes—right about now, but didn't say anything. He'd offered, but Sunday bloody Sunday, his house had been blown up. And it might not have been because of him. The Faction was after both of us. The fire was as much my fault as it was Sacha's.

Correction: it wasn't our fault. We were targets.

Sacha stopped on the trail and pushed aside a thick swath of evergreen that blocked the path. I hadn't smelled the clean scent of pine since leaving Scotland. I hadn't bothered to check out the parks in Paris, preferring to surround myself with asphalt, brick and steel. Not right, I knew. But the only thing the great outdoors did for me was to bring on homesickness and a longing I hadn't felt for decades.

Like now.

"We're close," Sacha said.

"Close to what? Hell? I thought we left the fires of hell. Shouldn't we be surfacing soon?"

His chuckle felt wonderfully exotic in the midnight darkness. Strange night insects chirped and chirred somewhere within the surrounding vegetation. The air smelled of smoke and grass and moist bark. Yet I was compelled by the huskiness in the man's voice and his constant checking to ensure my comfort.

"There's a road up ahead."

"Really?"

"It's not used at all anymore, except by the locals, but it will take us to the main road. The cell phone I gave you is in your bag."

"I don't think I get service out here. And if I did, what, do you want me to call for help? Who's going to come? It's not like I'm looking forward to a conversation with the authorities. We're on our own, Sacha. Let's just hope we don't walk right into the Faction's lap. They could be anywhere."

"I wish I'd taken along my night goggles."

"You've got all the fancy gadgets, eh? Come in handy

when you're kidnapping princesses?" I breathed out heavily. "I'm sorry. I'm just…sorry."

"You have every right. I'll never win citizen of the year, that's for sure—yeow!"

Sacha disappeared in front of me. Literally. There, then gone.

Between yelps and crunching branches, I heard his body tumble. The urge to spring forward and grab him was stopped by my healthy sense of survival.

Gripping the trunk of a skinny tree, I saw the demarcation in the soil where it suddenly stopped. The earth must have shifted, leaving a good four-foot drop. Sacha lay below. I couldn't tell if he was moving, or even alive.

"Don't be dead," I whispered. "You're not going to check out of this relationship like that."

Stepping over the edge and using the tree trunk to hang on to and lower myself, I managed to scale the short drop, then jumped to land on a crunchy bed of leaves just before the skinny tree snapped.

Sacha moved and groaned. He was still alive.

I bent over him. Don't move an injured person, I remembered from safety classes we'd been required to take in school. Yes, I'd paid attention in school. What else was there to do? "You okay?"

"Somebody get my mommy," he murmured, and I had to force myself not to laugh. He was obviously trying to make the best of an awkward, and likely painful, situation. "I'm fine. But I think I landed my ass. Ouch." He tried to sit up.

"Don't make any sudden moves." I squatted, and the muscles in the back of my calves pulled, but it felt good.

"I'll survive," Sacha offered.

"Keen. 'Cause I wouldn't know where to find your mommy."

"I said that, didn't I?"

"You know it. And I'll never let you forget it."

"Wouldn't expect you to." Shuffling his feet through the crunch of branches and leaves, he then wiped away clods of dirt that peppered his shoulder and legs. "My mom's in Brooklyn."

"New York?"

"Yeah, she's a nice chick. Settled down with a physics professor and just had another baby a year ago."

"You've got a tiny sibling?"

He pressed a hand to his back, stretching and grimaced. "Ava doesn't know about the baby."

"You and your mom are still close?"

"I call her once a week. I love her. She bugs me to move back to the States and marry a nice Brooklyn girl and have babies. I visit, for, you know…events."

"Seals?"

"How did you—" He winced. "Oh man, this is gonna hurt in the morning."

Sounded nice, having a mom who cared about you. I offered him a hand to stand. "So, when are you moving?"

"I'm not leaving Europe until I find my sister."

He was dedicated and possessed fierce integrity. Sacha Vital was ten times the man I'd thought Kevin to be. Stupid dimples.

"Tell me what Max knew," I prompted Sacha as he tugged my hand and forced me to settle beside him on the dirt.

He stretched his bare legs before him, galoshes heeling the path and dirt-smeared robe parting to reveal striped boxers.

If we hadn't had missile-wielding maniacs on our tail, I might have smiled at how ridiculous he looked. But the best I could manage was a grimace.

"I told you already, he hadn't time to give me details.

Whatever the Faction thinks Max might have told me, he didn't. But that won't keep them from killing me. Or you."

"You're such a comfort, Vital."

"Yeah? You impress the hell out of me, *la lapine*."

"That I'm still alive? Not for lack of your trying to kill me."

"I don't kill people, Jamie, get that into your head." Frustration was evident in his clipped tone.

So maybe I had formed assumptions about the man, and not the conclusions I'd tried to convince myself were a higher calling. He did deserve my disdain for kidnapping the princess from Spain; that was fact, and he'd admitted it. But that was all the solid evidence I really had on the man.

And since when had I ever detested the criminal ilk? They had been *my* ilk until very recently. Hell, they still were my ilk because the good job I'd thought I'd taken hadn't exactly gone down all roses and ribbons. I'd never found fault with them before. Had never thought myself so high and mighty that I was better than anyone.

"How many murderers have you driven from the scene of the crime?" he prompted in the still silence of the night.

"Well…" I'd never thought about that one.

Okay, truth? I have considered it, but it was a brief kind of thought one shoves away. Usually, I drove getaway from robberies, smash-and-grab jewelry thefts or some other getaway scheme. But to drive a killer away from the scene of the crime? Did killers do that? Hire getaway drivers?

"What about the freak who tosses a bomb and uses you to drive him away?" I countered. "Ever thought about how many dead were left in our wake?"

"Sorry," Sacha said. "I'm not trying to throw stones."

"You have every right to throw stones." I pressed two fingers into the soft cool dirt heaped near my thigh. "I'm not pristine, and I've never claimed to be. But I am trying. It's not as easy as I thought it would be."

"Driving for the good guys? What led you to believe the Faction are the good guys?"

"Max. He knew I wanted to go legit, and was keen on it." And yet, I had never officially gotten the all clear from Max regarding the Faction. He'd been meaning to meet with them, feel them out and then give me a report. It had been Fitch who'd ultimately hooked me up with the Faction.

No, I wasn't going to go there right now.

"Surprising. I didn't think the Network prided themselves on living the hard way."

"Well, I was never issued the handbook," I said. "What I know is only what I've been able to assume. Why don't you tell me what *you* know about the Network?"

"They're exclusive, and if you need a specific job done with discretion and accuracy, you call on them."

"You ever call on them?"

"Nope. But my father might have."

"How'd your sister get involved?"

"That's the thing. I'm not positive she is, though I have my suspicions she was cozying up with someone in the Network. The guy's name is Simon Quinn. Ever hear of him?"

I shook my head, genuinely having only just heard the name right now. "Names are not my thing. If you know the guy, why don't you go directly to him?"

"The Network isn't listed in the Yellow Pages. It's not like tracking down someone who does not mind being found."

"So you thought Max could find Quinn?"

"I knew he could. It was a matter of gaining Max's trust. That's why, in exchange for him digging up info on Ava and

Quinn, I'd suggested I might be able to get the goods on the Faction for him."

The goods being, checking them out to see if they were worthy of my time. Had Max died by exposing himself to unseen dangers all for me?

I swallowed back a thick clod of smoky bile and tried to keep from vomiting. Please, don't let Max's death be my fault. *Please.*

I searched the sky. A thick black cloud from the smoke seemed miles away. Had we trekked miles through the forest? It felt like it to my calves. I craved a hot shower and a huge plate of steaming spaghetti. Sardegna a Tavola served up some amazing marinara sauce and they flaked their parmesan so finely over the top it made me want to cry just thinking about it.

"What are you thinking about, Jamie?"

I sighed and stood to stretch my cramping legs. "Spaghetti."

"Sardegna a Tavola? On the rue de Cotte?"

"You like the place?"

"It's a favorite."

"Mine, too."

"Tell you what. After this is all done, I'll meet you there for a big plate of meatballs marinara and some chilled Sardinian wine."

"You tempt me, Vital."

"Even sprawled like a freak and wearing rubber boots?"

"Even." I offered my hand to help him stand up. The dirt that covered him sifted over my bare toes. "So what makes you think we're going to make it out of this alive?"

"I suspect the Faction may believe we're toast. You think anyone should have gotten out of that fire alive?"

"So how did we?"

"I don't know. I'd been sleeping for a while. Finally settled to sleep after checking on you."

"Checking on me?"

"You know, making sure you were tucked in."

"Looking at me?"

"Oh, sure. But I wished you were still wearing that sexy little skirt you had on the other day. It would have rode up your thigh, just to about there."

"Pervert."

"I confess! I'm sorry, I'm feeling a little vulnerable here. Where else does a man's mind go when he's in a freaky situation like this?"

"To sex?"

"Why not?"

"Come on." I started forward, spying the moon through a spiderweb of thin branches high in the sky. "You said there was a road nearby?"

Chapter 20

The trail did indeed eventually end at a gravel road lined with trees. I winced as my feet, which had become accustomed to the soft dirt trail, stepped onto gravel. My soles were tender—I don't think I'd ever had a blister on my feet before—but they were forming. Oh yeah, this was grim.

I eyed Sacha's boots covetously. Well, he *had* offered.

"Surprisingly, we're not far from the suburbs," he said. "I believe the freeway is about three kilometers off."

"Joy. A walk through the countryside." Forcing myself to wobble past him, I trudged onward, arms swinging lightly and head held high, unwilling to drop in an exhausted mess before the big handsome bad guy.

Correction: Was he really the bad guy? I believe his status had recently been upgraded to somewhere-in-the-middle guy.

Was it because I'd developed some twisted attraction to the man and wanted him to be good so I could act on that attraction?

Jamie, lass, when have you ever required a man to be good?

I have a theory about bad boys. They're just misunderstood little boys who want to do the right thing, but, because of upbringing or a terrible life event, they never learned what right really is. Sacha might be one of those bad boys. His father had been a kidnapper, and Sacha had known nothing else. However, there was his mother's influence. I knew little of her, but she sounded sane. And concerned. They talked once a week? Wow. I couldn't even imagine.

I'm not making excuses for the man, but I'd yet to see evidence he'd done anything other than kidnap one woman (whom he no longer had in hand).

Of course, there was the other woman—me—whom he'd had stuffed into the boot of my car. Subtract points for that little adventure. And strike off a few more for my horrors with chloroform.

"You want me to carry you? I could—"

"Don't even try it, Vital." Yeah, I'd forgotten about that crazy chloroform hangover. And my cheek didn't ache anymore, but that didn't mean I was going to forget the slaps.

"Call me Sacha. When you use my last name, it's so impersonal."

"We are impersonal, Vital. Get that into your head."

"You come like a goddess."

"What?" I stopped walking. I had heard him perfectly clearly, but the astonishment overwhelmed even my aching blistered toes.

He joined my side, rubber boots scuffing tiny pebbles of gravel against my heels. "Just making a point. We've been very personal, Jamie. I know things about you."

"Like what?" I regretted the question the instant it took shape.

"Like, you're a very aggressive kisser."

"Am not."

"Are too."

I resumed walking, and he stomped along in those sexy galoshes. Yes, they had reached sex appeal status. Right now, anything that could make the man's legs look so tasty *and* serve as protective gear was sexy in my book.

"You're a lazy kisser," I replied.

"Lazy?"

"You know, slow, taking your time."

"Nothing wrong with that. I enjoy tasting a woman, especially you. Vanilla!" he suddenly declared to the moonlight. Choirs of crickets sang hallelujah from the grasses.

"What?"

"Vanilla. That's what you tasted like. And you sparkled."

I laughed. I did have some vanilla body lotion I wore once in a while. When I wanted to sparkle. And attract a man's eye.

"Your shoulders were sweet," he said. "And your belly and your thighs. Man, so delicious."

"Sacha."

"And don't even get me started on your breasts. Oh, man, I—" Suddenly Sacha ran a few steps ahead of me, his head bobbing as he searched the horizon. "What's that?"

I spied what had captured his attention. "Hallelujah!"

Finding the energy to sprint, I set off for the abandoned car parked at the side of the road. I wasn't about to get my hopes up. No one abandoned a car, bonnet propped open, for any reason other than that it had stopped by itself or it had run out of gas.

But I never looked a gift car in the grille.

Tromping through overgrown grasses intent on taking over

the narrow country road, I slapped a palm on the boot. It was
a banger, a rusted old Renault Fuego that had certainly seen
its better days. Chipped blue paint conceded to gray and
crumbly bits of rust here and there. The windows were rolled
up and the doors locked. Must have taken a look under the
bonnet. The owner obviously intended to return.

I scanned the gravel road. Tire tracks were still visible in
the loose pebbles, so it may have been abandoned fairly
recently.

Sacha kicked the bumper. "Out of gas?"

"Maybe." I leaned against the rear quarter panel and
shoved hard with my hip, letting the car swing back to
position. "Hear that?" I said with a growing smile. "That is
petrol sloshing around in the tank."

I knew this car. It was a flaming piece of crap. Literally.
The Fuego had a tendency to suddenly burst into flame due
to a short-prone electrical system. Could be the problem. But
I wouldn't know until I checked under the bonnet.

"You got a flashlight, Vital?"

When he didn't answer, I looked over the bonnet at him.
He stood, highlighted by the gorgeous white moonlight, arms
crossed, looking obstinate.

"What?"

"The name is Sacha."

Rolling my eyes and hiding a smile behind the bonnet lid,
I corrected, "*Sacha*, do you have a flashlight?"

"Nope. I only had time to grab the most important
thing—and run."

The most important thing? What was that? Oh. Me. I
remained behind the shield of the bonnet, unwilling to look
at him. Did the charm naturally come to him, or did he have
to work at it?

I think it was natural.

On the other hand, it was me who had done the grabbing. If he had intended to turn around that little rescue in his favor…

"I'll take a look in the glove box." He peered into the car and tried the door handle.

And I let out my held breath. Oh, what was I doing? It slipped out; he hadn't meant anything with that remark. I was reading too much into it.

"Most important thing, my arse," I hissed. He hadn't bothered to offer me that important pair of boots, now, had he?

Drawing my dirty, achy toes up along the back of my opposite ankle, I leaned forward and gripped the edge of the car, stretching out the pulling muscles in the backs of my legs. I hadn't fallen down any dangerous dirt drops, but I'd be feeling this walk in the morning just as much as if I had fallen.

The flashlight would expedite matters but wasn't necessary. I poked around the engine. I could read an engine with my eyes closed, like Helen Keller reading a book in braille. I didn't smell burned wiring or even notice the taint of leaking oil. Must be the battery. Just needed a boost?

"Locked."

I straightened abruptly. Sacha stood right behind me. I hadn't noticed him come around, hadn't even heard the crunch of rubber soles on gravel. Man, when I had my head in an engine…

"Thanks. But I think I can boost it, and we'll be on our way."

"Seriously?"

"Yep. No fire damage that I can remark. Could have just flooded the engine. If I can break the steering column, and jimmy the lock, we're on our way."

"How'd you get to be so good with cars? You in your sexy

little skirts and T-shirts. You're quite the dichotomy, Jamie MacAlister."

Swiping my fingers across the hem of my white T-shirt left behind a trail of grease. I might be tired, smoke-riddled and a target, but now, I was in my element.

"I was born with a wrench in hand and greasy fingerprints on my bottle. My pa used to recondition classics. I drove in my first street race when I was fourteen."

"I take it you weren't fussing over your hair and picking out dresses for the prom like all the rest of the girls?"

Don't I wish I'd had a mother to keep me from buying that idiot turquoise dress with flounces and to make a fuss over my curly hair and inexpertly applied makeup. The woman was out there somewhere…wandering.

"I went to the prom," I said defensively, and then added as I wandered away from the car to scan the ditch, "I drove."

His laughter twinkled like stars in the midnight sky. "Baby, you can drive me."

"I have once."

"I haven't forgotten. You like the ride?"

"I did."

"So, if I understand things right, you're attracted to cars the same way men are?"

"If you mean because of the speed, gears and sex, yes."

I bent and splayed my fingers through the grass edging the ditch. Found what I was looking for…

"Oh yeah," Sacha said, "give it to me fast, and in a car."

The huge rock I'd lifted from the ground smashed the driver's side window with ease.

"What the hell? There are no keys, woman!"

Pulling up the door lock, I then opened the door, pushed the particles of safety glass from the seat and slid in.

"I've got a key. Now just be quiet for a few. I need to concentrate. Hand me my bag."

The duffel dangled from above the open car door. I grabbed it and shuffled blindly inside until my fingers curled about the torque wrench and the multitool. Jamming the heavy steel wrench hard against the lock cylinder, I torqued my grip and gritted my teeth.

"Come on, sweetie," I coaxed the banger. "I don't want to walk any further. Just give it up like a nice lass—" My fist smashed into the dash as the cylinder cracked. "Halfway there!"

"Now for the key." Leaning forward to catch a little moonlight on the multitool, I tugged out the screwdriver, then shoved it into the mutilated lock cylinder and turned it like a key.

The engine hacked out a protesting growl, but it ran, and that was all that mattered. "Yes. Thank you, darling."

Elated at the simple boost, I jumped out onto the gravel and grabbed the first thing to hand. Which was a half naked man. Pressing close, and pulling down his head with my hand, I kissed Sacha like I drove, with determination, drive and intention. Eyes on the prize, and don't stop until you've made it home.

He felt incredible. Muscles tensed and hardened under my fingers. Hot flesh. Sounds of satisfaction blended with the rumble of the engine behind me, like an angel's song. At this moment, the world became very right.

Snaking my left leg up and around the man's thigh, I drew him closer, so he had to lean in and press his palms to the roof of the car. The crazy reaction part of me wasn't about to free him.

The taste of freedom and darkness and utter abandon filled my mouth with his urgent kiss. I wanted more, more. *Give it all to me, baby.* This man had been born bad, but he wasn't bad to the bone. It would be so easy to let him into my life;

a life that craved companionship. I just wanted someone to care and not wander off.

"You're good," I muttered blissfully against his mouth.

Sacha abruptly loosened our embrace and pulled away. With moonlight flashing across his face, I could easily read his strange look. And it wasn't a happy one. "Don't even think about it, Jamie. I'm a nasty son of a bitch, and you know it."

Where had that come from? I knew he wasn't citizen of the year, but for him to suddenly push me away? After all the flirtation?

"Jamie?"

And then it hit me like a zap from a cracked spark plug wire. He was being more adult about this "relationship" than I could ever be.

"Right. Not playing on my team. I got it. Sorry. I was just happy about getting the car started. You know how things are."

"Sure. Sex, death, the rumble of a car engine. It's all the same, right?"

"You know it. Let's get out of here."

I slammed the bonnet shut, then strode to the driver's side, but the door was now jammed in place. Could be from the rock through the window; must have bent the frame. I could go around to the passenger side, but Sacha had already climbed in. So I dusted out the broken glass bits, and climbed through the window.

"Wish you were still wearing that skirt for that climb," Sacha commented.

"It's dark. You can't see a damn thing anyway."

"I know, but I have to wonder after admiring that short little skirt—"

"About what?"

"Bikini or thong."

I sat there, smirking and tapping the steering wheel. "Nasty son of a bitch."

"That's me." Yep, he had definitely changed colors after that kiss. "So, we off?"

Palming the stick, it rattled in my grasp—the linkage must be worn. I knew we should speed right on out of here, but something nagged at me.

The unknown.

The need to have just *a bit more*.

The only nasty thing in the vicinity was this car, not Sacha. And I wasn't about to let him play the bad-boy card after all I'd learned about him.

Twisting, I slid smoothly across the console, avoiding the shift, and landed in Sacha's lap, one knee to either side of his thigh. Before he could come up with another pitiful excuse for me not to kiss him, I laid another one on him.

His mouth was irresistibly soft and open. This time, his hands snaked up my thighs and caressed my arse. Sliding one finger inside the waistband, he toyed with the lacy trim of my panties.

"Bikini?" he whispered.

"Yep."

I wanted him to go further. I wanted him to touch me however he pleased, and then I'd see what reaction would come. It might be an affront. How dare he touch me so boldly? Or it might be a wanting moan, encouragement to continue toward the climax I knew he could bring me to.

I wouldn't push him away. I didn't want to. Pulling him closer was the only thought I had. Nestling into him, I sat in his lap. Striking out across his bare chest, my fingers skated over hard muscle.

"What the hell are you doing?" he murmured, but kissed me again, deeper, longer.

"Just play this game," I said. "You might win, you might lose, but you'll never know unless you get in the game."

He touched me at my nape, sliding his fingers through my hair and easing them up my scalp. I arched my back, responding involuntarily. Subtly, he controlled, with touch, taste and breath. I felt his fingers trace my jaw, and he drew back to show me his thumb. A smear of dark grease coated it.

I shrugged. "You don't like my perfume?"

Wiping the grease off on his robe, he pulled me back into the kiss.

"You know something?" I murmured. "Anything good that has ever happened to me has happened in a car."

"Is that why you spend so much time in cars?"

"Maybe."

Eating him like a rich dessert, I gorged myself on his masculine shape, his urgency, and the feel of him hard against my groin. I began to rock against him, rubbing him, coaxing him... I could bring him to climax, and take satisfaction in the moans of his orgasm. I wanted this. It was so close...

Did I trust this man?

Yes, I thought I did.

Whoa. Me and my reactive need to always jump into the fray.

I sat back and licked my lips. The loss of connection felt bold and final. Sacha slipped his hand down my neck and over my breast—the nipple was so damn hard—but didn't give me the strokes I desired, only rested his hand on my thigh.

"Let me guess," he said in a husky, kiss-drained whisper. "That was one of those kisses a woman gives a man to see if he's—" he did a wobbling gesture with his fingers "—the right one."

"Of course it was."

Feeling suddenly lost, and way off course, I navigated my way back behind the steering wheel. Safe here behind the wheel. *This is where I belong.*

Tucking a hair behind my ear, I tapped the accelerator, readying to drive.

"Well," he asked. "Did you feel anything?"

Gripping the steering wheel hard, I shifted with my right hand, and revved the engine. "No."

I owed the man the truth, but right now it wasn't as easy as I'd hoped.

Chapter 21

No sooner had the Fuego rolled into motion than one of my phones rang. I fumbled for it, and Sacha reached into the duffel to retrieve it for me.

"Where's the other?" I asked as he handed it to me.

He just shrugged. "That's the only one I see in there."

Hmm. I checked the screen. Unidentified caller. This was the phone Kevin had given me. I think.

"I think it's Eight."

Sacha laid a hand on my thigh. The heat of that connection rocketed directly to my groin. Something about escaping death and running for your life tipped my sexual desire scales to overload. And I was craving some skin on skin action.

He said, "If you answer it, you are alive, still in the game. And the Faction plays for keeps. If you let it ring…you're dead, free to start over."

Wrinkling my mouth, I stared hard at the cell phone as it

jingled a third time. Not only would I be dead, but Sacha neglected to mention he'd gain freedom from the Faction if I chose to let them believe I was a goner. We could both begin over without having to constantly look over our shoulders.

The entire reason I sat here right now in this banger car with a man I hated as much as I desired was because of the Faction. And that mysterious princess that everyone wanted to get their hands on. The Faction still had her. Likely they would torture her to get any information about the Network from her that they could.

They should have taken me into custody that morning of the pickup. Not that I could tell them anything more than I'd told Sacha about the Network, but it was likely more than the innocent princess knew. Why hadn't they?

And Kevin, he had had me in his apartment. Some things still didn't make sense. But others did.

I had been responsible for placing the princess in the hands of the Faction. Me. And while I hadn't a clue at the time, I couldn't step back from responsibility now.

There was no denying the truth. If I began to require more of myself—like obtaining all the information I could get for a job—then I'd start taking a more active role in the blame.

The poor lass. I could be her.

But I wasn't. And she needed a voice.

After six rings I clicked on. I glanced to Sacha as I said, "*La lapine.*"

"Jamie?"

"Eight." A ruby sunrise highlighted Sacha's dour stare.

"I've been trying to contact you for hours. What happened to me watching your back?"

"You've been tracking me, but as for watching my back—"

"Do you have Vital?"

"Maybe."

"Jamie, don't beat around the bush. Vital is a very dangerous man."

"Dangerous? What about the Faction? They're the ones who tried to blow me up. Not once, but twice. Don't deny it, Eight. Your men tracked us to Vital's home."

Kevin's heavy sigh carried over the crackling airwaves. "So you don't burn easily. Gotta give me credit for trying."

If I'd had lingering doubts about the man, he'd just blown them all out of the water.

"This has been a shell game since that first moment you picked me up for mochas, hasn't it? You've been hoping I would lead you to Vital, so you could take him out. And then you'd fry me, too."

"We need you alive, Jamie."

"I don't have any more information than Vital does."

I caught Sacha's irritated grimace, but ignored him. This was my game now. And I was revving for a furious start.

"We want to protect you, Jamie."

"My arse."

"Vital would have taken the princess in hand and then killed you. So long as the Faction kept the princess, Sacha had no choice but to keep you alive."

I now knew Sacha would never have harmed me—and never would. He wouldn't have harmed the princess, either. But right now, I didn't know if she was dead or alive.

"You killed Max, didn't you, Kevin? He knew too much about the Faction, and was threatening you."

"I didn't go near Max the morning of his death. Don't tell me Vital has convinced you he's innocent?"

"I happen to know Vital couldn't have possibly killed

Max." If the purchasing breakfast story was true. Which I was inclined to believe. No man murdered and then stopped to purchase *pain au chocolat* on the way home to cover his arse.

And how the hell did Kevin know Max had been killed in the morning?

"Whether you went near him or not, the Faction still killed Max."

"You have no proof."

"I'll find some." But how did one convict a man who didn't even exist? I was in deep, and wasn't sure if I could hold my breath for the duration. "What about the princess? Where are you stashing her?"

"She's…comfortable."

So they did have her. Now to play this right.

"What if I offer you a trade?" I met Sacha's eyes and held them. His emotionless gaze offered me no help at all. "The princess for Sacha Vital?"

I held my breath. The line remained quiet. Kevin was thinking.

"Ten seconds," I said. "Make your choice quickly, or you'll never hear from me again."

"Deal," Kevin answered. "Be at point zero in an hour. You'll receive further instructions then."

The phone clicked off, and I tossed it to the side. It landed Sacha's lap.

"What?" he asked.

"He'll meet us in an hour."

"With the princess?"

"Don't know." I shifted into Drive and spun out in a spray of gravel. "Buckle up and hold on."

"Where are we headed?"

"Back to Paris. He said to meet him at point zero."

"The Arago disks," Sacha answered. "We're headed for Notre Dame."

There are 135 Arago markers in Paris. Small bronze disks set along the zero longitude line in the city—that is, the former longitude line, until it was moved to Greenwich in the nineteenth century. A small N and S mark the north and south directions of the plaques imbedded in pavement. The disk set at point zero is right before the Notre Dame cathedral in the parvis.

Figures Eight would chose a very public place for the exchange. *If* he intended to make an exchange. He hadn't specified, and I wasn't about to start making assumptions. Assumptions got me nowhere, and usually down the wrong path.

The Fuego rattled into Paris around 10 a.m. I contemplated parking, and jacking the sexy red (with white racing stripes) Mini Cooper nestled outside a *pâtisserie*, but I wasn't a criminal. Not anymore.

From this day forward, I'd be doing my damnedest to keep away from sorts like Eight and the Faction and—

I swung a look across the car to Sacha. He sat with knees spread, which parted the robe to reveal his less-than-appropriate attire for a morning of sightseeing before the city's most popular tourist attraction. Exhaustion darkened the flesh under his eyes. I knew the feeling.

A curl of dark hair drifted over his left eye. He may not have been aware I was studying him because he kept his gaze to the street. I was great at dividing my attention between the street and my surroundings. But I didn't linger.

I turned my focus back to the road. A big smile pulled my mouth. Sacha's profile was imprinted in my mind's eye. A misunderstood little boy who loved his mother and wanted to protect his sister. There was not a single thing wrong with that.

"Pity, I'm not dressed for the occasion," he said as I pulled onto the pont d'Arcole that crossed before the cathedral.

"Don't worry, Sacha. You look so sexy in those boxers. Maybe Eight will cut you some slack. Perhaps he won't torture you quite as long. On the other hand, he could be a jealous bastard, and will prolong your agony just because you're cute."

"You think I'm cute?"

"No doubt about it."

"You're refreshing in your honesty. So I'll be frank. I have to tell you, I'm hornier than hell right now."

Downshifting, I slowed. Finding a parking spot would be murder during tourist season.

"I think it's the thrill of the chase and all that," he added.

"I love a man who gets off on adrenaline."

"And I love a woman who can drive a man to his death and make him enjoy every moment of it."

"My pleasure."

And you know what? It really was a pleasure—in a twisted, adventurous sort of way.

I parked in the shadow of the prefect of police and together Sacha and I vacillated on whether he should come along with me to point zero. His attire would attract attention, and that was the last thing I wanted to do.

"What time is it?" I asked.

Sacha still sat in the passenger's side, the door wide open, and I leaned against it.

He checked his watch. "We've got fifteen minutes."

I scanned the parvis before the church, already peopled by

myriad sorts. There were families with children and couples walking arm in arm. Groups huddled together and waddled like a flock of geese toward their photogenic destination. Two hundred tourists, at my guess; not a surprise for this early hour.

Along the edges of the courtyard, gift stands sold over-priced metal replicas of the church front, fake holy water in glass vials with blue, white and red ribbons, and maps of the cathedral, along with some belly-coaxing sausages on a stick.

"I could get you a Notre Dame T-shirt?" I suggested.

Sacha brushed at a smear of dirt that darkened the leg of his boxer shorts. "You don't notice anyone selling pants, do you?"

"Nope. But they've got some shiny plastic rain parkas. Those would be keen with your rubber galoshes."

He shook his head and smiled. What he did next, I wasn't prepared for, so I stumbled a little when he grabbed my hand and pulled me down to him. I landed on his knees, straddling his legs. The rough terry cloth robe I clenched in each hand, forcing myself not to touch bare flesh.

"Promise me one thing," he said.

I darted my gaze back and forth between his impossibly fathomless green-blue eyes. Dead serious; this was not a kissing moment.

"I'm not sure," I said. "Promises...you know..."

"Yeah, they're not exactly a commodity in our line of work. Listen, I'm playing along with this whole exchanging-me-for-the-princess thing, so I figure you owe me one."

I shrugged, reluctant to commit to anything.

"Just promise me, Jamie, you'll not let the princess out of your sight until she's handed over to her family."

I nodded. "I can do that." I wasn't sure I could, but I'd find a way. It had to be done. After surviving an attempted assassination, and then being kidnapped and transferred from location to location about Paris, the poor woman had suffered enough.

"And another promise."

"You're asking a lot, Sacha."

The slide of his hand along my waist, rising, embracing and becoming a part of me, disturbed me to the point I let out a little moan.

He leaned in, his cheek sliding alongside mine. Warm breath near my ear melted my insides. "Promise you'll try to find Ava? You've been carrying around her picture, the one in your duffel bag. I gave that photo to Max the night before he died."

"That's your sister?"

Sliding his palm along my left cheek, he wouldn't allow me to pull back. "If anything happens to me, she's on her own. She needs help, Jamie. Direction. Clear thinking. She needs…"

The utter agony of his emotional pain bled into my fast and furious heart. I bracketed his face with my palms and could only nod that I would. Again, I wasn't sure how, or why I even agreed, but I felt it was the right thing. *I just want to do good.* No woman should be alone when there was someone who could make her world right or, at the very least, steer her toward a new destination.

And maybe it would be a step toward making my world a little less wrong. I still clung to the destination. Now to make the journey head in the right direction.

"I won't stop until I find her. I promise."

He kissed me then. So softly, a gentle brush of his lips to the corner of my mouth. I wasn't sure if it was a kiss, or a pause to breathe and make contact with life.

He needed so desperately. And I was going to help him fulfill that need.

Because it might fulfill mine.

"Let's do this," he muttered. "I put my life in your hands, *la lapine*."

The statement rocked me backward. I stood, abruptly shaking out my hands and jumping in place as I blew out breaths, and summoned courage. "I can do this."

I think I said it more to myself than to him.

"You still got the gun?"

He patted his robe pocket.

"Give it to me. You're my prisoner, remember?"

He stood and slipped the gun from his pocket. Looking about to ensure the exchange wasn't witnessed, I slid it behind my waistband.

I looked us over. I was barefoot, dressed in dirty jeans and T-shirt and had just hiked through a forest. He looked like Hugh Hefner à la *Green Acres* after a long day in the field.

"We make a smashing pair," I said. "Come on, lover. We've got a date to meet."

Chapter 22

To say I was surprised that we, the motley duo, didn't attract more attention was putting it mildly. Sacha and I wandered, ever so casually, to the center of the parvis, stopping about fifteen paces away from the Arago disk, which was placed in the courtyard twenty meters from the cathedral. Surrounded by a circle of concrete, the octagonal bronze disk featured an eight-pointed star and north-south directional letters.

A bustle of Japanese tourists scrambled up to the disk, wielding cameras and chattering. Children, with seed purchased from a nearby stand, fed a flock of pigeons.

A small boy pointed out the funny man in the bathrobe to his mother, but she just tugged the child along, casting a sheepish grin our way. I waved, smiled and hooked an arm in Sacha's. Yes, we were comrades of the desperately weird, but we were on a mission to rescue not one, but two women.

"They probably think you're taking me for my afternoon stroll out from the mental institute."

"The hotel-Dieu is close," I said, with a glance to seek out the institution. "Centuries ago, the place used to treat the mentally insane."

"Don't get any ideas, girl."

Scanning our surroundings, I saw a *crêperie* sold thin crêpes wrapped about fruit and Nutella and enticed me with the greasy-sweet aroma of pastry. Next to that stood thin wire cages filled with peeping birds of every design, color and size. With hundreds of people milling about, I figured ninety-five percent had to be tourists. The remaining five natives blended well. Anyone could be suspect. The building tops, the ones I could see from this position, were clear. The cathedral blocked a lot of smaller buildings where snipers could easily hide and get a bead on their marks, the marks being us.

What was Kevin going to do? Just drive up and make the exchange? Toss out the princess of pink velour and grab the king of terry cloth? I still had the cell phone. It was about two minutes to ten. All I could hope was that Eight/Kevin would call with further directions.

"See anything?" Sacha muttered, lifting a hand to his brow to shade his view.

"Most everyone appears to be part of a family. Very few single pedestrians. I think we're clear on the ground."

"They won't come at us from the ground. Too many people." He looked up. "It'll come from up high, or as a drive-by."

"You talk like they're going to shoot us down in cold blood."

I looked to Sacha. For once, he didn't have a silly smirk or sexy grin on his mouth.

"You're out from behind the wheel," he said. "You confident with this scenario?"

"Not a hundred percent, no. But I've got you as a shield, remember?"

"That's what I admire about you, bunny rabbit. You're not afraid to use your resources."

I liked the way he called me *bunny rabbit*. Like a pet name. Not condescending or teasing, as Dove would put it. A little possessive, but more friendly.

"Monsieur, voulez-vous acheter un ballon?"

This was not good. A massive cloud of colored balloons blocked my vision of the sky and the rooftops. Sacha told the seller to buzz off in polite French, but just then, a flock of thigh-high children zoomed in for the kill. We became tangled in groping ice-cream-coated fingers and demands for "That one!" "No, the red one!" "Don't shove!" *"Moi, j'en veux!"*

"Let's get out of here. Too dangerous with all these kids," I said, as I tugged Sacha backward and away from the cavalcade of sugar-high innocence.

It was the piercing shot that landed the cement about an inch from my toe that made me duck. I jerked Sacha down with me to land in a crouch. A balloon popped and children screamed.

"Someone's firing," Sacha said.

"Not with all these kids!" I leapt to my feet and charged the balloon man and the children. "Get out of here! Danger! *Allez vous en!*"

The balloon seller cursed me, obviously unaware of the danger. Fortunately, the children's parents grabbed arms and lifted frantic crying half-pints into their embraces and sped off, only knowing some crazy lady was yelling at their kids.

Didn't they notice as the next bullet took out a divot in the concrete? I made a bone-jarring landing on the cement. Someone tumbled on top of my prone body. My hip bones hurt; I'd scuffed my palms raw.

Sacha's voice hissed near my ear just as a third bullet pinged the cement two feet to our left. "There's a sniper on top of that building to the west. We've got to get out of here."

"I'm with that. The longer we stay here, the more people we endanger."

I was literally dragged to my feet by Sacha's powerful tug. We broke into a run in bare feet and galoshes. Dashing down a few steps and through the parking lot, I headed for the parked car.

"No, this way!" Sacha tugged me to the right, away from the car. I stumbled behind him and down an alleyway that backed onto the hospital. "Better cover," he announced breathlessly as we took the narrow cobbled street past a crew of curious street sweepers. "Besides, you haven't got keys."

The man was thinking ahead.

Tugging my hand from his—my palm scuffed raw—I took the lead by a few steps.

The alley was clean and led to the back of a row of small shops and apartments. Cars lined the left side, while garbage containers and steps decorated the other side.

"Why would they do that?" I wondered as Sacha slowed and darted between two buildings.

"You didn't think we'd get out of there alive?"

I stopped, fingers clawing into my hips. Sacha surveyed the surroundings, huffing into my face.

"You expected as much?" I was stunned. And then I could have kicked myself. Sacha had expected this danger all along. And I'd naively bet Eight would make the trade.

A bullet knocked out dust of a brick from the wall right next to Sacha's head. I didn't look for the sniper. It had been a horizontal hit. Someone was on our tail.

"This way." I wasn't in a car, but navigation on the run was my forte.

The Conciergerie was close, but I didn't want to go into any buildings, especially any that contained officers of the law. But if we could lure our tail close to the police…

We made way for the waterfront skipping down the stairs to parallel the Seine. Trees shaded the area below the pont Neuf; I found a nook to rest in and tugged Sacha along. A wall, featuring a dribbling fountain, held our panting bodies up. Water glistened in waves of silver, for the opening was but thirty strides away. The river smelled awful, its stir of questionable ingredients heated to a brew in the summertime.

"You okay?" I said back to Sacha.

He didn't answer.

I spun around and found him poking at a red spot on his shoulder.

"You've been hit!"

He turned his back to me, but I spun him around and inspected the wound. The terry cloth had been torn away at the seam to reveal serrated skin and a little blood. No major damage. The seam must have lessened the impact. "It's just a surface abrasion."

"I'll be fine," he said. "I'm glad it wasn't eight inches to the right. I like my brain. It serves me well on occasion."

I rapped my fingers against the brain of the moment. "I like it, too. You're a good sport, Sacha. Not too many men I know would come along for such a goofy ride."

"The ride has been perilous and interesting, I must admit. But you're the goof, getaway girl."

"Getaway girl?"

"That is what you do best, isn't it? No matter on wheel or foot. You saved my ass just now. Thank you."

I don't think I had ever received a thank you for driving or running, or plain getting away. It felt...bloody good.

I drew in a deep breath and let it out in a sigh. For the first time, I actually felt as if I'd accomplished something.

Getaway girl? That was me.

But we weren't out of the woods yet.

While Sacha bent to slap some of the fountain water over his face, I tugged the cell phone from my pocket and tapped through the menus to locate the last number received. It was blocked. No way for me to call Kevin. "Where do you think they are?"

"Not sure." Sacha leaned against the stone wall and spread his legs. He closed his eyes and slumped down a bit. Water droplets dripped from his chin. I suddenly realized just how exhausted he was. The man might look to be in incredible shape, but he was no runner. And he'd taken a hit.

"Sit for a moment." I pressed on his forearm to get him to comply. "We've got to wait it out now, anyway. Eight will surely call once his thugs report back that we got away." I squatted near Sacha, stretching my legs out before me and wiggling my toes in the cool shade. "I can't believe they fired with all those kids around."

"A professional sniper would never have done that. Or rather, a professional would have hit his mark."

"Me? Or you?"

"Maybe that was the problem. He had two marks and couldn't decide between the two of us."

"Joy. Can't say I've ever been on anybody's hit list. And within the past few days, I've joined two of them."

"You're not on mine, Jamie. You never were."

"What about the ride in the boot?"

"That wasn't me. I don't know why you believe otherwise.

Sure, I had wanted to find you after I heard *la lapine* had driven the fouled pickup. But I would have never allowed my men to shove you in the trunk. That was another pickup the Faction beat me to."

"The Faction was responsible for the ride in the boot?"

This was the first time I'd even considered that option. It made enormous sense now that I knew the Faction was dirty. They must have made the decision to go back for the driver after the princess was secure. And yet…

"But you threatened Fitch. I saw the cut on her finger."

"Thom and Jacques. We tried to get you for a pickup, but Fitch gave us the runaround."

And all this time… So Fitch had been protecting me. But from the wrong bad guys.

"I'm sorry."

Sacha shrugged. "I've only ever been truthful with you."

And look what the truth had gotten him—this deadly chase.

The phone rang, and I was so startled at the interruption, I dropped it between my legs. Sacha laid a hand on it, right over my crotch. He didn't move. The phone rang again.

"If only this phone had vibrate on it."

That got him to smile. He released the phone with a sexy smirk and a wink. "I thought you saved your lipstick for that."

"I—what? My lipstick?" Had he been digging in my duffel bag? So I carried a lipstick vibrator. What of it?

Again, the phone rang. I answered. "Eight?"

"Still running, I see." Kevin's American accent did nothing but piss me off.

"I thought we had a deal!"

"Can't blame me for trying."

"Are you going to invite me to the party for real this time, or do we start blowing away all your men?"

"As you've done so far? Reports tell me you're unarmed and running about with a man in a towel."

"It's a robe."

"Ah. Did I interrupt something special?"

"Tell me where you are," I insisted.

"Quai d'Anjou. Number eleven. See you soon."

I hung up and told Sacha the location.

"That borders the Seine," he said.

"Yes, it's on the île Saint-Louis. Not so many people, and a bit of a sleepy neighborhood, if you ask me."

"Wish I still had my surprise package."

"The explosives? You're joshin' me, right?"

"You do have plans to turn me over in exchange for the princess. Don't know what the hell you'll do with her, but she seems to interest you more than I do."

"She's an innocent."

"And I'm not."

"Exactly." Well, sort of. In this situation, he was innocent. But not in life. "Please, if I knew I could actually get by with slipping you in for a trade…"

"You don't think I'll come along peacefully?"

"I know you will, and you'll be my backup, right?"

"Who's calling the shots?"

"I am."

"I don't usually take orders from women."

"Time to learn, Sacha."

"Back to first-name basis?" He nudged my leg with his knee. "You cozying up to me?"

"Will it get me an able backup man?"

"It might."

"Then yes." I leaned in and kissed him, pressing him hard against the concrete wall where the shadow of leaves danced above our heads. Arms spreading above and beside each of his shoulders I flattened my palms to the wall. The position of control. I liked it.

"Did I mention my hard-on?" he muttered, grimacing. "It's difficult to disguise with a robe."

"Should I stop kissing you?"

He vacillated, his eyes roaming across my face and landing my lips. "Maybe."

"Fine. I'll save it for later."

He gripped my upper arm as I stood back, stopping me still against his chest. "Will there be a later?"

"There had better be."

Chapter 23

The traffic was stop-and-go. A few bookseller stalls were open along the quay that paralleled the Seine. They sold mostly early nineteenth-century fiction not the hot and heavy kind of stuff I liked to read. I gunned the Fuego (heck, I still had the multitool. Screwdriver key, remember?).

Man, did I miss horsepower.

"Pity," I said, thinking of the fire that devastated Sacha's house—and the garage, where my brand-new Barrique Red Bimmer now simmered. "Two cars destroyed in so little time."

"Yeah," Sacha said, "and I'm feeling sixty grand lighter for it."

"Hey, I'm out a car, which, I will remind you, is my office, my way of life. How will I ever replace it when my only means to do so requires a car?"

"I'm out a new BMW. Barrique Red. What a loss."

"I thought it was a gift to me?"

"Oh, it was. I'll get you another one."

Pulling onto the pont St-Louis, I crossed the Seine for the smaller island. "Is it so easy for you to throw money around like that?"

"When it's for a good cause, yes."

"I'm working against you, Sacha. Remember?"

"What makes you think I'm on the wrong side?"

"Don't tell me you've suddenly seen the light and have decided to use your powers for good." I downshifted and turned left. "I don't buy it."

"What is it with you?"

The anger in his voice suddenly felt palpable, as if I could reach out and poke it. "What do you mean?"

"Why am I automatically labeled the bad guy, with no hope of redemption, and yet you get to rise above your past with the greatest of ease?"

"I—"

"Get over yourself, Jamie. We've both been there, done that. Am I not allowed the same consideration you are?"

Been there, done that. A chill prickled the back of my neck, and over my shoulders. He was so like me, it was scary. Was that why I continued to push him away, even while I was groping him for some skin on skin?

He had a point. If I was going to start believing my own journey had changed, I had to open the court for others to follow. I needed to go there.

"I'm sorry. I really am. Not the bad guy."

"I'm trying," he said. "All that concerns me, after we save the princess, is finding my sister."

"But you'll have to interrogate the princess to get any information out of her."

"Oh, sure. But I won't harm her."

"You don't think she's not damaged enough after all she's been through?"

Sacha sighed. "I don't do what I do for the thrill of it. Not like my...well..."

I remembered his heartfelt plea for me to find his sister after all had been hashed out with the Faction.

Who'd have thought the man I'd decided to trust would be the one I should stay far away from, while the man I'd tried to avoid, would turn out to be more heroic? Just proved I hadn't a clue when it came to men.

Get all the details. My new mantra.

"Almost there," I said.

"Cool. But I'm still feeling a bit underdressed."

I glanced to his open robe, the striped boxers and the ever-so-sexy galoshes.

"Don't tell me you want to go shopping before we dash in and rescue the damsel in distress? What sort of knight are you?"

He shrugged. "A tired one. A cranky one. Maybe even a little shy. This thing won't stay tied." He tugged at the robe ties.

"Works for me."

"Yeah? But every time I get close to you, people start shooting at us. I think that's a sign. Don't you? I do."

I chuckled. "Maybe. But take heart, I don't look much better." I glanced into the rearview mirror. Yikes, did my mop of dirty blond waves need a comb. "Besides, who's going to suspect danger from a man in a terry cloth robe?"

"This is punishment for the hell I put you through with the chloroform, isn't it?"

"It's a start."

I turned onto the pont de Sully and sighted the lush trees and shrubs bordering the expansive Square Barye. The apartment Kevin had mentioned had to be close. Sunlight kissed the treetops, and the whole area looked like a peaceful forest, save for the long yellow crane perched at river's edge and stretching over the calm green waters. The island was packed with shops and restaurants, but it still retained that cozy French village feel.

Driving slowly through the historic neighborhood, we both kept our eyes out for any sign of Faction rooftop snipers.

Sacha followed the movement of the crane as it swung slowly over the river and the heavy boom began to lower. I couldn't see from this angle, and through all the trees, what it held.

"Drive behind that sanitation container," he directed. "We'll get out and take a look around."

"I'm going to park on the quai d'Anjou." I would not take driving orders from anyone, let alone a man wearing nothing but his boxers and a robe. "There's only two cars on the street. Maybe we'll get lucky. Eight could be one of them, along with the princess and thugs."

"You counting on thugs?"

"There's always thugs."

"What have you got against thugs?"

"Besides the unimaginative couture? Nothing. Love 'em. Especially when they're running *from* me, not to me. Here we are."

I parked the Fuego, and it sputtered, rocked and died before I could even turn off the ignition.

"Looks like this old lady has breathed her last breath. Thanks, sweetie." I patted the dashboard and then looked to Sacha. "You got any cash on you?"

He gave me a bewildered look and lifted his hands in mock surrender.

"Sorry. Just thought to leave a few euro notes in the glove box as payment for use of the car."

"You really are turning a new leaf. But no, no cash."

"Ah well. Let's go. Hopefully the police can trace the registration to the owner."

"And our fingerprints?"

"Clever." A swipe of my sleeve around the steering wheel and across the stick shift would do little good. Sacha followed by wiping the corner of his robe over everything he may have touched.

"Must be tough for you," I commented. "Sitting in this filthy old wreck."

"Why do you say that?"

I shrugged. "I have been witness to your compulsive wiping and tapping, OCD Boy."

"OC—" Doing a double take, the man then twisted on the seat to face me fully, and—exploded. "I do not have OCD. Is that what you think? I've just got a few…quirks, is all."

"If that's what you want to call it." Most people didn't get so defensive about a nonexistent condition. "I'm not throwing stones. But now that you mention it, what's the deal with the stones and tapping them?"

He settled back in the seat as I opened the driver's door and stuck out a foot to stretch. "Stones are a focus object. Part of my anger management process. My therapist prescribed the ritual for me."

"You're seeing a shrink?"

"Shrink is not the proper term. She's a licensed psychotherapist, who specializes in serenity seeking. And yes, I have…issues."

I lowered my forehead to the steering wheel. This man had issues? I didn't know whether to agree or giggle. Serenity seeking? I had to press my lips tightly to keep back the giggle. Next he would tell me they sat around cross-legged and hummed *om* to the gentle lull of a stone fountain.

"When I get angry I tend to lose focus and…"

"Slap women around?" I offered.

"Yes! But you're all right," he said quickly. "I mean, I didn't hit you too hard, did I?"

He was genuinely apologetic about that little incident in his office.

"Sacha, you're freaking me out."

"I'm freaking—woman, I had sex with you. We had this amazing night of anonymous sex, and we were great. You're cool. I'm cool. Then, two months later, you're my enemy. You think you're freaking? I'm the one who's freaking here, lady."

"Yeah? Well, rub some stones, buddy."

"I do! I've been rubbing them a lot since I thought I'd never see you again. But it's hard to focus when the anger rises." He clenched a fist. A flash of white teeth glinted.

"Are you angry now?"

"No. I mean, I don't think so." The fist stretched out to five splayed fingers. He released a breath. "Relaxed, yeah, I'm good."

It was all I could do not to shake my head in pity. But he must have sensed my disbelief.

"Hey, don't knock the therapist. You'd be fucked up, too, if you used to toddle down the stairs when you were only five to see some man in the living room, tied to a chair and dripping blood from his nose, while my father paced around him. He used to have these metal instruments, you know. Torture devices. Damn it! And poor Ava…"

Sensing his rising anger, I jumped out my side of the car and searched the ground.

"I need a focus object!" Sacha declared to the world, as I slid around the front of the car and to his side.

I pulled open the passenger door and displayed my find for him on the palm of my hand. "Here. Rub away."

Sacha took the egg-sized stone I'd grabbed from the street. Turning it about, his eyes crossed, then focused. He tossed it once and caught it smartly. Nostrils flaring rapidly, he breathed fast and heavily. I wasn't sure if he would throw it at me, or send it through the windshield.

His burst of laughter relieved me more than you can know.

"Oh, this is just sweet, goofy girl."

"Goofy?"

"You are! And I love you for it. Thanks." He tucked the stone into his robe pocket and got out of the car. "Sorry to freak you like that, Jamie. I shouldn't have gone there. My childhood was one nasty nightmare."

"I'm sure it wasn't easy for you as a kid."

"Bizarre, actually. But we don't need to go there, right?"

"Sounds keen to me. Ready?"

"Behind you all the way."

"Right." I touched the gun I'd tucked into the back of my jeans and looked back to Sacha. Tension pulsed in his jaw. "Do keep a hand on the stone. Just in case."

He gave me an all clear with two fingers to his brow.

I scanned the front of the building. It wasn't large, three stories high and probably twice as long. Windows on the bottom floor were boarded over—must be remodeling—and bright white and red graffiti declaring the revolutionary slogan *liberté, egalité, fraternité* dashed along the brick facade.

Every building was nestled snug against its neighbor. This was not my dream scenario for bursting in and laying the enemy out cold. There would be witnesses, there had to be. So I kept a keen eye on my periphery.

Sacha tightened the belt on the terry robe with a determined tug. With a shake of his arms and fingers, he shrugged off the nastiness that had visited him and assumed a staunch stance. "I am your prisoner."

"You got it." And to make it look good, I gripped him by the collar and poked the gun into his back. "Let's rock this joint."

An iron staircase clattered with each footstep, so we took it slowly. Not that my bare feet made much noise, but Sacha's boots clopped like horse's hooves. We reached the third floor, which curved close to the windows that overlooked the Seine. I peered out at the crane, and saw it held a car by a massive circular magnet and was slowly swinging back over the river.

"Oh my God!" I pressed a palm to the dirty window. My heart suddenly slid into overdrive; I had to swallow to counter the adrenaline flow.

"What?" Sacha paused a few feet away.

"That's Max's Audi!"

"Told you I didn't steal your car."

"Yes, but—so that means…" It really was the Faction that had dumped me in the boot. I swung a look back at the dangling car. "Why would they—?"

And in the next instant, I knew exactly why a mere car would hold so much sway over me. There was something valuable inside that car. A princess.

Walking swiftly, I set my jaw and passed Sacha. "That bastard is going to pay."

"Jamie, be careful."

I tugged my arm from Sacha's reaching fingers. "Don't touch me. You just play your part, Vital. The Faction is going down for this one. Eight killed Max. And now he wants me dead, and will likely take down you and an innocent woman in the process."

A deft move by Sacha pushed me against the brick wall. I

lunged forward and lifted a foot, but he countered by slamming his whole body against mine, a move that chuffed out my breath.

"Rub the stone, you arse—"

"I don't need any stones, but maybe you do. Slow down," he said. "See me."

"I see you. You're standing close enough to kick."

"Yeah, but do you *see* me?"

"You're an idiot."

"I may be, but at least I'm not wearing blinders." He breathed lowly. "The Faction does want you dead. And me. So play this one close, and don't let your anger get the better of common sense. Jamie! Look at me."

I knew that behind us, on the other side of the wall, stood my nemesis. Max's murderer. A man who would toy with human lives for reasons I had yet to completely understand. All I wanted to do was wipe those dimples from Kevin's face—with a bullet. I wasn't a cold-blooded killer, but in this case I wanted an eye for an eye.

But Sacha was right. I had to settle down, calm myself.

"Take a deep breath," Sacha directed. He leaned in so the robe dusted my leg and one of his sideburns tickled my forehead. Too gentle a touch, ridiculous for this moment. "Focus."

I pressed a hand against his chest to keep him at a distance. "I'm breathing." A few demonstrative inhales.

"Yeah, well try this." He dug in his pocket and presented the stone, holding it between two fingers before my eyes.

For a moment, we both just stared at the stupid gray thing. Then I smiled and nodded. "I'm chilling. I've started to coast."

"You sure? Be one with the stone, baby."

I gave him a shove and smirked. "I'm cool. How many do you think are inside?"

"Likely two or three, beyond Eight. They'll all be armed, that's a given. Are you an expert shot?"

I didn't answer.

"Jamie, give me the gun."

"But you're the prisoner."

"Doesn't matter. Just give it to me."

I pulled it from the back of my waistband and handed it to him. It was difficult, handing over a portion of the control. But, I knew it had to be done. I wasn't an expert marksman. I didn't know if Sacha could pull it off, either, but right now, I was willing to place my bets on the boy who'd grown up in a household focused on the criminal and the bizarre.

He stepped back to give me some room as he checked the magazine for bullets. "Do you have any skills beyond your driving expertise that can save our asses?"

"I can street fight."

"Really? That means you'll have to get close enough to connect, and I don't think I want you doing that."

"Yeah? Well, you're not calling the shots. This is my game now. You remain back by the door."

I watched as he swept back the robe and tucked the gun in the waistband of his boxers. The front of the boxers sagged to reveal dark hair. He tugged out the gun and tried it behind him. "This isn't going to work, I'll have to keep it in my pocket."

"So long as you stay by the door, I can distract. I'm good at distraction."

"Oh, I know it, sweetie, I know it. Hey, Jamie, can I tell you something before we go inside?"

A glint of sun on steel caught my eye. Just outside, the Audi hung precariously. If the princess was in there, she had to be freaking.

Please, let her be freaking, because that would mean she wasn't dead.

"Make it quick," I said.

"Okay." Eyes half-green and half-blue fixed me like no factory-new shiny red Porsche 911 (with a race button) ever could. "I think I like you, Jamie."

"Like?" I feigned being affronted. "No love?"

"I've only known you a few days. Give the guy a running start. You…want me to love you?"

"No," I blurted. "I was just checking the waters. You wouldn't say something unless you mean it."

"Damn straight."

"Like is fine. And a hell of a lot safer than love." Shrugging a hand along my arm, I wondered if I should reciprocate the warm huggy compliment—and then decided, what the hell. "I…like…you."

"Yeah? Well, I like kissing you."

"Oh yeah? I like…having sex with you."

"No kidding? I promise a repeat performance should we get out of this alive."

"I thought we were doing spaghetti?"

"That, too."

"But according to Mister Macho, who pushed me away from kissing him, I wasn't supposed to have anything to do with your nasty self."

"Yeah, well, you know, I don't want to hurt you."

"So that little speech about me not calling you a bad guy was hot air?"

"No. I'm trying, Jamie, I really am. But I'll always need my stones."

Who wouldn't smile at such a confession?

He leaned in and kissed my forehead. "You're only interested in the sex anyway, right?"

"Don't forget the spaghetti."

"Sounds like a date to me."

Chapter 24

I opened the door carefully and walked inside the upper-floor room which was as vast as a warehouse. Twisting Pa's ring about my thumb, I surveyed the scene. Wall-to-wall windows surrounded an open floor. Sunlight beamed ultrawhite swaths across the dusty hardwood floors burned black by decades-past machinery. No machinery now; the place was empty, save for three figures fifty paces away from me.

Kevin stood in the center, hands on his hips. He wore a suit today, no jeans, but not your standard thug couture. Cream linen, like something you'd wear to the beach, hung from the man's frame, and a peek of light blue shirt popped between the crinkled lapels.

To his left, a thug wielding a freakin' machine gun and looking as if he could eat VWs for breakfast sneered. To Kevin's right, a smaller version of the VW eater assumed a stoic, thug pose. He didn't hold a weapon, but I guessed he was packing somewhere in that ill-fitting black suit. I recognized them both. Things One and Two.

Just because they were bigger than me didn't give them the advantage.

"Good morning, sunshine!" Kevin announced with a grand splay of his arms to encompass the room. "So glad you could make it, *la lapine*. And Sacha Vital, in…a hell of a bit more flesh than expected."

"He stays by the door," I interrupted Kevin's glorious speech. If you let the villains go off on their wicked I-rule-the-world spiel, the whole day can be ruined—not that it hadn't already reached suck status, but I was holding out for a brilliant finale. "Let me see the princess."

"She's close."

"You promised a trade."

I stopped about a quarter of the way into the room. Kevin stood a good ten paces from me. Even from here his dimples broadcast loud and clear. Thing One and Thing Two flanked him at ten paces each. Everyone was too spread out. Not good.

"I don't hand over my prize until you show me your prize," I said.

He slid a hand inside his suit coat. I wished I had a weapon. If he wasn't armed, I could take out Kevin, or at the very least, incapacitate him. But could I count on Sacha to back me up? Could I *really* rely on the man?

Why, oh why, was I even thinking this now? Of course I could trust angry OCD Boy.

Slowly, Kevin drew out a walkie-talkie from his inner suit pocket and displayed it before him.

"Not good enough," I said. "How do I know you haven't prerecorded something?"

"It's a monitor," he explained. He clicked a button and a static distorted buzz echoed in the room. "You there, sweetie?"

A female scream was abruptly cut off with a flick of Kevin's finger. He nodded toward the window and the car dangling outside.

"I think you'll recognize the vehicle," he added. "She's in the trunk. You play me wrong, she drops. You hand over Vital, and I order the crane operator to set her down nice and gently."

I glanced back at Sacha. He stood before the closed door, legs spread and hands inside the bathrobe pockets. Now was the time to play it stone-cold serious.

"Nice look, Vital," Kevin said with a cool sneer. "You'll have to hook me up with your designer."

Those dimples were so wrong on his face now. I mentally kicked myself for ever considering having sex with the man.

Sacha didn't return the remark. Smart man. My man.

Yes, well, a girl goes there when she's under duress.

"Let's cut the crap," I said. "You put the car down gently, and then I'll step aside and let you do whatever you wish with Mr. Vital. But you must realize that I know you're not going to let me out of here alive. I know as much about what Max had going on with Vital as he does. I'm dangerous to you, Kevin."

"So good of you to remind me. But I beg to differ. I've been on a joyride with you, if you'll recall. I know you pack heat. But I also know you won't shoot, because you haven't got it in you."

Gulp. He had an advantage, knowing that about me. Fine. Game tilted in his favor. Now, to pass him along the outer edge and take the lead.

"But I have made a deal," Kevin continued, "and I'm nothing if not a fair dealer. You'll walk away from here, princess in hand. I promise."

"Yeah? How far will I get before Thing One puts a bullet in the back of my head?"

"You're worth more to me alive than dead, Jamie. I know you don't have any direct contacts to the Network now. But Vital does."

I flashed a wonky look at Sacha. Couldn't be helped. In that moment, I was so startled by what Kevin had said, I dropped all pretense. Sacha held my gaze, not moving. He wasn't going to give me anything.

Kevin was playing us against one another. He had to be.

"I've had enough." I swung around and stepped forward— but two strong arms grabbed me from behind.

Ah, *merde*.

With a gun barrel firmly pressed to the underside of my chin, I managed to mutter, "What the hell?"

Myriad thoughts raced through my brain, the strongest being, *Did he really know more about the Network than he had let on?*

"She gets it if you don't set that car down nice and easy," Sacha commanded.

"You're not going to kill her," Kevin challenged. "Besides, my men can put a bullet through your brain as fast as you can put one in her mouth."

Double gulp.

"But then you'll have no one to lead you to the Network," Sacha said. "That is what this is all about. The boys in the Network wouldn't let you join their club, so you took one of them out. Now you hope to find them and finish them off. I'm guessing the princess either didn't talk, or didn't have the information you need. Now, you can't do it without Jamie's help. She's your only connection to the Network. So what's it going to be? We make a fair trade, the princess for the driver. Or do I splatter her brains?"

Yikes! Right now I was beginning to think my trust-o-meter had never worked properly. Sacha sounded dead serious. And the gun barrel pressed hard against my jaw brought the meaning of serious to a whole new level. With his other arm wrapped around my chest, I wasn't about to struggle free.

"I don't need the driver," Kevin said. "I know exactly where to find the Network, and Ava is going to lead me there."

Sacha breathed, "Fuck", but it wasn't loud enough for anyone but me to hear.

So the princess had talked. And she'd had information about Sacha's sister. A name? How would the princess know the name of her alleged assassin?

The gun barrel was momentarily removed from my jaw.

"Tell me what you know!"

I bit my tongue as the gun slammed back into my flesh. It was hard to believe Sacha was on anybody's side but his own right now. Rage clenched his fingers into my ribs. I stumbled as he stepped and brought me forward a few paces. My fingers slid over the robe belt, and I tugged it, gently.

"So that brings the fire to your eyes," Kevin said, ever so calm. He hadn't moved an inch at Sacha's outburst. "I shall take great pleasure in killing you, Vital. And then I'll tell your sister all about it."

Kevin hadn't just pressed Sacha's anger button—he'd stomped, beaten and whacked it beyond recognition. And not a stone in sight—thank goodness.

Sacha shoved me. Robe belt running through the terry cloth loops, it detached from the robe, and I stumbled toward Kevin. From the corner of my eye, I saw Thing Two kept a keen bead on me, but Thing One concentrated on Sacha. Good, they were divided.

Now to conquer.

Knowing a thug wouldn't risk taking out his own boss, I lunged and snapped the robe belt before Kevin, wrapping it about my hands to use as a weapon. I pressed it to his neck and we went down. Thing Two hissed out an oath, but he didn't fire.

Gunfire rattled from the machine gun. A body dropped, a gun clattered. As I struggled with Kevin, I allowed him to roll me to my back. Keen. Now his back was to Thing Two, and that provided protection for me. I had the belt around his neck and pulled both ends tight.

"Sacha?" I called.

Kevin's fist barreled into my gut. I choked but directed a wodge of spittle at his chest. I didn't let go of the belt, only tightened it.

"Get Vital, I've got her under control," Kevin ordered Thing Two. He choked and his face turned purple.

If I could just pull harder, but the soft terry cloth wasn't proving too dangerous to the man's breathing.

Out of the corner of my eye, I saw the massive body of Thing One lying inanimate on the floor.

Snapping up my knee clocked the back of Kevin's thigh, setting him off balance. Releasing my shoulders, he wobbled, and slapped a hand to the floor. My grasp on the belt slipped free.

I shimmied away from his grip and stood, snapping the belt like a whip. "Why Max?"

Kevin jumped up, holding his fists in front of him like a boxer. He must not have been packing heat, because he would have pulled it on me by now. The playing field was level. So long as Sacha kept the remaining thug busy...

A bullet whizzed so close to my cheek I felt the heat of its wake. Taking advantage of my surprise, Kevin delivered a high kick that skimmed my jaw much closer than the bullet had. The move made me flinch, but I shook it off like a pro. Bending, I swung up my right leg and kicked out behind me, using the force of my body. Kevin ran right into the kick. His body bounced off the attack, but he didn't fall.

"So the Faction isn't as benevolent as I thought?" I asked, rhetorically.

"It's the Faction's rule to keep the bad guys under our thumb," Kevin said. "Max was a bad guy. End of story."

"The only bad guy I've met in the past few days is you."

I winced when another gunshot seemed to connect with Sacha's shoulder. His left arm flew back and he hit the wall by the door where we'd entered.

Too late, I saw the fist as it zoomed toward me, blocking my vision.

Stumbling backward to take the blow and not allow it to fell me, I saw Sacha fire again. Thing Two took a bullet, his body doing a dancer's pirouette toward Kevin and me as he went down.

Thing Two fired, not aiming; it was a dying reaction. Even as I tried to move, I knew it would be too late. The bullet burned through my hip, like a million iron particles prickling my flesh. My stance wavered.

Kevin lifted a hand greased with my blood and grinned. Caveman-like and with dimples deepening, he stumbled before me.

"You should have left Vital and walked away." He pulled the walkie-talkie from his inner pocket. "First your mentor. And now you lose again, Jamie."

As Kevin spoke into the walkie-talkie—"Let her drop,"— Sacha fired.

Kevin's body took the bullet in the back. Arms flying out

to his sides, he stood there momentarily, poised like a manic savior prepared to deliver a mass, staring at me. Then he dropped.

Gripping the pain at my hip, I felt for the wound. It had ripped through my jeans, but it didn't feel deep. There was blood...

Let her drop?

I jerked my head toward the windows facing the river at the very moment the Audi was released from the crane's magnetic boom.

"No!"

Chapter 25

Sacha stood in the doorway. Blood dribbled down his left arm, bright against the white terry cloth. He straightened and spread out both arms to me as I charged toward him.

"No time!" I shoved him out of the way, dashed down the hall, and took the iron stairs at autobahn speed.

"Oh shit!" Sacha took up behind me, obviously having seen the car drop, as well. "Jamie, there's nothing you can do!"

I pushed open the building's doors and hit the cobble-stones at a run. "The river isn't that deep. The car won't sink fast!"

"The windows were open!" Sacha called. "I'll go after the crane operator. Maybe he can hook the car and pull it out."

Out was the last word I heard as I scrambled down the stone stairs to the river's edge and dived into the water. I hadn't come all this way just to watch an innocent drown.

Didn't matter what the woman was worth to Sacha or Kevin, or even me—I'd somehow been responsible for getting her into this mess; I was going to get her out. Alive.

The tail of the Audi slipped under the surface as my hands cracked through the sun-silvered waves and my body swiftly submerged. The water was cold, shockingly so. Surprising, for a French summer. I had always thought the river would be warm. Pity I had to find out like this.

If I got too close to the car, would the downward motion suck me along with it? That suddenly became the plan.

The water was murky, but I could see the chrome glinting in the sunlight that broke through the surface. Water entered the car, filling up under the wheel wells and gushing into the engine.

Kicking, I swam to the car, and though I was close, the suction did not tug at me as I'd hoped. Slashing my legs and pulling myself through the water with the breast stroke, I finally reached the vehicle.

The windows were down, but the princess was in the boot. A plan instantly formed in my mind, and I dove for the open passenger window.

I gripped the metal rim and poked my head inside the car, but had to wiggle to get inside. My body wanted to float and rise to the surface. Using the headrest as an anchor, I pulled myself in. I choked and exhaled.

Panic trilled in my chest. I wasn't an expert swimmer, and I really did like to breathe.

Gliding over the headrests and into the backseat, I frantically mined for the small pocket of air that blessedly remained near the back window. My nose emerged into the sweet spot and I tilted my head back to gasp in air through my mouth. Pushing my feet against the driver's headrest, I held there, taking in as much air as I could. But the water rose mercilessly.

I'd once watched an episode of the American TV show *Fear Factor* where one of the contestants had held his breath for more than two minutes in an underwater coffin. Much easier done when one is lying there peacefully.

When only three inches of air remained, I sucked in a deep breath. Pushing my body down, I groped about the murky backseat. As the car sank, the sunlight receded, and it was becoming more difficult to see.

I ran my fingers along the seam of the seat. It had to be here. This model definitely had one—yes! My fingers landed on the tag to pull the seat forward. I found the tag on the other seat as quickly, and soon had the backseat open to the boot.

A pair of bare feet slipped through the opening. My fingers glided over the sodden velvet jogging suit. She wasn't struggling. I attempted to pull her out, but after a few tugs, I realized that wasn't going to work.

Feeling as if I had gulped in the entire algae-green river, I realized my lungs were filling. My eyelids fluttered. It was difficult to keep my mouth closed, because I impulsively wanted to gasp for air. Tired, so tired. Shivers trickled up my arms and over my shoulders.

Pushing the princess's body to the right, I nudged my head through the opening and into the boot. It was a tight squeeze. My back skimmed along the upper cage of the boot, but I spied what I was looking for. The good old glow-in-the-dark release tag.

One would think if a thug were serious about kidnapping, he'd cut that puppy off.

Thankful for the low IQ level of thugs, I grabbed it and yanked. The muffled sound of the boot catch releasing sounded like heaven's angels from above. Shoving hard, it opened, but I had to push against the pressure of the water. Oh yes, angels. The white glow beaming from above beckoned with an imagined heavenly chant.

I felt the swish of silken hair upon my lips. Reaching over, I weaved my fingers under her arm and, using my own head, pushed against the boot lid. It opened, and my body began to float upward.

My passenger weighted us down. Bubbles trickled from my nose. I hadn't much more than a whisper of air left.

I lost my grip on the prize. It was too dark to see. A flash of something glinted. Jewelry. I grasped for the glint, but in the process let out my last bubble of air. It was a bracelet, and attached to that, an arm. Gripping her forearm, I kicked for the surface, fighting the urge to scream, and the strange compulsion to surrender and let go.

Thank God for the body's ability to float. With all my breath gone, I had little struggle left, yet managed to kick. Kick for life. The sky glittered in a wavery silver sheen. Just a few more kicks.

I want to touch the angels.

As my head broke through the surface, I panted for air. The princess's weight tugged me back under. I swallowed water and slapped at the surface. With a few backward thrusts of my shoulders, I managed to tilt to my back and float. Staring up at the sky, huffing, I gasped in life-saving air.

Feet kicking madly and wishing for solid ground, but only swishing through murky nothingness, I had a hold of the woman beneath her chin. I shifted my grasp to hold a clump of hair and an arm. I didn't want to hurt her, but I didn't want to drop her, either.

The river was walled with stone, and there was a cobbled

walk that stretched most of the way—but I didn't see that right now, only an imposing wall.

"Jamie!"

An angel in a dirty white bathrobe and galoshes waved to me.

And the next sound I heard was the plop of a rescue ring landing a blessed three feet away from me.

An ambulance arrived, and as medics loaded the princess into the back, I made way to the other side of a line of shrubbery, a hundred metres away from the scene.

The police had also arrived to tote the thugs out in body bags and arrest Kevin. Yep, still alive, that bastard, but not looking so good being carted out on a gurney. Whether or not the Faction had special privileges when it came to police investigations, I'd never know. I don't know who had made the call to the authorities. Must have been Sacha. I wasn't hanging around to ask. No sense in giving them another suspect by walking up and introducing myself. I had developed a healthy need for distance from law enforcement over the years.

Sacha walked by the police without a care. Though his attire should have drawn some suspicion, a few officers glanced at him but then turned their attention to their police radio.

"You're going to start a new fashion, you know," I said as he stepped around the hedge and stopped inches in front of me.

He tucked a clump of my wet hair behind my left ear. "It's rather freeing."

"Didn't the police want to question you?"

"I told them I heard a ruckus and that I lived across the street, which explained my hasty costume. I work nights, you know. Was just getting ready for a shower."

"Clever."

"I thought so. How are you? Cold? You can have my robe—"

"No!" Then I giggled, because I'd said it so loud and quickly. Sacha leaned back to scan the scene. No one had heard me.

"The pecs are great, Sacha, but I don't think we need burlesque so early in the afternoon. I'm not cold, maybe, well…" A huge shudder traveled from head to toe, branding me a liar. "I wonder about that river. One hears stories. You think my ears will turn green and fall off?"

"It's not as toxic as everyone makes it to be. The fish don't mind."

"Yes, but if you're born to it…" I sighed and slumped against him. Not a planned move, more like a semicollapse. I was just glad I hadn't fallen flat onto the sidewalk. A warm arm wrapped around my shoulders. My head fit neatly against his neck, which was also so warm he seemed like fire burning against my icy flesh. "She going to be all right?"

"I'm sure. Won't know until the doctors take a look at her, but the emergency techs resuscitated her just fine."

I had done it. Something good. I'd actually saved a life. And I hadn't given a second thought to what it would mean for me, how much I'd get paid for the job or even if it would earn me a bit more.

And the male ghosts of my past joined hands and said in unison, *Jamie MacAlister, you're going to be just fine.*

Sacha tilted my head to look at him. He stroked my jaw with his thumb as he silently gazed into my eyes. It was one of those silver screen moments where the audience stops munching popcorn and waits, open-mouthed, for the big kiss.

I fluttered my lashes and allowed my eyes to close. Expecting a kiss? You bet. But tired, as well.

"I, um, think I'm going to accompany her to Casualty," Sacha said.

A shake of my head dismissed silly images of romantic endings and happily-ever-afters. "Of course."

Sacha couldn't let the princess out of his sight. There were things he needed to hear from her. Kevin made it clear he'd found out about Ava from the princess. I hoped Sacha could get the information.

"So I guess this is it." I forced myself to push away from him. A glance around the shrub counted three police vehicles and the ambulance. The crane was currently hoisting the car from the river.

I didn't want to look at Sacha. It was weird, but for some reason this felt like goodbye. Hell, it *was* goodbye. And why did saying goodbye to a man I'd known less than forty-eight hours bother me so much?

Because it isn't ending the right way.

I paced a few steps widely around him, avoiding the heat of him that seemed to want to pull me back like filings to a magnet. Bare feet still left wet tracks on the concrete because my clothing was soaked from my dip in the Seine.

"If a man wanted to get in touch with you, could he contact Fitch?" Sacha asked.

I shrugged, centering my gaze on the line of the hedge that neatly cut across the heads of the emergency personnel rushing about. It would be easier to make a clean break. Sever him from my life. Because he didn't mean a thing to me. Could never—

I was making excuses for my new reality. Was it a better reality than I'd had up until now? What had happened to the journey? And my destination? Cripes, the map had been altered so thoroughly over the past few days. But I knew the destination remained. I would walk away from my past. I felt the power within me. It had never left; it had only been challenged.

And maybe the past few days had needed to happen. For if it hadn't been worth working for, perhaps I'd never truly learn to appreciate the hard life.

"Jamie."

I swayed my head toward the coaxing tone of his voice. But sensing him reach out to me, I curved my shoulder away from his grasp.

I didn't have wanderlust. I wasn't like my mother. I could accept new things and people into my life. All I had ever wanted was to feel safe and to be able to trust. I didn't want to walk away.

Sacha had given me truth. He'd protected me in the warehouse when Kevin could have blown him away. He'd been unselfishly generous.

"Yeah, I should be going," he said.

I still didn't turn.

"A girl like you doesn't need an asshole like me hanging around, steering her life off the road. I know you have plans to drive the straight and narrow. I wish you luck."

All the muscles in my body tightened. I wanted to turn and protest. And I wanted to grab him and pull him into a hug, but instead I managed, "Right. Bye. Thanks, Vital."

"No problem. All in a day's...ah, you know. The ambulance is pulling away. I gotta go."

I listened to the plodding thud of rubber galoshes against the cobbled walk. He was walking away.

Walking away!

My body turned. The white terry robe billowed as Sacha jogged and flagged down the ambulance. He was allowed to ride in the passenger side. As he got inside and closed the door, he didn't turn to look at me.

"Bye," I whispered, rubbing my hand up my arm to dispel the chill of his departure.

No one to blame but myself.

I'd be much better off not having the man in my life, anyway.

Right?

Chapter 26

Fitch felt the gun at the back of her head and quit typing. Fingers leaving the keyboard, she held her hands up near her shoulders. "Didn't hear you come in," she tried, but the nervous timbre of her voice gave away her fright. "Take your shoes off. Sit a spell."

"Kennedy Fitch?"

A British accent. Male. Fitch couldn't place the voice. Damn, she so frequently dealt with people who used voice-altering software when calling that she really had set herself up for this one.

"Maybe," she said. "Who's asking?"

The gun barrel impressed a perfect circle at the back of her skull. To her right, another person moved into her peripheral view. That person navigated the cluttered floor without nicking a single DVD or tossed empty coffee cup.

Fitch turned her head slightly to the right. A slender,

gorgeous woman, with straight dark hair falling to her shoulders fixed a cool stare on her. "Do I know you?"

"You with the Network?" the Brit asked from behind.

"Never heard of 'em." That was the practiced answer. "Seriously, set a spell. Get comfy. Remove the nasty gun from my head, and we'll chat. Get to know each other."

The trigger cocked.

"Or not."

The woman approached, and the man behind Fitch pulled back the wheeled desk chair, with Fitch in it. Gun still firmly placed at her head, Fitch remained like a statue as the woman leaned over her keyboard and began typing.

She hadn't been wise enough to shut down—hadn't had time—so access to all her files was right there. Easy as apple pie. But she never kept sensitive information in easily accessible files. And all names and numbers were coded—

"Jamie MacAlister," the woman said in a cool voice that didn't sound foreign. At least not European foreign. Was she American? Who the hell? Why did they want info about the Network? And why Jamie?

"You're *la lapine*'s handler, yes?" the woman asked.

The dilemma. Lie and risk blowing her cover, or tell the truth and put Jamie in trouble? The poor girl wanted freedom from her past. Hell, this morning after her swim in the river, she'd walked away from the best thing that had ever happened to her, only because she'd thought Sacha Vital couldn't change. She'd been lying to herself, poor girl.

"Ever hear of Christian Lazar?" the man behind Fitch asked.

"I don't…hmm…" Her connection with the Network was priority red. No one, but no one, knew how deeply she was involved. Not even herself, sometimes. "Maybe."

The woman turned and sat on the desk beside the keyboard, crossing her long legs at the ankle. She tilted up Fitch's chin with a finger. "I'm Rachel Blu. I used to be with Lazar. I'm looking for the other women in the Network, and I think you can help me."

"Haven't a clue, ma'am."

"Ever hear of Ava Vital?"

"Nope." Truth.

Maybe.

"We're on her trail, and I need a driver."

I'd gotten off the phone with Fitch about thirty minutes ago. And here I sat, on the city bus again. A humiliating step down for one who'd once thrived behind the wheel. But it would last for no more than the fifteen minutes it took to cross the river and skip on over to the chop shop. My sweetie waited for me. She'd be thankful I hadn't gotten her involved in the ruckus of the past few days. Her new paint job would appreciate it.

Though I had minimal cash in hand, I did have a stash that would see me through a few months. Max had kept most of my money in a Swiss account. But how to access that was beyond me. I'd have to check with Fitch—yes, I still trusted her. After all was said and done, even if I didn't have a home, I had a car—and that was all that really counted.

I'd taken a bullet to my right hip, which must have popped out while I was swimming. Surprisingly, there wasn't much blood or pain. Either that, or the toxins in the Seine had numbed it and I would be dead within the hour.

The bus stopped at the courtyard before the hôtel-Dieu and, though my planned stop wasn't for another few miles, I got off. An impulsive decision.

I couldn't let it end this way.

Or maybe it was because I couldn't let my new life *begin* this way.

I didn't have to wonder if I should stroll into Casualty and start searching rooms. I'd been on the street no longer than a minute when a vision walked out from the south entrance of the hospital. Said vision wore a terry cloth robe and galoshes.

Instead of rushing to him and wrapping my arms around his bold shoulders and torso, I started to laugh. Couldn't be helped. He just looked too goofy. Laughter segued to a belly rumble. I bent at the waist and gasped in air. But this lack of air felt a world better than a drowning breath.

"Come on," Sacha said as he approached. He spread his hands out from his body. "I know you think I'm sexy."

The robe slipped open to reveal the striped boxers and— had I *not* noticed those six-pack abs before? Foolish girl.

"You're right. You are a sexy man, Sacha Vital."

"And don't you forget it."

"Hard to when you're flashing the entire city."

"Oh, come on, the French embrace nudity. A half-naked man won't even make them blink."

I blinked, batting my lashes coyly.

The move earned me a devilish grin and a suggestive lift of brow in return.

"So, what are you doing here, Jamie? Come to get that bullet wound stitched up?"

"It's just a graze." I eased a palm over my hip. Nothing a Band-Aid couldn't cure. "More blood than horror, really."

"Not grim?"

"Not grim," I answered.

He knew things about me. Could he surmise that I stood here right now subtly shaking with nervousness? *Because it hadn't ended right.*

"So if it's not for emergency aid, then what?"

I cocked my head and assumed a casual pose, hands to hips—one of them crusted with dried blood—and unkempt hair, but I worked with it. Inside I was a mess, but the more I concentrated on looking the part, the more my body followed suit. "Thought you might need a driver."

He made show of scanning the street behind us, then looking me up from feet to face. "You don't have a car. And I thought we were through."

"I do have a car. And we are through."

He gave me a so-what's-the-deal shrug.

"I…have some new information on Ava Vital."

"You do?" His entire body changed to open, pleading. "How'd you get that? Where? Who from?"

"Another member of the Network has surfaced. She contacted Fitch an hour ago. Seems she's determined to sniff out all the women in the Network and, well…set them free."

"Sounds ambitious."

"I'm in. It's a good thing."

"I'm in, too."

"Sacha, I don't…" Hell, who was I to tell the man what he could or could not do? We were in the same boat, as he'd made clear to me earlier. "You weren't able to speak to the princess?"

He shrugged and shoved his hands into the robe pockets. "I hung around, close to her room, just to make sure she'd be all right. But I couldn't bring myself to go in and talk to her. She's been through so much. I made sure the nurses were aware she was the missing princess the papers had been talking about."

"But if you showed her Ava's picture…?"

"You know, I was thinking about that. There's no way the princess could have known my sister's name. It's not like an assassin is going to introduce herself before attempting to kill you, right? So, Eight must have gotten that info somewhere else. Or he just researched me and tossed that morsel out, in hopes to get me."

"Which worked."

"Get me angry and…" He sighed, swiping a hand over his jaw. "I need to book a session with my therapist."

"Let's do it after we find your sister."

"You're serious? You'll really help me find her?"

"I wouldn't have come here if I wasn't interested."

"You're trying damned hard to keep this impersonal and professional."

"How am I doing?"

He squinted against the sunlight, but smiled broadly. "Let's walk."

I took up his side, the bedraggled carless driver alongside the hunk in a tattered robe. We walked to the right bank, toward the Bastille area in the 12th *arrondisement*. I followed Sacha's direction for some time, content to just be at his side. Conversation wasn't necessary.

I tried to decide what our theme song should be. "Come What May"? Maybe. Perhaps a bit too romantic for this furious heart. Try "Radar Love." Yeah, that would work.

Eventually we turned into a residential area. Rich and quiet, there were high-rises here that Trump couldn't touch with his gold checkbook.

"Going to visit your rich uncle?" I wondered. "I do have a car to pick up…"

Sacha clasped my hand and tugged me into a quick walk. "I told you I have homes all over. A man can't become complacent in my kind of work."

"And just what is your kind of work?"

He stopped, one hand at his hip. I was so accustomed to the bare chest and hard abs by now that I didn't even look twice. No, I just lingered, that first look being a good long one.

"This is my truth," he said, pressing his palms together and punctuating his words with beats of his hands. "So listen up, because I'm only going over this once. I've been convicted of grand theft auto and some minor betting scams. Five years ago, I served eighteen months in a Brooklyn minimum security lockup. While I was in, I decided I wasn't my father. I've been following his trail, trying to clean up his mistakes ever since. I never expected Ava would succumb to the profession. I should have stayed in touch, but I thought distance would keep my influence away from her. The princess was the first time I've kidnapped. It was necessity, Jamie, you have to believe me. I would have never harmed her."

"I know that."

"I'm not clean. You need to know that."

"Neither am I. Just because I never committed the crime doesn't mean I'm not an accessory. But from this day forward, clean is the new me."

Sacha placed both palms on top of my shoulders. Emerald, his eyes. I decided that blue was his cool and angry look; green meant he was focused and real. "What if devious means are required to help this woman track the Network?"

"If the end result is finding your sister, I'll do what I have to."

He nodded. "I trust that you will."

Scanning the neighborhood, I noted the leaves on the maple tree behind us had begun to turn yellow. Tourist season was almost over, and the streets would return to the usual lighter tie-ups.

"So, where are we headed?" I wondered.

"We're here."

He walked up to a garage nestled below a newer model town house fronted in red brick and pressed some numbers on a digital entrance pad. The steel garage door rose on a squeaky chain drive. Not your standard garage door; he must want to keep whatever was behind it safe.

"Now for the finale." Sacha abruptly gripped me by the shoulders. He turned me from the garage door as it rose and kissed me—hard, long and as if he meant it.

You know how to tell the difference between a casual kiss and one that really means something?

I do.

As far as finales went, this one bordered on brilliant.

When I rose from the gentle assault, I simply pulled him back for another. Twining my fingers up through his hair, I wasn't about to let him break the kiss until I had gotten every last bit of breath from him. I took it into me; it was Sacha inside me, swirling about and making himself at home.

"I like you," I murmured against his mouth.

"Me, too, getaway girl. But before we go all mushy on each other, I've got something to show you."

"What? You do burlesque?"

"Something better."

He stepped aside and splayed out a hand to display what sat inside the garage.

Forget bordering brilliant. Sacha had just smashed through the gate and released the bulls.

My heart fluttered. I walked like a zombie until I reached

the sexy curve of a car. The bonnet, roof and boot were midnight black, the sides a deep velvet red.

"Be still, my furious heart. A Bugatti Veyron 16.4."

These beauties had only recently hit the market with a limited edition of a mere three hundred cars. Sixteen cylinders, four turbochargers. Its carbon body streaked at 350 kph, and the 1001 horsepower took it from zero to sixty in three seconds. And it had low-end torque that promised to push you back in your seat.

I leaned over the hood, drawing in the incredible power that sat quietly beneath me. I could feel it, the acceleration, just waiting to take me on the ride of my life. "I love you, Sacha."

"So now it's love, eh? Sure it's not the car?"

I shrugged. "Probably is."

Yeah, it was. I couldn't be responsible for anything I said when standing over this gorgeous beauty.

I spread my arms and embraced the bonnet. The cool, glossy paint kissed my palms, teasing coyly. This baby cost well over a million euros, and every inch of her felt like it.

"I haven't had a chance to take her out on the road yet," Sacha said. "Maybe you'd like to do the honor?"

Oh baby, one speed orgasm coming right up!

"Yeah," I said dreamily. "I could thrash in this sweetie."

I sensed Sacha lean over me to say lowly, "Despite your attraction to cold steel beasts, I still like you."

"Mmm," I murmured, and had to force myself to stand up.

Every part of me hummed, set to rush over the edge and fly. I was absolutely ready for the brilliant finale. Only with great reluctance did I drag my eyes from the Bugatti.

All right, so there were two bits of brilliant within my

grasp. I wanted to drive them both; I'd already test drove the one. But one should never purchase until they've taken it around the block a time or two.

Walking around and opening the passenger door, I flashed Sacha a suggestive wink, and said, "Want to go for a ride?"

"Can I change first?"

I looked him over. Skin on skin action? Coming right up. "Don't think so. I'm going to take you for a ride you'll never forget."

"Promise?"

"Have a seat and push it all the way back."

He lifted a brow. "I am so with you right now."

Sacha sat in the passenger seat and I, resisting the urge to linger on the car's luscious red flash, instead unbuttoned my jeans. They'd dried during our walk and were a little crunchy, so I had to wiggle to lower them over my hips.

"So nice," Sacha said. "Come here, getaway girl."

I stepped out of the jeans and swung a leg inside the car, over Sacha's lap. There wouldn't be much head room, but I didn't plan to go bronco riding.

"Who am I kidding?" I murmured. "This isn't going to happen. Not like this. Come here."

I pulled the tall bit of brilliant outside, but wouldn't allow him to move away from the car. Bracketing my hands to either side of him, my fingers swept over the satin smooth exterior of the third party in this ménage.

A warm hand slid up my back, under the T-shirt and around to cup my breast. Sacha kissed the corner of my mouth. He flicked out his tongue, tasting me. "I thought we had plans to do spaghetti?"

"You want to eat or you want to break in this beauty?"

He tilted his head in thought. "I'm not too peckish. Breaking in, it is. You know this car does zero to sixty in three seconds?"

"Yeah, but she's going to have to push it to the floor to catch up with me 'cause I'm already there, lover."

Hooking a leg up near Sacha's hip, I kissed him the only way I knew how—hard and quick.

Drive, baby, drive.

* * * * *

Set in darkness beyond the ordinary world.
Passionate tales of life and death.
With characters' lives ruled by laws the everyday world
can't begin to imagine.

Introducing NOCTURNE, *a spine-tingling new line from*
Silhouette Books.

The thrills and chills begin with UNFORGIVEN *by*
Lindsay McKenna.

Plucked from the depths of hell, former military sharpshooter
Reno Manchahi was hired by the government to kill a thief,
but he had a mission of his own. Descended from a family of
shape-shifters, Reno vowed to get the revenge he'd thirsted
for all these years. But his mission went awry when his target
turned out to be a powerful seductress, Magdalena Calen
Hernandez, who risked everything to battle a potent evil.
Suddenly, Reno had to transform himself into a true hero and
fight the enemy that threatened them all. He had to become
a Warrior for the Light....

Turn the page for a sneak preview of UNFORGIVEN *by*
Lindsay McKenna.
On sale September 26, wherever books are sold.

Chapter 1

One shot...one kill.

The sixteen-pound sledgehammer came down with such fierce power that the granite boulder shattered instantly. A spray of glittering mica exploded into the air and sparkled momentarily around the man who wielded the tool as if it were a weapon. Sweat ran in rivulets down Reno Manchahi's drawn, intense face. Naked from the waist up, the hot July sun beating down on his back, he hefted the sledgehammer skyward once more. Muscles in his thick forearms leaped and biceps bulged. Even his breath was focused on the boulder. In his mind's eye, he pictured Army General Robert Hampton's fleshy, arrogant fifty-year-old features on the rock's surface. Air exploded from between his lips as he brought the avenging hammer down. The boulder pulverized beneath his funneled hatred.

One shot...one kill...

Nostrils flaring, he inhaled the dank, humid heat and drew it deep into his massive lungs. Revenge allowed Reno to endure his imprisonment at a U.S. Navy brig near San Diego, California. Drops of sweat were flung in all directions as the crack of his sledgehammer claimed a third stone victim. Mouth taut, Reno moved to the next boulder.

The other prisoners in the stone yard gave him a wide berth. They always did. They instinctively felt his simmering hatred, the palpable revenge in his cinnamon-colored eyes, was more than skin-deep.

And they whispered he was different.

Reno enjoyed being a loner for good reason. He came from a medicine family of shape-shifters. But even this secret power had not protected him—or his family. His wife, Ilona, and his three-year-old daughter, Sarah, were dead. Murdered by Army General Hampton in their former home on USMC base in Camp Pendleton, California. Bitterness thrummed through Reno as he savagely pushed the toe of his scarred leather boot against several smaller pieces of gray granite that were in his way.

The sun beat down upon Manchahi's naked shoulders, grown dark red over time, shouting his half-Apache heritage. With his straight black hair grazing his thick shoulders, copper skin and broad face with high cheekbones, everyone knew he was Indian. When he'd first arrived at the brig, some of the prisoners taunted him and called him Geronimo. Something strange happened to Reno during his fight with the name-calling prisoners. Leaning down after he'd won the scuffle, he'd snarled into each of their bloodied faces that if they were going to call him anything, they would call him *gan,* which was the Apache word for *devil.*

His attackers had been shocked by the wounds on their faces, the deep claw marks. Reno recalled doubling his fist as they'd attacked him en masse. In that split second, he'd gone into an altered state of consciousness. In times of danger, he transformed into a jaguar. A deep, growling sound had emitted from his throat as he defended himself in the three-against-one fracas. It all happened so fast that he thought he had imagined it. He'd seen his hands morph into a forearm and paw, claws extended. The slashes left on the three men's faces after the fight told him he'd begun to shape-shift. A fist made bruises and swelling; not four perfect, deep claw marks. Stunned and anxious, he hid the knowledge of what else he was from these prisoners. Reno's only defense was to make all the prisoners so damned scared of him and remain a loner.

Alone. Yeah, he was alone, all right. The steel hammer swept downward with hellish ferocity. As the granite groaned in protest, Reno shut his eyes for just a moment. Sweat dripped off his nose and square chin.

Straightening, he wiped his furrowed, wet brow and looked into the pale blue sky. What got his attention was the startling cry of a red-tailed hawk as it flew over the brig yard. Squinting, he watched the bird. Reno could make out the rust-colored tail on the hawk. As a kid growing up on the Apache reservation in Arizona, Reno knew that all animals that appeared before him were messengers.

Brother, what message do you bring me? Reno knew one had to ask in order to receive. Allowing the sledgehammer to drop to his side, he concentrated on the hawk who wheeled in tightening circles above him.

Freedom! the hawk cried in return.

Reno shook his head, his black hair moving against his broad, thickset shoulders. *Freedom? No way, Brother. No way.* Figuring that he was making up the hawk's shrill message, Reno turned away. Back to his rocks. Back to picturing Hampton's smug face.

Freedom!

* * * * *

Look for UNFORGIVEN by Lindsay McKenna,
the spine-tingling launch title from Silhouette Nocturne™.
Available September 26, wherever books are sold.

nocturne™

Save $1.⁰⁰ off

your purchase of any Silhouette® Nocturne™ novel.

Receive $1.00 off

any Silhouette® Nocturne™ novel.

Available wherever books are sold, including most bookstores, supermarkets, drugstores and discount stores.

Coupon expires December 1, 2006. Redeemable at participating retail outlets in the U.S. only. Limit one coupon per customer.

RETAILER: Harlequin Enterprises Ltd. will pay the face value of this coupon plus 8¢ if submitted by the customer for this specified product only. Any other use constitutes fraud. Coupon is nonassignable. Void if taxed, prohibited or restricted by law. Void if copied. Consumer must pay for any government taxes. Mail to Harlequin Enterprises Ltd., P.O. Box 880478, El Paso, TX 88588-0478, U.S.A. Cash value 1/100 cents. Limit one coupon per customer. Valid in the U.S. only.

5 65373 00076 2 (8100) 0 11265

SNCOUPUS

Save $1.⁰⁰ off

your purchase of any
Silhouette® Nocturne™ novel.

Receive $1.00 off
any Silhouette® Nocturne™ novel.

Available wherever books are sold, including most bookstores, supermarkets, drugstores and discount stores.

Coupon expires December 1, 2006. Redeemable at participating retail outlets in Canada only. Limit one coupon per customer.

52607136

SNCOUPCDN

THE PART-TIME WIFE

by *USA TODAY* bestselling author

Maureen Child

Abby Talbot was the belle of Eastwick society; the perfect hostess and wife. If only her husband were more attentive. But when she sets out to teach him a lesson and files for divorce, Abby quickly learns her husband's true identity...and exposes them to scandals and drama galore!

On sale October 2006 from Silhouette Desire!

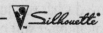

SPECIAL EDITION™

Experience the "magic" of falling in love at Halloween with a new *Holiday Hearts* story!

UNDER HIS SPELL

by KRISTIN HARDY

October 2006

Bad-boy ski racer J. J. Cooper can get any woman he wants—except Lainie Trask. Lainie's grown up with him and vows that nothing he says or does will change her mind. But J.J.'s got his eye on Lainie, and when he moves into her neighborhood and into her life, she finds herself falling under his spell....

Silhouette
BOMBSHELL™

COMING NEXT MONTH

#109 DRESSED TO SLAY by Harper Allen
Darkheart & Crosse
On the eve of her wedding, trendy society-girl and triplet Megan Crosse found out about her mother's legacy as a vampire slayer the hard way—when her fiancé turned on her and her sisters, fangs bared! Now it was up to Megan to trade in her bridal bouquet for a sharp stake and hunt down her mother's undead killer....

#110 SHADOW LINES by Carol Stephenson
The Madonna Key
Epidemiologist Eve St. Giles had never seen anything like it—an influenza outbreak that *targeted* women. But this was no natural disaster—someone was manipulating the earth's ley lines to wreak havoc. Could the renowned Flu Hunter harness the ancient healing rites of her Marian foremothers in time to avert a modern medical apocalypse?

#111 CAPTIVE DOVE by Judith Leon
When ten U.S. tourists were kidnapped in Brazil, the hostages' family connections to high political office suggested a sinister plot to bring American democracy to its knees. Only CIA operative Nova Blair—code name, Dove—could pull off a rescue. But would having her former flame for a partner clip this free agent's wings?

#112 BAITED by Crystal Green
Pearl diver Katsu Espinoza was never one to turn down an invitation to cruise on multimillionaire Duke Harrington's yacht. But when her dying mentor announced he was disinheriting his assembled family and making Katsu his heir, the voyage turned deadly. Stranded on an island in a raging storm, with members of the party being murdered one by one, Katsu had to wonder if she was next—or if she was the bait in a demented killer's trap....

SBCNM0906